Books by
FLORENCE CRANNELL MEANS

PENNY FOR LUCK
A BOWLFUL OF STARS
A CANDLE IN THE MIST
RANCH AND RING
DUSKY DAY

PENNY
FOR LUCK

A Story of the Rockies

BY

FLORENCE CRANNELL MEANS

with illustrations by
PAUL QUINN

BOSTON AND NEW YORK
HOUGHTON MIFFLIN COMPANY
The Riverside Press Cambridge
1935

𝕿𝖍𝖊 𝕽𝖎𝖛𝖊𝖗𝖘𝖎𝖉𝖊 𝕻𝖗𝖊𝖘𝖘
CAMBRIDGE · MASSACHUSETTS
PRINTED IN THE U.S.A.

CONTENTS

ILLUSTRATIONS

I. POLISHING THE PENNY

PENNY shifted the dog from one aching arm to the other and took a fresh hold on her bundle. The bundle was tied up in cotton cloth printed with faded roses.

'It does seem like you needn't 'a' been so big,' she protested to the dog. 'Land knows you ain't got no meat to spare; but you do stick out every which way.'

He was an ungainly, whiskery pup. He hung over Penny's arm, sighing patiently at her when she addressed him. One of his legs was wrapped, like the bundle, in faded rose print. It prodded Penny whenever she moved him.

The day was warm, for March. Before Penny, behind Penny, the hot gray ribbon of cement pavement stretched on and on, unshaded by a tree. She was straining toward the service station ahead. The station and the house behind it stood stark in the gray-brown prairie, without trees or shrubs. But she could rest under the portico; and perhaps some motorist would pick her up there.

The dog slipped and slipped. Penny clutched him against her till he grunted.

'I never seen nobody awkwarder to tote,' she muttered, easing him down onto the road when he had slid till his

nose pointed upward over the crook of her elbow. 'But
— there now! I got no call to fault you for it, pore thing.
I'm jest as overgrowed myse'f.'

She pushed back her hair, which sprang up defiantly
from her fingers, mopped her hot face with a grimy handkerchief, and gathered up the dog.

Cars passed Penny: whizzed by, purred by, rattled by.
Some drivers turned to stare after her, unbelievingly;
some hooted with their horns. Penny plodded on, eyes
to the front. She hadn't had much luck thumbing rides,
and she wasn't going to beg any more till she'd tried this
service station.

Just as she reached it, a long blue car drew up in its
arcade. The car had elegant lines and a mirror finish,
but Penny noticed that it stopped with a shriek and
settled to rest with a clatter. That was significant. She
studied the people in it as she came at last to the patch
of shade and lowered the dog into a corner.

The driver peered at the gasoline gauge, dragged out a
worn wallet and peered into that, studied the gauge again.

'Three more gallons ought to take us in,' he said. 'No,
not the super gas. We ain't so stuck up.'

He clambered out, opened the hood of the machine to
look vaguely at the engine; closed it with a shake of the
head, put water into the steaming radiator.

'It ought to get us to Denver safe enough, Mamma,' he
said reassuringly, 'though I own I don't like that little
smack it's making.'

Penny glanced from one to the other of them. The
driver looked like a real father; and 'Mamma' was all
right, in a stylishly lean and worried-looking fashion; but
best of all Penny liked the grandpa and the little boy in
the back seat.

She cleared her throat and addressed the service-station man. He turned a cold eye upon her as he held the pump-nozzle in place.

'Hain't you got a job so I could earn enough to get to the next town?'

He glanced from her to the pump, shut off the gasoline, put the cover back on the tank.

'Job?' he asked scornfully.

'Wouldn't your woman like he'p with the spring cleaning?'

He shook his head with harsh finality.

This was no fun. If Penny had guessed how aching and dusty and hot and cold and hungry and frightened she was going to be, she would have thought twice before running away; even from the Home; even after all that had happened. Yet what else could she have done?

Penny was thirteen, going on fourteen, though she was so big that everyone thought her older. Up to last Christmas her life had been a plain gray road, like this highway; only that the highway went somewhere and her life didn't. But in the past three months the road had suddenly changed into a whirligig.

The first thing she could remember was living with her father and mother in a mountain town, Central City. That memory was little more than a fuzzy-edged dream of being put to bed and kissed good night. She held on-to that good-night kiss fiercely; she was almost sure she hadn't just made it up. She was almost sure, too, that she had been trotted on a large booted foot, 'Nim, nim, nim, nim, this is the way the ladies ride.' That was the whole of her memory.

Her father and mother had both died. Pewmony,

A'nt Sally said. Penny had gone to live with A'nt Sally and Unc' Jeff, up a mountain draw way off from any-where: Four-Mile Draw, its name was. She was five then, and she had lived in Four-Mile Draw till last Christmas time, when A'nt Sally had died, and people had come and taken Penny down from the hills and stuck her into an orphanage. Since then Unc' Jeff had died, too.

The Home was terrible to Penny. She was like a wild pony suddenly forced to trot in harness all day and every day. The children giggled at her because she hadn't even seen a street car before and was frightened by a water faucet. The matron heaved exasperated sighs once an hour: 'The girl never wore a nightgown — just her under-clothes. And her table manners —!'

Then there were the women who came to the Home to look for children to adopt. When the first one came, Penny began to dream dreams.

'If you like the looks of one of them, you act as sweet as sirup,' Maybelle instructed her. 'Be wiping one of the little kids' noses, darn 'em; there's always one that needs it. Or something like that. Then they think you're kind and helpful.'

Maybelle was small and quick and fourteen. She had a reckless, impish little face and large mysterious eyes. Penny followed her with admiring wonder, for Maybelle seemed to know everything.

'Like this,' whispered Maybelle. She flipped open the top button of a small orphan, and then buttoned it with lingering fingers. The orphan twisted around and gaped at her when she patted him. She was so much more likely to pinch.

This first visitor was a comfortable woman with a double chin. Penny 'liked her looks,' even though she

was the kind who should keep to plain colors and wears
flowered prints and triple-strand necklaces instead. Her
face was a mother's face. Besides, Penny could see the
woman's car from the window, and on the back seat of it
a wire-haired terrier loudly demanded his mistress, with
only occasional panting pauses. Next to a father and
mother, Penny had always desired a dog. She would have
liked a cat; but a dog 'always loves a body so.'

The woman smiled approvingly at Maybelle as she
fussed around wiping noses and patting rompers. The
woman lingered over all kinds of children: little round
ones and tall skinny ones and rosy ones and pale ones.
But Penny she didn't even see.

Penny was so big. She was so red-headed and freckled
and lumpy. Her face had its points, she felt, looking
secretly into a pocket mirror. Though a funny color, her
eyes weren't homely: she'd seen pansies of the same
reddish-brown. And she had heard that some people
liked red hair; but not Penny's red hair. As to her
mouth, there was nothing wrong with it except the size,
and when she smiled experimentally it showed fine
teeth.

There wasn't much to smile about, though; and there
was a great deal to make a lonesome big-little girl cry
into her wadded-up pillow until it was hard to get her
breath without waking the girl in the next bed. To long
with every inch of you for a family of your own, and to
have nobody want you — ever ——

Then came Mrs. Henley. And wanted her.

Mrs. Henley was a member of the board of directors
of this small orphanage, and an important person. Mrs.
Henley was small and brisk and dark and had a high nose
and pearl earrings. At first Penny couldn't read the look

with which Mrs. Henley surveyed her, drawing back her lips from a hard white china smile.

'—— absolutely untrained,' the matron was saying dubiously.

'All — the — better!' nodded Mrs. Henley, pulling out her eyeglasses from a spring affair pinned to her shoulder and tapping the air with them. Even the air seemed to click when she hit it. 'In six months you will not know her, my dear woman. In six months she will scarcely know herself. And for what are we here, Miss Fleming, if not to make the world a little better than we found it?'

Penny went home with Mrs. Henley. A few weeks later Mr. and Mrs. Henley were called abroad on a business trip and returned Penny to the Home for safekeeping till they should be settled again — 'When I *believe*,' said Mrs. Henley, 'if conditions are as we expect them, we may decide to take the young girl into our home permanently.'

Even in those few weeks Penny had begun to doubt who and what she was. Surely not Penny Adams of Four-Mile Draw: wild Penny Adams, who could shinny up the tallest pine and ski the steepest slope and snare rabbits and catch shining strings of trout. No: a lump of a girl who was being clipped and prodded, without a moment's relenting, toward something like Mrs. Henley's glittering decisiveness. It wouldn't matter to Mrs. Henley how much of Penny was lopped off in the process. So much the better!

All her life long Penny would remember the prickling wretchedness of her first days in the Henley home: the opening pages of a month-long chapter of prickling wretchedness.

First, Mrs. Henley showed Penny her room. A chart hung on its wall, indicating with ruled lines and type-writing just how Penny should use her hours.

'Our precious, precious hours!' Mrs. Henley had clicked, baring her shiny white teeth in a businesslike smile.

A similar chart hung in the kitchen. Penny flinched from those charts, stealing glances at them when Mrs. Henley was not looking. Could she spell them out on the sly, so that the Henleys needn't know that she couldn't read them right off easy?

The kitchen was as white and shiny as Mrs. Henley's teeth. Not so much as a match was where it shouldn't be. — 'A place for everything and everything in its place,' smiled Mrs. Henley. — Naturally there was no dog lying under that gleaming porcelain stove. A dog would have been impossible in that spotless house.

'And now I am sure, Penny ——' Mrs. Henley paused as if she found the taste of the name unpleasant. She frowned and thrust out her lower jaw to click her teeth in meditation — 'We do not care for nicknames. We shall call you Pauline. I'm sure you will like to become one with us at once by helping prepare the dinner. Go up to the bathroom, Pauline, and wash your hands. Thoroughly. We do not use the kitchen for personal toilet.'

'Did you find the right towels?' Mrs. Henley asked briskly when Penny stole into the kitchen again. 'The rack which I showed you behind the door, Pauline?'

Penny had dried her hands furtively on her slip, not daring to sully any of the orderly ranks of towels. She looked at Mrs. Henley dumbly, trying to shrink. There-upon Mrs. Henley tapped her sharply between the shoulder blades. Mrs. Henley was not wearing a thimble, but the tap felt like a thimble, and Penny jumped.

'Buckles in, brooches out!' Mrs. Henley admonished playfully.

Helping prepare the meal was bad enough.

'Pauline!' said Mrs. Henley. Penny didn't recognize the name. 'Pauline!' Mrs. Henley repeated. Penny jumped, and found herself looking down at the fragments of two cups and saucers she had taken from the china closet.

'Tk tk tk!' Mrs. Henley clicked, and sighed. 'Brush them up, Pauline. Who would suppose you had a nerve in your body? A great girl like you.

'I was about to say,' she went on, while Penny coaxed the pieces into a dustpan clumsily, not being used to the long-handled contrivance — 'I was about to say that we do not throw the tea towels around our necks like that, Pauline.

'And Pauline!' she chided her smilingly a moment later, 'an abundant supply of clean holders hang in that container beside the stove. Never use the dishcloth for a holder again. It is a slovenly habit.'

'No, mom,' Penny stuttered. 'Yes, mom.'

'And Pauline! do stand on your two feet!' Mrs. Henley tightened her lips over the shining teeth in a thin smile of patience.

Penny came down abruptly. It was an old barefoot habit of hers, that of standing like a crane and scratching one knee with the other foot. Again she tried to droop into herself and so escape more attention. Again — tap-tap-tap — the finger beat its tattoo on her quivering spine.

'Buckles in!' said Mrs. Henley.

By the time dinner was served, Penny was jumpy.

The moment she sat down she emptied her glass of water over the fresh tablecloth. She had never used — she had never even seen — a tall stemmed goblet before.

'Hit's turrible tipsy,' she stammered, sopping at the pool with her damask napkin.

'*It* is easily tipped,' Mrs. Henley corrected.

'Yes, mom, hit shore is!' Penny agreed heartily.

Mr. Henley wasn't bad. He was an abstracted gentleman with pouched eyes and blue lips and thin hair combed over his bald spot. He was always taking a small memorandum book from his pocket and making hasty notes in it. He was the town's principal banker.

Penny had been hungry when she sat down. As soon as her plate was served, she picked up her knife and fork eagerly.

'Observe how Mr. Henley and I hold our silver, Pauline,' Mrs. Henley said wearily, 'and do as we do.'

Even more bitter was the next day. Penny was sent back to her room before breakfast to put on the dark blue serge school dress hanging in her closet. It was a neat dress, of good quality. Mrs. Henley had taken her measurements, and the dress fitted.

'A size eighteen frock,' Mrs. Henley informed Mr. Henley when they sat down to the table.

'She looks eighteen,' Mr. Henley said absently.

'But how absurd to try to have her look thirteen — a great girl like Pauline,' reasoned Mrs. Henley.

At school they tried Penny in the seventh grade, with children up to her shoulder. They tried her in the sixth; in the fifth; in the fourth. They gave her an intelligence test, to make sure that she was mentally fit.

Penny couldn't think how to explain to them about the little schoolhouse two miles from Four-Mile Draw:

a school with two or three mountain children as pupils.
Gilpin County was particular about its schools, and
would have one for a single child, if necessary. But when
the snows came, A'nt Sally kept Penny home; and when
it was very cold, and when there were heavy rains, and
when A'nt Sally had rheumatics, and when Unc' Jeff had
a touch of misery in his side.

A'nt Sally and Unc' Jeff Adams had no use for schools.
They themselves could not so much as scratch their
own names — 'And hain't we-uns made out good enough?'
It had been a proud day for Penny when she had been
able to spell out the headlines in a newspaper pasted on
the cabin wall.

She couldn't explain all this. She only slumped lower
in the third-grade seat and glowered sullenly at the wall
while the principal conferred with the teacher.

'If it was anyone but Mrs. Henley ——' said the
principal.

'Well, of course, since it is Mrs. Henley —— ' the
teacher shrugged.

At recess Penny stood in a corner of the school ground
in her size eighteen dress and wished with all her heart
for an earthquake to swallow her. At noon she broke
down and begged Mrs. Henley not to send her to the
school again. Hands hanging clenched at her sides, she
stood before Mrs. Henley, who knitted and rocked
swiftly.

'I can keep on learning myse'f to read and write, Mis'
Henley. I don't need no schooling, honest. I can work
harder for you-uns if I don't have to go.'

'One-two-three and purl,' frowned Mrs. Henley.

'Mis' Henley, I cain't go along with them little kids.
I cain't!' Penny's voice rose wildly.

Mrs. Henley ran the needles carefully into her knitting and laid it in her lap. She studied Penny calmly. 'I'm sorry, Pauline,' she said, 'but I think it is best for you to continue. I had considered engaging a tutor, but, no, I think not. I wish to see exactly what can be accomplished, in our public schools, with a case like yours. It is a trial, but by trials we grow, Pauline. We grow. Do not permit yourself self-pity. A great girl like you.'

These, in brief, were the first two days. The remaining twenty-two were not unlike them. Of course Penny grew hardened to some things; on the other hand, a chestnut bur under a horse's saddle grows no more comfortable as the hours pass.

'I won't go back yonder,' Penny declared to Maybelle when she had been returned to the Home. 'I rather die first.'

Maybelle stared curiously. She had never seen Penny's feelings uncovered before. 'Didn't lick you, did she?'

Penny shook her head. 'Nope. She — she won't leave me be.'

That didn't seem enough, so she tried again: 'She don't like me. Not even *like* me.'

She gave it up. You couldn't make Maybelle understand.

'Well, you got to get taken out by somebody else before this dame comes back, then,' Maybelle suggested. 'She didn't have you for keeps, did she?'

Penny shook her head, groaning. 'She aims to, though.'

Maybelle studied her with unflattering attention. 'We could fix you up a lot,' she decided. 'A permanent, now. If your hair was all curly and wavy, wouldn't it make an awful difference?'

Penny considered it thoughtfully. Almost every child

who was taken out had curls or large dark-fringed eyes or rosy cheeks or *something*. It seemed reasonable to suppose that waves and curls would help.

'They couldn't make it any *worse*, could they?' Maybelle demanded.

No, it didn't seem possible that anything could make it worse. The two girls scanned the advertising cuts in the small-town newspaper, and Penny's heart beat thickly as she visioned those lustrous waves, those round and luscious ringlet ends, on her own head. There was a special price, good for a limited period only. $1.98.

$1.98. Penny's eyes grew glassy with thought as she calculated rapidly on her fingers. That would leave a dollar and twenty-four cents of the hoard she had been gathering for years and years. Mostly by pennies she had gathered it, with a rare nickel and a rarer dime. Only once had she acquired a quarter: an unsuccessful fisherman had paid her two-bits for six darkly shining trout.

Penny took a deep breath of resolve and dedicated the major part of her life's savings to the winning of a home and a mother. It was worth trying.

II. GILDING THE PENNY

THE two girls slipped away on a Saturday morning and walked past the small beauty 'shoppe' three times before they could make their feet enter it. Penny's heart continued to stifle her during the hours of the ordeal. She was sustained only by the thought of the results.

She could imagine mothers irresistibly drawn by her burnished curls. There were several kinds of mothers that Penny especially liked, but almost any sort would do, as long as she was not hard and brisk and clicking; as long as she looked at Penny motherwise.

Penny's nose tickled saltily at that thought and she gulped and sniffed. Maybelle looked up at her from her movie magazine.

'Look at yourself!' she giggled.

Penny turned her eyes toward a mirror. No wonder Maybelle giggled. Penny's auburn eyebrows rose high in an expression of anguished inquiry, and her hair writhed upward like a hundred petrified snakes. ('You've got an awful heavy head of hair,' the beauty operator had grumbled, 'and finer than red hair generally is.')

At times the heat grew intense, and she sprayed her head with cool air from the nozzle the operator had left

with her, holding tensely still for fear she should pull
something loose and be burned or maybe electrocuted.
And at last, when she began to think she was forgotten,
the operator came briskly from another room.

'Now, girlie, I guess we can tend to you.'

With growing disappointment Penny watched the
undoing of those bundles. Multitudes of small red pick-
aninny frizzes burst upon her gaze. She turned alarmed
eyes on the operator.

'Now don't you worry, honey. Wait till I get through.'

She washed the red frizzes again and attacked them
with a furious comb that drove into Penny's skull, ram-
ming wave after wave into place. Miraculous scallops
were firmly pinned; curlers clamped on hair-ends; a tight
net cap tied on; an inverted nickel bowl like a lampshade
adjusted to pour warm air down Penny's neck. Another
half hour dragged by.

When the nickel bowl was swung aside and the net cap
lifted off, Penny held her breath. She gazed into the
mirror.

She saw an Easter egg, with moulded ridges and
painted scallops and varnished rings of red.

Dumbly she paid her $1.98.

'It don't look like I figgered,' she mumbled, as they
scurried Homeward.

'Well, naturally, it's got to be combed out,' Maybelle
reminded her.

Unseen by the powers, they gained the refuge of the
dormitory.

'Now are you game for the whole works, Pen?' Maybelle asked, her sea-green eyes sparkling.

'Huh? What whole works?'

'Like movie stars. Rouge and lipstick and mascara

— that black goo for your eyelashes. You've got no idea
what a difference that's going to make, Penny. Nobody
looks good with eyelashes and eyebrows you can't hardly
see.'

It was little that Penny knew about rouge and lipstick
and mascara. They had not been used in Four-Mile
Draw, and when Penny visited Central City with A'nt
Sally and Unc' Jeff, the old woman had called those
cosmetics by very hard names. If Mrs. Henley used
them, Penny did not know it. Penny's eyes rounded with
fear of the unknown.

'*Ev*-erybody uses them!' Maybelle scoffed at her fear.
'Everybody but these old horse-and-buggies at the
Home.'

Penny still stared doubtfully, and Maybelle stamped
her foot with angry impatience.

'Look, I try to help you and you're just a big cowardly
custard. What harm could it ever do anybody to have
pink cheeks and red lips and black eyelashes? You're a
scaredy-cat, that's all.'

'But where'll we get the stuff?'

Maybelle drew a deep breath of satisfaction and,
looking furtively around, pulled a bundle from under
her mattress.

'These aren't the regular bought stuff. Miss Fleming
took ours away — me and another girl's that used to be
here. So we fixed up some of our own. Gosh, but we
had to sneak! — Now this is rouge. Hold still.'

With a bold finger she applied a spot to Penny's
cheek, hurrying lest Penny should weaken. Doubtfully
she regarded it, sitting back with head on one side and
eyes half closed. Then she blended it out toward ear
and eye.

'That was what I was reading about in that movie magazine,' she murmured, 'while you were having your permanent. About where was the right place to put it to make you look younger and all.'

Still regarding the finished cheek dubiously, she attacked the other.

'It needs the mouth matched up to make it look right,' she decided, applying the rouge with a small paintbrush. 'Keep still, Pen. Kind of hold back your lips so I won't get it on your teeth. This is real fast color.'

Penny rolled her eyes toward the clock. 'You got to hurry, Maybelle,' she quavered. 'It's almost supper time. Maybe you better leave the black stuff till morning.'

'It — kind of needs the black stuff,' Maybelle insisted, dipping the brush hastily into the gummy darkness. 'Here, shut your eyes and hold this paper underneath your eyelashes. I wouldn't want to get any of the black onto your face. It don't wash off easy. — For goodness sake, hold still!'

'I think I better do the eyebrows,' she said, after a moment's survey.

She had traced the first brow when the bell began to clang. With haste she drew the other, and they hurried at once to the dining-hall. Her heart thumping, Penny took her place behind her chair at the oilcloth-covered table. At the clang of the gong she sat down. She reached for her fork — and dropped it with a nervous clatter.

'*Penny Adams!*' The matron's voice slashed through the subdued clink of china and silver. It smote, bleak yet thunderous, on Penny's ears. 'Penny Adams, stand up!'

Penny stood, her eyes fixed on her plate. The subdued click gave way to frozen stillness. The stillness was breathed upon by a sighing breeze of laughter. The breeze of laughter swelled into a gale. Penny stood burning with mortification and longing to cover her head with her arms and flee.

'Go and wash your face and comb out your ridiculous hair,' ordered the matron.

Blindly Penny stumbled through the dining-hall and up the stairs. Blindly she dragged her comb through the varnished ridges of her hair. She combed and combed, screwing up her face. Then she sped to the bathroom and soused her rouge and mascara with water, rubbing on soap with a lavish hand. She came up dripping, to look for the first time into the mirror. At sight of the image there she stood immovable.

Sharp black eyebrows winged surprisingly upward at the corners, one higher than the other. Lashes stood out in thickly gummed rays. Cheeks and mouth were streaked with a shade of red that warred against golden freckles and creamy tan, and warred still more violently against the mass of red wool that stood on end above them, defiance in every kink.

After a long, desperate stare, Penny tiptoed to the head of the stairs and listened. The eaters were still eating.

Dashing back, she poured Dutch Cleanser recklessly into her palms and scoured her face with it. Its pinkness showed that it had removed some of the color; but it was also removing some of the skin. Penny dared not persist.

She ran the bowl full of water and stood with her head in it, then wrung her hair with frantic hands, wrapped

it in a towel which she pinned turban style, and scurried
into the dormitory. She pulled on her nightgown over
her clothes, took off her shoes, and crept into bed.

When the girls began to come into the room, she was
lying with her face to the wall, the sheet over her head.
When the matron marched up, purpose in the stride of
her low-heeled oxfords, Penny seemed to be fast asleep.
Not in vain had she learned to feign that sound slumber
in the days of A'nt Sally's rawhide.

The matron stood looking down at her for a space of
minutes. It might have surprised Penny to see the telltale twist of the matron's lips. The matron might once
have been a plain little girl herself; she might have been
remembering the clothespin she used to snap on her nose
at night to persuade it to straightness and dignity.

But Penny did not peer through her thick lashes. She
risked nothing, but breathed steadily, eyes tight shut.
The matron passed on.

It seemed hours and hours that Penny lay there,
stubbornly pretending sleep until she really did drift
off into early slumber. When she woke, the dormitory
was darkened and still. She raised herself cautiously on
her elbows and looked up and down the gray length of
the room, where small mounds lay quiet or flopped and
muttered.

Satisfied that everyone slept, she tiptoed to Maybelle's
bed. Maybelle's innocent cheek was pillowed on her palm.

Penny shook her gently, holding a hand ready to clap
over her mouth.

'Lemme be!' Maybelle mumbled; and then, opening
her eyes, 'Oh, Penny! Oh — *Penny!*' An uncontrollable
snort of laughter escaped her, and the hand descended,
ungently.

'You shut up!' Penny commanded. 'Listen here. Had you ever tried thisyere roodge and the black stuff on anybody elset?'

'Penny, we thought sure it would work all right.'

'You tried it out on me, didn't you?' Penny gave the other girl a despairing little shake. 'D'you know if there's any way to get loose of it?'

Maybelle shook her head dumbly.

'And the hair. Feel of it.' Penny jerked off the soggy towel. Her hair lay in crinkly damp strings, but wherever a strand had begun to dry, it rose erect and kinky like twisted wire. 'Why would my hair have to do me this way?'

'Some hair don't take a permanent very good,' Maybelle said feebly. 'I guess they don't know how to manage the different kinds — little hick town like this.'

'It would have to be *my* hair,' Penny said bitterly. 'D'you reckon anything'll take out the kink?'

'They — they do say you just have to outgrow it.' Maybelle threw up her arm as if to ward off a blow. 'Honest, I never once thought it would turn out like that, Penny.'

Penny gave her a final shake, made a terrific face at her, and stole back to her bed. A little longer she lay there, thinking hard. One thing was sure: she would not meet the laughter of the kids again. She would not face the matron's icy frown.

Stealthily she gathered her belongings. They were few, for what she had acquired at Mrs. Henley's she left in her locker. Her comb, her toothbrush (she was proud of this first toothbrush), her broken-bladed jackknife, her old mouth-organ, her rabbit's foot, her underwear and nightgown — all these she wrapped in a faded print

dress. She pulled on her other dress, picked up her shoes
and her bundle, and went to the nearest window.

A mighty old woodbine climbed the wall close beside
it. With its stout woody trunk to break a fall, the ten-
foot drop looked slight to Penny. She opened the screen,
dropped her bundle and shoes to the ground, listened
tensely to make sure that their soft plop had not roused
anyone. Then she clambered out onto the sill and made
her way down.

The night terrified Penny. Sometimes when A'nt
Sally had been in a talkative mood, she had knocked the
ashes out of her pipe and sat staring into the fire while
she told tales of ha'nts and hoodoos and the terrors that
lay in wait in the darkness. Some of the stories Penny
sturdily rejected, but life was nevertheless woven full
of signs and omens: moons over left shoulders, spilled
salt, dogs that howled sinister warnings.

She made her way watchfully through the starry night.
Whenever a truck loomed on her sight, or the headlights
of any car bored a tunnel of light through the darkness,
Penny ran and hid. But a more breath-taking panic
came upon her when a small black animal slipped softly
across the road ahead of her. She stood still, in an
anguish of uncertainty.

'I hain't got the time to go clean back and start over
again,' she murmured. 'But — a black cat a-crossin'
my path! Great Jawns!'

She set down her bundle, squatted on the road, and
drew a cabalistic design with a stick. Then she rose and,
more or less by guesswork, hopped on one foot from section
to section of her sign. Rapidly she muttered the words
A'nt Sally had taught her. Solemnly she leaped and
turned. Three times she repeated the mystic formula
before she picked up her bundle and fared onward.

'I could'nt see to do it just right, but that had ought to take the hoodoo off,' she consoled herself.

As to trucks and cars she was even more cautious in the gray dawn than in the night. The world was no less lonesome, and it was a harder place to hide in. She could have danced with joy when the sun rolled rosily above the horizon and smoke rose straight into the blue sky from every chimney, and children played in the door-yards, and there was always at least one Sunday morning car in sight on the highway.

At the peak of the forenoon she came upon the dog by the wayside. He had evidently dragged himself there after a car had broken his leg. Such a thin, overgrown puppy! With such suffering eyes!

'You're so plain, too!' Penny said with passionate fellow-feeling.

She hunted a tin can out of the dry weeds, and brought him a drink from the irrigation ditch.

'You're homely as a mud fence,' she crooned, while he noisily lapped the water. 'But maybe you're nice, too, when anybody takes the trouble to find out.'

She was glad that she had doctored wounded wild things around Four-Mile Draw. A berry crate which she found in the weeds gave her strips of wood for splints. The sleeve of the rose-flowered dress made a bandage. She took her best safety pin to fasten it, for 'Great Jawns, the pore thing might have to get along for a coon's age with jest one bandage.' That left only a very shaky pin to fasten Penny's broken garter; and neither in Four-Mile Draw, nor in the Home, nor at Mrs. Henley's, had Penny learned the art of rolling her hose. 'But a stocking ain't much to a broken leg.'

When she had done her best for the fracture, she

dragged the dog to the shelter of a culvert, refilled the can and set it beside him, well propped so that he would not tip it over, and started away. He whined piteously. She walked faster, keeping her eyes ahead.

For a half mile she walked without glancing back. But when she stopped to invest five of her pennies at a hamburger stand, something moist touched her ankle, and she looked down with a start to see that the dog had dragged himself after her.

His eyes adored her. 'My life is in your hands, O Almighty and Glorious Being!' prayed those eyes.

'Great Jawns!' she protested, 'I'd have to tote you every step!'

And so she had done, the rest of the day. It was four o'clock when she reached the service station near Colorado Springs. The dog had grown heavier with every hour, until now Penny was near the end of her endurance. Desperately she turned from the cold-eyed service-station man to the long blue car.

That long blue car loomed like a haven to Penny: like a home and a family. The grandpa was gazing over his spectacles at her, puzzled but kindly. The little boy stared steadily at the dog, which lay with its bandaged leg sticking straight out, its tongue hanging. The little boy craned to look, whitening his painfully puckered forehead against the window. Penny gulped.

'Cain't you give me a lift to the next town?' she asked. 'I'd — I'd clean your otto for you. Or anything.'

'Certainly not,' snapped Mamma. 'We don't pick up hitch-hikers under any circumstances whatsoever. Not in any way, shape, form or manner.'

Penny stooped and gathered up the dog again. As

she straightened, two things happened. She saw her reflection in the station window: a large girl whose long rumpled dress made her look full grown, and whose face was a comic mask of red and black, topped with wild red wool.

And as if to give point to the enmity of the whole world, the decrepit safety pin opened again and gave her a vicious dig in the knee.

It was too much for the tired child. Without warning her face puckered and she burst into tears.

III. PICKING IT UP

THE blue car family stared at Penny in complete consternation. Grandpa broke the silence.

'Why, that ain't no young lady!' he ejaculated. 'It's jest a overgrowed kid. And she's plumb tuckered out.'

Penny had crumpled down and hidden her face against the dog's dusty body. He whined and wriggled round to lick her with a lavish tongue.

Grandpa reproached Mamma over his spectacles. But Mamma no longer needed reproaches: she was out of the car and bending over Penny. She may have looked like a toy fox terrier mothering a Saint Bernard pup; and the hand she laid on Penny's heaving shoulders may have hesitated. But her voice was motherly, and so were her eyes when Penny looked up into them. Mamma could be cold to a grown-up hitch-hiker. A desolate child was a different matter.

'Why, how old *are* you?' asked Mamma.

'I'm going on fourteen.'

'*Fourteen?*' Mamma looked dazed.

'I'll *be* fourteen, my next birthday,' Penny corrected honestly. 'Next Feb'uary.'

'*Thir*teen! My word! — Where do you live?'

'I — don't live nowheres. And if I got to go back to that old Home I jest as lieves die.'

'You run away from some orphanage or other?' guessed Papa, standing helplessly by. 'Where is it, little girl?'

'I jest as lieves die,' Penny choked.

The little boy began to cry. 'Let's take the g-g-girl home with us,' he begged, crying and coughing. 'And the doggie, Mamma. And the doggie.' He reached out and caught her skirt with skinny little hands. 'Please, Mamma, let's us.'

'We can't leave no young un gallivantin' round the country like this. 'Tain't anyways safe,' reasoned Grandpa.

'But we haven't enough gas to go back any distance,' the father worried.

He and the mother exchanged glances.

'We'll just have to take her along to Denver,' the mother concluded, 'and then notify this Home, wherever it is. — All right, then. Climb in.'

She eyed the dog as Penny clambered into the car with him.

'Is he shedding very bad?' she asked.

'I'll hold him on my dress,' Penny promised.

Penny sat in a happy daze while the car sped along the highway, swung closer to the long range of blue mountains, came into the region of pine trees, chugged and steamed up the Divide.

Junior — the little boy was called Junior — was beside her, staring into her face and giggling when the dog gave his hand a languid lick. Grandpa hitched forward whenever the car labored and choked.

'I bet you I could find out where that trouble's at,' he chirped to the front seat.

'We'd look fine, letting you get out and work with the engine, Father,' Mamma countered shortly.

'I always knew this car was a mistake,' said Papa. 'We picked a lemon when we bought this car. It was too good-looking for the price. I always knew there was a catch in it, but of course Virginia ——'

Virginia wouldn't give them any peace till they bought it, it seemed. Virginia, Penny learned, was the daughter. She hadn't come with the Smiths because she was invited to a house-party in the mountains. 'And catch Virginia stringing along with the family when the other kids are off on a lark.'

'That's only human,' soothed Grandpa. 'Young uns is young uns.'

'And birds of a feather flock together,' muttered Mr. Smith. 'But that bunch don't strike me as the kind of birds for Virginia. That Zip Spencer, especially.'

'Now, Papa, they're some of the most popular seniors at East, I'm sure,' Mrs. Smith objected. 'From nice families, all of them, Virginia says.'

Penny dozed off, sitting wedged in the middle of the back seat. Again and again she jerked awake. She answered questions with 'No, mom,' and 'Yes, sir.' She listened sleepily and patched together what she heard.

Mr. Smith was a bookkeeper in a large office, working only part time during the depression. Mrs. Smith was a beauty operator. Penny's eyes snapped open at that information, and she felt of her woolly waves with a remembering hand. Mrs. Smith owned an interest, evidently, in a small shop. Her business was slack, and so was business in Mr. Smith's office. He had been laid off for a week, and they had taken a trip during spring vacation.

On and on and on went the car. Once it had topped the Divide, it rolled smartly downhill for miles. Penny ate a banana and a Hamburger, giving the dog a bite for each of hers. She blinked drowsily at the lights that sprang up on each side of them and gradually clotted into a white blaze.

'Is they a circus, or what's all the crowd?' gasped Penny, brought wide awake by the glare.

'This here's Denver!' Junior singsonged, jouncing up and down. 'It's Denver. It's Denver. Purty soon you'll see my house, Penny.'

They rumbled between miles of houses, little ones and bigger and biggest, more than Penny had dreamed of, before the car stopped with a loud squeal of brakes in front of a building that looked magnificent to Penny. They all went in at a wide entrance, their arms piled high with belongings, and mounted two flights of carpeted stairs. Mr. Smith set down his tipsy pile and fished out his key ring. He threw open the door, and stuffy darkness greeted them. He reached in and pressed a button that sent the darkness leaping into light.

'Be it ever so humble!' he announced contentedly. 'But speaking of home, Mamma, hadn't I better go down to the telephone and send a night message to that Home the kid's run off from? They'll have notified the police, of course.'

'What's the address, child?' Mrs. Smith asked. And Penny unwillingly gave it.

'This is my house, Penny!' Junior was shouting, capering with pride. 'How d'you like it, huh, Penny? Huh, Penny? Huh?'

Penny stood squarely in the way, clasping the dog. The small apartment living-room dazzled her. With its

Oriental-pattern rug, its overstuffed set, its Maxfield
Parrish pictures, its beaded and rose-painted lampshades,
it was even more gorgeous than Mrs. Henley's, if not
so large.

'Bet you don't know where my bed's at, Penny!'
chanted Junior. 'Give a guess! It's in this room. I say
it's in this room. Penny, I say it's in this room. Where
d'you guess, huh?'

'Oh, for goodness' sake, hush!' ordered Mrs. Smith,
throwing open a window for air and turning on the steam
for warmth.

'But I want her to give a guess!' insisted Junior, hop-
ping around on one foot and holding up the other in his
hand.

Penny pointed a free finger at the davenport, deep
and soft.

'Uh-uh! That pulls out and makes V'ginia's bed.
She won't let me sleep with her. I'm a nervous child
and get nightbears. Give a guess where's mine, Penny.'

'Oh, do show her, Junior, and get it over with,' advised Mrs. Smith, moving wearily to put things away.
'But don't you dare take it down, you little imp. Virginia'll be coming, and ——'

Junior dashed at the door in one end of the room,
gruntingly tugged at it, and brought a bed revolving into
view, fully made, and standing, as Penny thought, on
its hind legs. Blithely disregarding his mother's com-
mand, he brought it down on all fours and stood grinning
proudly at Penny's astonishment.

'Put it up this minute, Junior,' his mother ordered
sharply. 'Virginia's likely to be coming any time.'

She herself was studying Penny, and Penny involun-
tarily scrooged behind a table and spread her hands over
her hair. Mrs. Smith laughed.

'Poor child!' she said, 'who on earth gave you that permanent?'

'Ain't they a thing that'll take the kink out?' begged Penny.

'Not so far as I know,' Mrs. Smith said regretfully. 'You can brush it a lot, and use hot oil, and that ought to make it grow faster. And tonight — as soon as you've taken a nice hot bath — we'll rub cream on your face and vaseline into your eyelashes and eyebrows. The red and black won't be permanent, anyway.— No beauty shop on earth gave you a facial like that?'

'Facial? The roodge and the black stuff? No'm. It was me and another girl.'

'What ever possessed you to do such a thing?'

'I wanted to look nice,' Penny muttered.

Mrs. Smith gave her a brisk pat. 'Well, now you scoot along into the bathroom and get a good bath,' she said, glancing at the mantel clock. 'Here. I'll find a clean towel for you.'

Before Penny could reach the bathroom, a triple knock sounded at the door, and Junior darted to open it to a troop of young people.

Penny looked this way and that and turned her back. She could not have these smart, nonchalant, beautiful boys and girls see her in her comic mask. Even with her back turned, she could feel their eyes upon her, while they politely greeted the Smiths: 'How do you do, Mrs. Smith?' 'Good evening, Mr. Smith.'

'Well, hello, folks,' a clear young voice cried breezily. 'You just get home? — Oh, sure we had a good time. Did you? — Good heavens, who *is* it? This isn't Hallowe'en.'

Penny felt her cringing shoulders grasped by impera-

tive small hands, and she was wheeled around to look
down into a laughing small face. The laugh was wiped
away by blank incredulity.

'Why — why, I thought it was Dick. He's — he's
always monkeying. I certainly beg your pardon ——'

'Virginia, this is Penny Adams' — Mrs. Smith, who
had tried to edge in a word before, now succeeded in
making this introduction — 'Penny, I know you're too
tired to meet strangers tonight. Run along, child.'
She shoved her gently into the bathroom and closed the
door.

Penny turned on the water in a steamy blast, but she
could still hear stifled laughter and wisps of talk through
the light walls. Her face burned, and slow tears oozed
from her hot, tired eyes.

'Mother, what under the sun?' the cool voice demanded. 'Has this family gone absolutely nuts?'

('I feel like a cow!' Penny addressed the steamy bathroom in passionate silence. 'A great big painted-up cow.
But Mis' Smith — ain't she kind?')

The outside door banged and there was stillness for a
moment. Then Virginia's voice rose, clear and penetra-
ting.

'And that awful, smelly dog, too. I was never so embarrassed in all my life. What Zip Spencer's going to
think of me now — I don't care: I tell you it isn't fair
to make me ridiculous. — No, she can't either hear me;
and, anyway, I don't care if she does ——'

The high voice was trembling, but it went on, punctu-
ated by remonstrances in a lower key, until it was
muffled by the closing of another door. Someone had
evidently urged Virginia on into a more distant room.

IV. THE HOUSE OF SMITH

PENNY occupied the door-bed that night and Junior, delighted with anything new, curled up like a puppy on a pallet in his parents' room.

Penny slept heavily, though she seemed always struggling up through strange and dreadful dreams. She was wakened next morning by the bang of a door and a petulant voice beyond it. Her sleep-blurred eyes sought the Maxfield Parrish pictures and the beaded lampshades. She was really here; not in the Home; not at Mrs. Henley's; not plodding endlessly along the oil-striped band of cement highway.

She listened to the voices from the kitchen, her sharp hearing aided by the thinness of the partitions. Smells of bacon and coffee seeped through those walls, and so did words and whole sentences.

'You care more about a great ———'

'Shh!'

'Well you do. You care more about a girl you never saw till yesterday than you do for your own daughter.'

A subdued crackle of replies, broken by brisk steppings to and fro.

'But, Mother, I ask you! Do you want me to go

around with nice people, or don't you? — Fat chance I have, at the best. Not even a decent living-room to entertain them in. — You must think I *like* to run Granddad off to the kitchen, and you and Dad. And there's Junior, yawning and whining around by nine o'clock and howling by ten. And now this ——'

The kindliness of Mr. Smith's voice had acquired an edge when he broke in: 'Now look here, daughter. Kindly remember who it was that wouldn't give us any peace till we took this apartment. We all said it was crowded. — Lord knows we didn't have much home life before, Mamma working at the shop every day and you gadding every minute you were out of school. But now it's like housekeeping in a canary bird's cage.

'We all said it was crowded. You knew it when you nagged us out of our wits about it. Just because it had more class and was hanging on to the edge of a swell residence district. You can't have class and comfort, see; not on our wages.'

'Yes, your wages! You don't get half what you're worth, Dad. Hoot's father and Betty's — they haven't half your sense, but they've got — oh, a lot of bluff — and they pull down loads of money. If you'd only stand up for your rights, Dad! I'm so sick and tired of being poor!' Virginia wailed. 'And now you have to lug home this great ——'

'For goodness' sake, hush, Virginia!'

'Well of course you're going to send her back to her old Home by the first train. My heavens, you've simply got to!'

Rap-rap-rap! The partition could not even muffle the purposeful rap of a knife-handle. And now Mr. Smith's voice was all edge. Penny, lying on her stomach, rose to her elbows and listened, wide-eyed.

'Since when has our seventeen-year-old daughter been handing out the orders in that high-and-mighty style?' he asked icily. 'Got to send her back, have we? Now listen here, Virginia Smith: While your mother and I are slaving like we are to put clothes on your back and keep you in school, it's us that says what's going to happen, see? Anyway, once in a blue moon it is. And that poor kid's going to — stay — right — here.' He underlined the words with three more blows of the knife handle. 'At least for the present,' he added, as if his declaration of authority might have carried him too far.

'Till we can get that terrible paint off and maybe tame down her hair,' Mrs. Smith added.

Penny drew a deep breath and collapsed into her pillow. That was *some*thing. She lay still for a few blissful minutes before she rose and drew on her clothes, taking her one change of underthings, clean though forlorn, from her bundle, and putting on her dusty runaway dress distastefully. She was sitting on the edge of the bed wondering what to do next when Mrs. Smith opened the door a crack and peered in.

'Oh, good morning, Penny!' Her greeting had the cheerfulness that often hides unease. (How much had Penny overheard?) 'You come out to breakfast any time. Grandpa and Virginia are having theirs. Papa and I have to go to work now. We'll talk things over tonight, and write a letter to the Home. Papa thinks maybe they'll let you stay a while and make us a little visit. Would you like that?'

Penny nodded, her throat choking back her words. Then she went shyly into the kitchen. Grandpa, neat and well-combed, though collarless and coatless, sat at the small table in the alcove, and Virginia, in an orange flannel bathrobe, opposite him. From his folded rug under the gas stove the dog thumped his tail in greeting.

Grandpa gave Penny a slow, smiling nod and hitched over to make room for her on the painted bench. He waved his fork at the platter of bacon and eggs in front of him, while he hastily chewed the mouthful he had just taken.

'V'ginia, you switch on the toaster and put in a couple slices for Penny,' he said, his voice husky with bacon. 'You take coffee, Penny?'

'Yes, sir, thank you,' said Penny, watching Virginia with shy admiration.

Virginia shrugged ever so slightly at her grandfather's request, snapped on the electricity with a thrust of a red-flashing finger-tip, and slapped two slices of bread onto the metal leaves that let down on each side of the toaster. 'This toaster's about kapoot, Granddad,' she observed. 'I never saw such a house. Everything's always coming to pieces.'

'I guess mebbe I can fix this up so it'll work a while longer,' promised Grandpa.

Virginia broke another bit of toast, jeweled it with orange marmalade, ate it, sipped a cup of black coffee. Penny thought her little neck the prettiest she had ever seen: a small, smooth column with a delicate hollow at the base. Penny watched wistfully, wishing Virginia's curved dark lashes would lift and Virginia's small set mouth would smile across the narrow table. But Virginia set down the emptied cup, slid out from her side of the table with a general nod of good-bye, and hurried to dress for school.

'Oh, tunket!' Grandpa exploded softly, 'that toast!'

A wisp of acrid smoke curled out of the toaster. Grandpa stood up and reached over to open it and turn the too-brown slices.

The door creaked open and Junior pushed through, scrubbing his eyes with his fists and twisting his face in a huge yawn. Junior's hair was matted like fur; his faded pajamas gaped, buttonless, on his thin little body; his bare toes curled up from the cold linoleum. He blinked from Penny to the dog under the stove, shook with a spasm of coughing, and then smiled elfishly, bewitchingly, a smile with a hole in it where an upper tooth was out. He made a little rush at Penny and snuggled up against her.

'See if you can't get a decent breakfast down him, Penny, sence he's took sech a shine to you,' Grandpa suggested. 'Mostly he don't eat enough to keep a fly alive, the little shaver don't.'

Penny buttered a slice of the toast, which had announced itself with another trail of smoke, spread it lavishly with marmalade, and handed it to Junior. He ate it slowly, turning wide eyes from her entertaining hair to the dog, which lay with his nose on his paws and his eyes pleadingly following each mouthful of food. Junior slipped off the end of the bench and took him a morsel of toast, which he snapped up hungrily.

'Now — now — now!' Grandpa urged. 'Little boys got to eat their breakfast or they won't grow to big strong men. Eat your nice bacon and egg, Junior.'

'Nasty ole bacon and egg,' Junior whined, his face abruptly losing its interested smile. He took a bite of bacon, chewed it with open mouth expressive of acute disgust, and manufactured a cough which grew into a real one and left him limp against Penny's shoulder. Grandpa looked at him anxiously.

'Penny, would you mind reaching into that paper
sack in the vegetable rack behind the door?' he asked.
'Like a banana, Junior? They ain't so ripe, are they?
But the young un's got to have *sumpn* to eat.'

Junior ate the banana, making little jabs at the dog
with his bare toes and giggling till he coughed again.

'Tunket, Junior, if it ain't half after eight!' Grandpa
exclaimed, looking up at the green alarm clock. 'You
hustle yourself into your clothes, young man, or you're
going to get late for school again.'

Junior swallowed the last chunk of banana with exaggerated gulps and sauntered into the other room.
Penny could hear him singing and coughing as he dressed,
playing with the water as he washed, and making fre-
quent excursions to his box of playthings throughout
both processes. He broke a shoe-lace, and Grandpa
had to knot and lace the pieces for him. He scrambled
down the stairs in a wild hurry twenty minutes later,
buttoning his shirt as he went.

Grandpa turned back from the door with a deep sigh.
'I alluz feel kind of like a cyclone's passed over, time the
folks is off,' he confessed. 'I generally takes a squint at
the *News* to get my breath before I do up the dishes and
the beds.'

'I'll redd up this morning,' Penny offered eagerly.
She felt relaxed and at ease, almost talkative, with
Grandpa.

'I guess likely you can find where things is at,' Grandpa consented. 'You best give your dog the scraps, hadn't
you?'

It was fun to wash the dishes, with plenty of soap and
water and nobody to watch her with critical eyes. Dishwashing at the cabin had been a rough-and-ready matter,

but Mrs. Henley had taught her proper methods in that prickly month.

'Kind of short on dish towels,' Grandpa apologized over his paper. 'She don't have no time to look after sech things. Seems like a woman can't get a holt of the handle and really run her house when she's got to get out and earn money too. 'Tain't right.'

'Cain't I rench out some things, after I've redd up?' Penny asked diffidently. 'Is there tubs?'

Grandpa jerked his thumb toward the stationary one with its cover forming the drainboard.

'Ain't things handy?' Penny admired.

'Handy!' Grandpa snorted. 'If you like everything to be making out it's what it ain't. If you like to turn your bed into a sofy and a door — tunket! a *door!* — and set down to meals by turns or else give the parlor table a yank and stretch it out to eat on. And all for show. Faucets leaking and doors squeaking and windows rattling and every shade in the place crooked. Not a sliver of good honest quality in the whole shebang.'

Penny could find no answer to that. She disappeared, and came out presently in the faded print dress with its sleeve missing. She carried the dress she had taken off, and a slim little garment, all clever biases.

'D'you reckon she'd mind if I washed up thisyere dress of hers? She left it laying on her bed.'

She was scrubbing away, with equal degrees of enthusiasm and awkwardness, and Grandpa was tinkering with the electric iron, when Junior burst in, crying and coughing.

'She sent me home,' he said, hurling himself dramatically on his grandfather. 'She says I got hoop and cough and I got to stay home in a korromteen.'

'Whooping cough? I ain't heard no whoop,' Grandpa said mildly.

'I did one, though,' Junior claimed with mournful pride. 'This morning. Sumpn fierce.'

In spite of her sympathy for Junior, Penny had never known so happy a day. She still slid past all mirrors with averted eyes, however. Her face was fading rapidly, but the change had not yet worked any great improvement: she looked like a drawing in colored chalks, half erased. And the crinkly masses of her hair had mounted higher and higher as she worked over the steamy tub.

But she was happy with Grandpa and Junior, and she pretended she was there for keeps and that they were her grandpa and her little brother. When she had finished 'redding up,' she and Junior bathed the dog carefully in the laundry tub, despite his shivering struggles. She ripped out her other sleeve to make a clean dry bandage. And while he limped around in circles trying to escape his own wetness, they discussed a name for him. Penny was ironing her dress and Virginia's, now. Ironing was another art she had learned since she came down from Four-Mile Draw. A'nt Sally thought it was enough if clothes were washed.

Penny had thought of the name Adam, so that the dog would seem more like a relation. Junior, on the other hand, was a follower of the comic strips, and solemnly enjoyed Uncle Elby and his blundering dog. He begged for the name Napoleum.

'Adam ain't no dog's name!' he pouted.

And when Penny hesitated, he broke down in such a storm of crying and whooping that she hastened to give in.

'I had water sprinkled onto me,' Junior suggested,

his breath catching in left-over sobs, 'when I was Christianed. I was Christianed James Henry Junior Smith. Let's us Christian Napoleum.'

He solemnly dipped his fingers into a saucepan of water and dripped them over the shrinking victim. And then three jabs sounded at the doorbell. Penny stood tense a moment, and dashed for the one clothes closet while Junior ran to open the door. She could hear Virginia and one of Virginia's friends, and she stayed hunched there, patiently waiting till the visit should be over.

The closet door opened a crack, and Junior peered in.

'I found you, Penny!' he whispered hoarsely. 'Say, Penny, I got to be amused, and Ginny won't amuse me while that ole Dot Hooper's around. Say, Penny, you want to hear how good I can read in my reader?'

He edged in, showed her how to turn on the electric light, and curled himself against her knees to read.

'"Once upon a time,"' he began, '"they was four little rabbits. Their names was Flopsy, Mopsy, Cottontail and Peter."'

With suspicious fluency he raced through the story, coming out at least four words ahead at the end of each page. Penny followed him with solemn attention, right to the 'bread and milk and blackberries for supper.'

'Now you,' he commanded, climbing over into her lap.

'"A mer-chant had done a good bus-i-ness,"' Penny began reading obediently.

'Why, you don't read very good, do you?' Junior demanded, wriggling around to stare into her face.

Penny shook her head, but plodded on, keeping her place with her forefinger.

Dresses drooped from sacheted hangers: Mrs. Smith's dresses and Virginia's. The men's few suits hung stiffly, Mr. Smith's smelling faintly of tobacco. The shelves were stacked to their very tops, for it was the only closet in the apartment.

The place gave Penny a comforting sense of intimacy: you couldn't get much deeper into a house than this. She didn't mind if it was a little close and a little over-warm, and a little too strongly scented with leather and rubber from the rows of shoes and galoshes. She read, and Junior dreamily listened and twisted a lock of her hair as he liked to twist his mother's. His mother never had time to hold him any more.

After a long while, the door opened a crack again, but neither of them noticed. Penny was reading a poem:

'"Hun-derds of but-ter-flies on the lawn;
    But on-ly one moth-er the wide world o-ver."'

Junior jumped out of her lap. 'Oh, Ginny! Me and Penny's been reading, and I can read better than her and I got hoop and cough and we named the dog Napoleum.'

Penny looked up, startled. Tears were running down her nose. She sniffed and crooked her arm to wipe them off. 'It was jest thisyere sorry piece in the book,' she mumbled.

Virginia's clear little face was serious. Seldom had Penny seen laughter or smiles upon it, but this seriousness was unlike its usual sort. Virginia opened the door wider, holding the dress Penny had laundered.

'It's too stuffy in here,' she said soberly. 'And anyway Dot's gone. Granddad says you did up my dress. It's the dickens to iron, isn't it? Thanks, Penny.'

V. THE ELEVATOR GOES UP
—AND DOWN

TO PENNY, the next weeks were a blissful and unexpected gift. She worked hard; but nobody nagged; and while she and Grandpa and Junior were alone, she could pretend she was in her own home. It was fun, anyway, to work with modern equipment.

Grandpa had to tinker with the vacuum sweeper almost every day; it was old and decrepit and always shorting. Yet pushing it along over the rugs and watching it gobble up the shreds and dust was vastly different from sweeping A'nt Sally's splintery floor with a stub of a broom and sending the sweepings flying out the one door of the cabin. And it was much pleasanter than using Mrs. Henley's shining instrument under Mrs. Henley's watchful eye.

To be sure, Penny made mistakes. The brush of the sweeper caught the fringe of the Oriental-pattern rug and had chewed off six inches before she could stop it. She emptied the kitchen dustpan unconcernedly out of the window until a wrathful tenant below complained to the janitor. She laboriously cleaned all the knives, forks, and spoons (with Dutch Cleanser), collected them by kinds and patterns, and neatly bound them in bundles with the rubber bands that came around the daily papers. Next day she was horrified to find the silver darkly tarnished by the rubber.

In the evenings and over week-ends, she was timorously silent, with a silence that appeared almost sullen. At such times she did nothing on her own initiative.

Her red-gold eyelashes and eyebrows were themselves again, and her lips and cheeks free from the raucous rouge. Her hair Mrs. Smith had shingled in the back; the rest of it she had cut into as good a boyish bob as possible, and she set Penny the task of brushing it two hundred strokes a day. She bought her a wash silk dress at a sale, so that she would have something suitable to wear outdoors, and a beret to cover her hair.

Penny treasured the dress as something miraculous. It looked fourteen years old instead of eighteen, and it was of a shade of peacock blue that discovered remarkable qualities in her own coloring. As far back as she could remember, she had never before owned a pretty dress.

Her improved appearance was not wholly a delight to her. She was beginning to study the mirror anxiously, for the Smiths had said they would keep her till she looked respectable again.

A case worker had come out from the Associated Charities, inquiring into the conditions in the home, and looking up Mr. and Mrs. Smith's positions and standing. She had evidently reported favorably to Miss Fleming. Miss Fleming wrote that they might keep Penny at least until Mrs. Henley's return from Europe, and she told them what a rare opportunity Mrs. Henley's home would ultimately offer a girl like Penny: music and travel and college, if she made good.

Even Virginia had ceased prodding them about letting

her stay for a visit. Virginia seemed to understand about Mrs. Henley better than Maybelle had, and, besides, she had grown to like Penny a little. Penny would do anything for Junior, and though Virginia supposed she loved her small brother, she found him a serious nuisance. Penny took the nagging bother of him from her hands. More important, Penny would do anything for Virginia, and gazed upon her delicate and capable prettiness with her heart in her eyes. As Napoleum looked at Penny, so Penny looked at Virginia.

'Hardly know you for the same girl we picked up a month ago!' commented Mr. Smith, on a Saturday afternoon when she was dressed in her blue frock, ready to go downtown with Grandpa, since Virginia was for once willing to stay home and look after Junior.

Penny looked anxiously from him to Virginia and swallowed hard. 'You-uns — oh, cain't you-uns leave me stay for six months?' she whispered. 'If Miss Fleming would let you? I can do more chores than I been. And if I was to go back now, as soon as that Mis' Henley came back, she —— I can do heaps more of the chores, and I don't have to eat as much as I been.'

Mr. Smith cleared his throat and looked at Virginia.

'I don't see why not, Dad,' she said, applying scarlet lacquer to the delicate ovals of her nails. 'For six more months.'

Penny flashed her a glance of passionate gratitude. She knew quite well that she had relieved Virginia of tasks that Virginia had half done or done not at all. But she wanted Virginia's tolerance at any price.

'Well, I'll tell you what, Penny,' said Mr. Smith — 'that is, if Mamma agrees. If the boss gives me a raise, we'll let that settle it.'

'Oh, Dad, are you going to ask for a raise?' Virginia demanded. 'It's about time. I should think those old men would be ashamed of themselves, the way they've cut you and cut you.'

'It's bad, with Mamma not even making expenses, hardly. Folks can't afford to be beautiful any more, I guess,' he chuckled mildly. 'Yeh, I'm going to beard the lion in his den. This very afternoon.' He squared his stooping shoulders and tightened his gentle mouth to pretended grimness.

'Granddad,' Virginia interrupted, 'did you remember about the iron's going kapoot again?'

'I shouldn't wonder if I could tinker it up myself,' Mr. Smith offered, a certain eagerness in his voice, 'while you're gadding, Paw.'

'Now, now, Son!' Grandpa rebuked him. 'That's my job. Only thing the old man's good for, these days. You leave it till I git home. You'll leave it, won't you?'

'Sure, Paw, I'll leave it,' Mr. Smith conceded. 'Likely I'd fix it so good you couldn't do anything with it, if I did try.'

Penny could see that there was a wistfulness about him. She had already wondered whether Mr. Smith didn't *like* to tinker. He watched his father, over the top of the newspaper he was supposed to be reading, with such rapt attention.

The walk downtown from the apartment was nothing to Penny, used to mountain trails and enthralled by these vistas of streets lined with apartment houses of brick and stone and stucco, lawns greening over with spring, trees and bushes swelling their leaf buds. But for the old man it was a long pull. Penny had continually to shorten her steps to match his. Four car fares, though, were well worth toiling to save. They amounted to more than thirty cents. And thirty cents would do wonders.

They divided the sum equally, and shopped at three of the big red-and-gold-fronted 'dime stores,' before they had spent it all. The dime store offered everything Penny could imagine, and more. By the time they had traversed all the aisles of all three and exhausted their wealth, Grandpa was getting shaky in the knees and blue around the lips; so they went to one of the department stores — the Denver — and sat in easy-chairs in the balcony, watching with wonder the surging crowds below.

Grandpa had used one of his nickels for candy: smooth golden circles of butterscotch. 'We'll passel 'em off into fourths,' he said.

Penny spread a clean handkerchief on her lap, emptied them out, and counted them. 'Ain't we-uns lucky?' she beamed. 'They's eight!'

They each took two, and Grandpa folded the top of the paper bag tight and thrust it into his pocket, and they sat and savored the satiny sweet rounds, sucking them contentedly.

'Don't you want to ride that there escalator now, while I rest a mite longer?' suggested Grandpa, who had noticed her steadfast gaze at the moving staircase.

'Reckon I do!' she murmured.

'Don't you be in no hurry. Jest take everything in,' Grandpa said indulgently. 'Run across the street to the May, if you want, and try the revolving doors. They're quite a show, them revolving doors. Only watch and walk by the lights when you cross. And they's elevators, too: scare you out of a year's growth, some of 'em. Lots of free shows, town as big as Denver.'

Penny rode up on the escalator, walked timidly down the stairs, rode up again. She soared to the top floor on the elevator, and dropped to the basement, clutching the rail with delicious terror at the downward swoop.

Venturing out into the street, she stood long on the curb, fascinated by the shift of the traffic lights. At length when the green blinked on for the tenth time, she started across with the crowd, only to be swept back on a wave that surged out of the way of a stream of cars rolling interminably around a corner. She was gasping when she gained the opposite curb.

Two blocks down the street she found the store with the revolving doors Grandpa and Junior had described. She hung back, watching shopper after shopper enter the deadly looking whirligig, before she drew a deep breath and hurled herself into it.

'I shore wish A'nt Sally could have seen thisyere!' she thought, walking through to another door, and around and in at the revolving one again. 'Wouldn't her eyes have bugged out!'

A'nt Sally and Unc' Jeff had made their way Northwest in the seventies, and had thereafter never left the heart of the Rockies. A'nt Sally had been sure folks were mocking her when they told her of modern wonders. While Penny had lived with her and Unc' Jeff, she, too, had been bound to a narrow circle of hills. Once in a long while they had hitched the old mule to the older cart and gone to Central, where there were electric lights and telephones and a movie theater. Those visits had marked the extent of Penny's contact with the outside world and with the twentieth century.

Here, too, Penny rode the elevator until the uniformed girl operator looked back at her over her shoulder too inquiringly. Then she braved the traffic and rejoined Grandpa, who sat nodding in his chair above the hurly-burly.

They reached home, tired but happy, just in time to let Virginia go out to a dinner, and Penny hurried to pare the potatoes and start the creamed dried beef.

Dinner over, she and Grandpa brought in their booty, in small brown dime-store envelopes, and spread it out among the emptied pie-plates on the table.

'Oh, Penny! Oh, gee! you got a litty-bitty blue auto!' shrieked Junior. 'I didn't know big girls liked little autos. A blue Packard — that's one kind I ain't got,' he added.

Penny shoved it over to him, her teeth flashing in a transient smile, her pansy-brown eyes aglow with happiness.

'It's yourn,' she said.

From her other envelope she drew out a card with a butterfly pin. This way and that she turned it, to catch the light.

'Looked to me like it was mighty sightly,' she said hopefully, 'for a dime.'

'It *is* pretty,' Mrs. Smith commented absently. Mrs. Smith ate and worked in a state of abstraction, as if she were constantly adding up rows of figures without getting any results. 'Very pretty, Penny.'

'You — you reckon she'll fancy it?' Penny's words stumbled with eagerness.

'She?' Mrs. Smith paused in scraping dishes.

'Her. V'ginia,' Penny said, flushing.

'Child, didn't you get a thing for yourself?'

Penny wished she could explain the treat it was for her to be able to bestow blue Packards and iridescent jewels on those she adored.

'Papa,' said Mrs. Smith, leaving her rows of figures for a minute, 'she's spent all her fifteen cents on Junior and Virginia.'

Mr. Smith smiled at Penny, and sat watching Grandpa, who was shaking out his own treasures. Grandpa spilled out half the butterscotch circles into Junior's cupped hands, and then complacently displayed a gadget for holding a safety razor blade so that it might be used without cut fingers for a handy household tool.

'Can't see why I couldn't have figgered out sumpn like that myself. Little idea like that — might bring a man thousands,' Grandpa approved.

Mr. Smith went on watching, as distrait as Mrs. Smith. While Penny was doing up the dishes, and Mrs. Smith worked on a class-day dress for Virginia, and Junior ran his new car busily around among their feet, and Napoleum lay under the table thumping the floor with his tail, Grandpa attacked the problem of the defective electric iron.

Penny loved hours like this. If Junior hadn't been kept away from his playmates by whooping cough, he would have been out racing the streets, till at eight or nine, Mrs. Smith had called three or four times: 'Junior! Hoohoo, Jooonior!' Virginia was never at home, except once in a while with some of the 'gang.' But this was very like Penny's warm secret picture of a family; and she was in the midst of it.

To be sure, Mrs. Smith was tired and abstracted and Mr. Smith was somber. He was often somber, but tonight he should have been twinkling-eyed; he should have been joking his kind, stale jokes, if he had asked for a raise and received it. That thought lay icy cold at the pit of Penny's joy.

He sat watching his father take the iron apart, the old hands deft and knowing, though they trembled. Penny saw Mr. Smith's own fingers twitch in small, unconscious movements.

'You're good, Paw,' he approved, when Grandpa had finished and attached the iron and held his hand over its flat surface, nodding contentedly when it began to heat. 'Seems like mechanics was born in us Smith men.'

'Us!' Grandpa mocked gently. 'You gone a step higher, Son, jest like your maw alluz meant you should. Tunket! how she did hate and despise to have you tinker anything, didn't she? She was so scaret you'd get to be jest another greasy mechanic in overhalls, like your paw and grandpaw before you.'

Mr. Smith didn't smile. 'There's Virginia at the door, Junior. Run let her in. Go *along*. — Remember how bad I wanted toy trains? And a little steam engine?'

'I hankered to get you those kind of do-dads, Son. She made me get you books. And a dinky typewriter. Recollect?'

Mr. Smith laughed shortly. 'And was she ever sore when I took that typewriter to pieces and couldn't get it together again! Had parts enough left over for another machine.'

'Well, I guess your maw knew best.' Grandpa sighed and polished the bald crown of his head with a slow palm. 'If it hadn't been for the world's turning upside down like it has, I guess you'd been consider'ble further along than you are; but at that ——'

'At that,' Mr. Smith said heavily, 'as a bookkeeper I'm a pretty fair chauffeur, if you want to know the truth.'

They all stared at him, arrested by his tone. Virginia, coming into the kitchen, closed the door.

'Dad,' she demanded, 'did you? Did you get your raise?'

Penny held her breath.

Mr. Smith's shoulders sagged as if flinching from an expected blow. 'No, Virginia, I didn't get any raise.'

'Dad! I bet you didn't ask for it! I bet you got humble again and didn't ask for it. Did you ask for it, Dad?'

'No, Virginia, I didn't.'

'I might have known it,' she stormed, half crying with disappointment.

'Because the boss beat me to it.'

'You mean — ?'

'I mean when I got my pay envelope it had a two weeks' notice alongside the check. I'm fired.'

VI. UNTO THE HILLS

FIRED!

Mrs. Smith dropped her tissue-paper pattern with a soft rustle and sat staring. Penny went on washing the cooking dishes. After her first glance at Mrs. Smith's face, she kept her eyes turned away; but her hands moved slowly, softly, and her ears listened.

'Dad! Oh, Dad!' wailed Virginia. 'Oh, Dad — maybe it'll mean you'll get something better. They didn't appreciate you. Maybe it was time you cut loose from such a poor job. It *was* a poor job.'

'Something better.' Mr. Smith laughed without mirth. 'This isn't 1929, Virginia. I guess you've forgotten what year it is.'

Virginia cleared her throat. 'Well, — I've got to go, folks. I'm — awfully sorry, Dad. I'll — be seeing you.'

Her voice wavered on the last words. She stood poised an instant, her back toward them, and then was gone.

'Don't you feel bad, old girl,' Mr. Smith comforted his wife. 'I guess we won't starve.'

'Henry,' said Mrs. Smith, 'I hate worse than ever to tell you now: but we'd just decided to shut up shop. We're in the red a little worse every month, and it don't

look like sense ——' Her voice was muffled in another
rustle, as if her head had plunged down into the tissue
paper.

'Whatsa matter, Mamma?' whimpered Junior, scram-
bling to his feet. 'Mamma, don't do that! Did you stick
yourself with a pin? Don't do that, Mamma!'

Grandpa shuffled his feet helplessly, and Penny stood
with her hands in the cooling dishwater, staring at the
wall. For it needed no words to make it clear that without any income at all the Smiths could not afford to keep
a chance orphan any longer.

Grandpa and Penny went to church next morning.
Grandpa missed the homely friendliness and warmth of
the little churches he had always known, where everyone
was acquainted with everyone else; but a Sunday without any church at all he could scarcely have imagined.
The old man and the young girl had sat side by side in
the cushioned pew these Sunday mornings. This experi-
ence, too, Penny had liked.

Her mind soon wandered from the sermon, for she was
unused to giving continued attention. It came back,
today, when the minister repeated the words: 'I will
lift up mine eyes unto the hills.'

The hills. Penny listened to hear what this man had
to say about them.

He went on to explain the question and answer that
followed the stately sentence. '"From whence cometh my
help?" Not from the hills,' he said, 'splendid and
strengthening as they are; but from the God who made
the hills and who can aid his children when nothing else
can. "From whence cometh my help? My help cometh
from the Lord, who made heaven and earth."'

Penny was not well acquainted with God. A'nt Sally

and Unc' Jeff had used his name only as a handle for
hard words. But the hills she did know, and her mind
fled away into their fastnesses.

Longing swept up through her like waves of sickness.
She'd never thought about loving the hills. She'd never
thought about them at all. But suddenly she was feeling
as if they were a part of her, as if she were a part of them.
Or as if she were a brook trout tossed up out of their cool
water to die in the underbrush. And as if she would
stifle if she could not fill her lungs with piny air. Unconsciously she nodded her decision.

'If they go to send me back to the Home, I'll run off.
I'll run off to the mountains. I could make out by myse'f
in the mountains.'

She sat with her face lifted toward the preacher, eyes
fixed on the colored rose window above his head — like
a mountain sunrise, that window — and thoughts running swiftly back to her hills.

If she could get overalls, she could pass for a boy,
especially with her hair so short. She could fish, and
snare rabbits, and ——

Suddenly her hands gripped each other in her blue silk
lap, and her breath quickened. She had a new thought.

When they came in from church, Virginia was just
getting up, heavy-eyed and cross because the dinner
dance had been late. They all hurried to make the beds
and straighten the living-room and pull out the leaves of
the living-room dining-table. The Smiths made it their
aim to have Sunday dinner in the living-room.

'Eating in the kitchen all the time,' Mrs. Smith
complained, 'we're getting the manners of heathens.
You're bound to get sloppy ways. Junior won't know what
a napkin's for, or how to sit properly through a meal.'

More often than not, they failed of their aim. With
Virginia usually sleeping till noon, and the living-room
stale and unaired; with Saturday the busiest day at the
beauty shop, so that Mr. Smith must do the food-shop-
ping because Mrs. Smith was not through till after the
cash-carrys had closed; with all these hindrances, Sunday
dinner, like the others, was customarily a makeshift con-
coction from tin cans and paper bags, partaken of by
relays in the 'breakfast nook.'

Today, however, Mrs. Smith had a savory roast of
beef, and baked potatoes, and biscuit, and pineapple
upside-down cake.

'Awful good dinner, Mamma,' Mr. Smith congratu-
lated her.

'You ain't lost your knack after all,' chirped Grandpa,
who often said the wrong thing in the kindliest way.

'Meaning that I don't practice much any more, I
suppose,' Mrs. Smith responded tartly.

'We never did throw that up to you, did we, Mamma?'
Mr. Smith apologized hastily. 'It only makes me mad
as the dickens that I'm not man enough so we can live
on my salary, without you wearing yourself out at the
shop like you've done.'

Mamma forced a smile for him. She was too tired to
laugh, Penny could see that. Tired all the time. And
Virginia didn't help. Virginia went to school, and had so
many friends, and all. And besides, Virginia was scarcely
formed for hard work — so pretty and slim; and her
mother hadn't brought her up to it.

Beneath the tiredness, Mrs. Smith was an honest-to-
goodness mother. Penny felt that she had cooked this
company dinner as a special treat because Penny was so
soon to go away. That thought took the flavor from the
food and made it hard to swallow.

Junior stared up at her wanly as she gave an audible gulp. He had had a bad night, coughing every time he fell asleep. Virginia was silent and moody. The rest of the family were resolutely cheerful.

'Good preaching, Paw?' asked Mr. Smith. 'Won't you have just another little slice of the meat? Here's some of the brown part you're so keen about.'

Grandpa passed his plate, peering in pleased anticipation at the crusty brown slice on his son's raised fork. 'I'm afraid I wa'n't paying such good attention as I'd ought to,' he confessed. 'I got to figgering, kind of.'

Penny moistened her lips. 'They was one part about lifting your eyes,' she mumbled. 'Lifting your eyes to the hills, he said.'

They looked at her in surprise. Penny usually froze into complete silence when they were all present. Flustered by their regard, she picked up her fork backward, in the banjo grip she had been used to, remembered the Henleys and Virginia, and laid it down quickly.

'It don't cost hardly nothing at all to live up yonder in the hills a summer,' she said desperately. 'You-uns could take your otto. I can catch fish. They's even a heap of old houses a body can live in for nothing.'

This was the new thought that had blazed upon her in church that morning.

The Smiths looked at each other. 'Why, we couldn't very well do that, Penny,' Mrs. Smith deprecated. 'Just pick up and leave. We never could afford a summer's vacation like that.'

'It don't cost hardly nothing at all,' Penny repeated.

'Mamma,' whined Junior, 'why can't we go to the mountunes, like Penny says? You always said maybe we could some day. Why can't we go now? Huh, why can't we?' He burst into violent coughing.

'My word!' Mrs. Smith said crossly. But her eyes were thoughtful as she followed the child to the kitchen to assist him with the difficult task of whooping.

'If I couldn't find a job,' Mr. Smith observed, when she returned, and Junior, wet-eyed and pale, had climbed to his chair beside Penny, 'why, then it might be something to tide us over the summer, Mamma. Of course I've got to find a job; but if —— Well, by next fall things ought to be looking up. Good gosh, they've *got* to be looking up, by that time.'

Penny went on chewing. She had reached the dessert and it was delectably sirupy under its cream, but Penny couldn't seem to get the taste of it; she could only chew and swallow.

Grandpa was sitting with knife and fork gripped hard looking at his daughter-in-law over his spectacles, his kind old eyes bright.

'I do believe I could tinker up that old automobile so't she could carry us up there all right. Seems like it would make a fellow over new, being out in the mount'ins all summer. Cooped up like this ——' He waved a disparaging knife at the crowded room — 'And it's going to be hot as tunket here this summer.'

'Jones, down at the office, he made a trailer that works as good as a bought one. Got some wheels off a junked car, see, and ——' Mr. Smith narrowed meditative eyes.

Virginia's face had gone mutinous. 'I don't suppose it matters about me,' she stormed, pushing back her chair. 'You know perfectly well that if there's anything in this world I hate and despise, it's camping out and all that sort of thing. Ugh! Sand in your food, and getting rained on at night, and always looking tacky —— You can just count me out of any such scheme as that.'

She left the table, stepping on Napoleum's tail in her wrathful haste, so that he set up a shrill yelping and limped to lay a moist nose on Penny's knee for comfort.

Later, Virginia looked sharply, suspiciously, at the pencil sketches her father was making on old envelopes.

'Dad, you surely aren't thinking seriously of any wild plan like that?' she flamed out at him.

Mr. Smith dropped his ruler with a self-conscious clatter. 'I should think a person could figure out a trailer if he wanted to,' he said defensively, 'without having everybody jump on him!'

That night was a bad one for Junior. Mrs. Smith lighted a croup lamp in the living-room, where he slept in his door-bed again, while Penny shared the davenport with Virginia. The lamp thickened the air with an aromatic haze; but every time Penny dozed off, Junior's strangling cough wakened her.

During an especially sharp attack, she stumbled over to his bed and held him erect so that he could get his breath. Virginia, tossing impatiently in her half-roused sleep, realized only enough to blink across at them and say, 'Poor Junior!'

Penny was dizzy with sleepiness, yet she did not altogether dislike the ordeal. Junior's little pajamaed boy-body, damp and limp and babyish, rested against her so confidingly when a spasm of coughing passed, his tousled head rolling drowsily against her shoulder.

They fell asleep so, Penny braced against the bedpost and holding him comfortingly in her arms. Mrs. Smith tiptoed in at dawn and found them.

'You're an awfully good child, Penny,' she said gently, sliding Junior down under the covers and giving Penny an awkward pat.

Penny, waking to the mothering words, the mothering touch, crept into bed beside Virginia, and flopped over on her stomach to hide her emotion.

'I'm going down awhile this morning,' Mrs. Smith said at breakfast. 'To the shop. Get things ready to close up. But this afternoon or evening I really think we'd better have the doctor drop in. The way Junior's losing weight ——' She paused behind him to lay her palms along his spindly neck. 'He's feverish, too; I don't like it. And I don't suppose we ought to take him to the office; he might run into other children.'

'I'll be seeing if I can't land one of these jobs,' said Mr. Smith, punching with a blunt finger the list of 'Help Wanted — Male,' from the Sunday paper. It was a short list, while 'Positions Wanted' stretched on and on.

When evening came, and dinner time, it was unnecessary for him to tell them that he had not found a job. 'Spring was the deuce of a time to get laid off,' he said. 'Unless, of course, we really should strike out for the mountains. And of course that don't look reasonable.'

'It certainly doesn't,' said Virginia.

'Let's get the dishes out of the way quick' — Mrs. Smith changed the subject — 'before Dr. Brown gets here.'

Dr. Brown took Junior on his knee and examined the boy while the boy examined Dr. Brown's watch charms. He slipped down the child's shirt and ragged underwear and listened to the bony little chest with his stethoscope while Junior giggled and wriggled and coughed. He popped the thermometer into the small parched mouth and told a story till the two minutes had ticked past. He ran gentle fingers over the lumps, like an uneven

string of beads, that ran along the sides of Junior's neck. He plumped him down on the floor and gave him a nickel and a dismissing spank.

'Run along, skeezicks,' he said, and waited till Junior had sought Virginia in the other room to show her the nickel.

'Nice little fella,' wheezed the doctor, leaning plumply to open the bag that stood between his feet. 'But he's at a stage where he needs lots of outdoor air and sunshine. These pills' — he was writing a prescription — 'they'll help. But medicine won't do the work. Got a yard? Back yard you can turn him loose in?'

'Well, no, Doctor, you know how apartment houses are.'

'I know they're no place to bring up youngsters like Junior.'

'You mean Junior is —?' Fearfully Mrs. Smith left the question dangling.

'A little temperature. Skinny as a rail. Pulled down by this darned cough. Yes, of course. But it's the glands I don't like. Frankly, I don't like the glands.' He waved his prescription blank to dry the ink, and handed it to Mr. Smith. 'He'll be first rate, though, if he can live about twenty-four hours a day outdoors. We won't insist on the twenty-four being all sunshine, even in Colorado. Have to let the stars have their turn.'

'Looks like mebbe we better go on to the mount'ns,' Grandpa ventured, after the doctor had gone.

'It might be our best bet, at that,' Mr. Smith nodded, his tired eyes almost eager.

'Well, then, I'll start hunting a job!' flared Virginia.

VII. THE VENTURE

MR. SMITH continued to look for work, but during only a part of each day. The rest of the time he was toiling away in a friend's back yard (no room at an apartment house) building a trailer. In spite of worry about his job and about his little son, he looked more contented than Penny had ever seen him. His evenings he spent poring over books on the internal arrangements of automobiles.

Grandpa sometimes went nodding, while his son pointed out parts, and jerked himself up guiltily when his nodding head woke him. Grandpa was so busy these days that he was worn out at nightfall. He and Penny spent hours away from home whenever there was anyone to look after Junior. Their explanations were vague: they'd been down along the Platte; they'd been to the library. From the library they brought home books, but these they hid securely.

'Anybody'd think you were kids with a bunch of dime novels,' protested Mr. Smith.

Mrs. Smith and her partner were trying to sell the beauty shop. Between-times Mrs. Smith worked on Virginia's clothes. And through all their varied activities ran the phrase, 'If we should spend the summer in the hills.' That phrase changed little by little to 'If we spend the summer in the hills,' and at length, 'Since we're going to spend the summer in the hills.'

Penny's climbing hopes were several times dashed backward. Aunt Retta, a distant relation of Mrs. Smith's was going East for the season and offered the Smiths the use of her apartment in Park Hill. Apartments are safer when occupied, and Aunt Retta had been unable to rent hers furnished.

'The dog, of course,' she had asserted without fear of argument, 'must be disposed of, and the girl will be going back to the Home.' She surveyed Napoleum through an invisible lorgnette, with hostile amazement.

'We ain't either going to expose him!' shrilled Junior, clasping the rough brown neck convulsively. 'And the doctor said I got to go to the mountunes. I got glams. Ain't I got glams, Mamma?'

Aunt Retta turned the lorgnette on Junior.

'Dr. Brown does think we should have Junior outdoors all summer,' Mrs. Smith placated. — 'Junior, you'd better take Napoleum into the other room. Go *on*, Junior. — We certainly appreciate the offer, Aunt Retta. You mustn't think we don't.'

Aunt Retta ignored 'glams' and doctors. 'I'll wait a few days before I make other arrangements,' she reproved. 'I'm leaving Denver about the twentieth of June.'

Aunt Retta's apartment remained threateningly in the back of Penny's mind. Yet plans went on, and her hopes crept upward again. The Smiths would store a few treasured pieces and a trunkful of small articles in a friend's attic. A few other pieces they advertised for

sale. The rest would go back to the stores from which
they were being bought on the installment plan. It gave
Penny a curious shock to know that the Oriental-pattern
rug and the overstuffed set, the refectory table and the
radio, were none of them paid for.

Part of the beauty-shop equipment was sold, and Mrs.
Smith's half of the remainder was stored with the trunk
and the furniture. The money from the sale of goods was
small. Half of it had to be used to placate the grocer.
Even with the Smiths' Saturday purchases at the 'Pig,'
the grocer's bill was frightening. Penny had often
wrinkled her brow at its total, stuck askew on top of a
thick pad of daily bills above the sink. How could so
small a family ever eat over a hundred dollars' worth of
bread and potatoes and such?

Virginia put in applications for work everywhere,
dashing downtown in her spare moments. She was
caught up in the whirl of Commencement time. She had
a part in the senior play; she was on the committee for
the senior prom; she had been on the staff of the senior
annual.

Zip and Dot and Fran and Hoot — Penny had got
that many sorted out and tagged with their names
because they came oftenest — were in and out of the
Smith apartment at all hours, on all sorts of class business.
Junior often had to be put to sleep in his mother's bed
and transferred to his own late at night.

Between-times there were the fittings of Virginia's
class-day dress and graduating gown. Mrs. Smith made
them herself, having time for both since she was not
working at the shop.

Penny watched the fittings with delight. She would
have liked to tell Virginia how she looked in those flower-

like frocks. With her pointed olive face and brown amber
eyes fringed with black, she was clear and flashing and
cool and frail.

Commencement was a splendid pageantry to Penny,
sitting in the city auditorium and watching six hundred
graduates pass between blossoming aisles of junior escorts
to receive their diplomas.

Later, Penny pored over the columns of graduates'
names in the Sunday paper and the groups of photo-
graphs. There were pictures of head boys and head
girls; winners of scholarships and prizes; class officers.
Virginia's was among them. She had accepted a scholarship for Quentin University. She supposed she might as
well, she said, though she didn't think she'd ever want
to go and grind away any four years in college. If she
could have just a little money, like the other girls in the
gang, she said bitterly, and go into a sorority, it would
be different, but when you were poor —— The kids in her
gang would every last one 'go fraternity,' and wouldn't
she feel like a poor fish if she couldn't?

Until the day before the Smiths' departure, she continued to hunt for a job. By that time she had decided
that there were no jobs in existence, and that she had no
choice but to go with her family. Her disappointment
was softened by the sport clothes her mother had found,
reasonably priced, at a sale: smart jodhpurs and leather
jacket.

It was the middle of June when the Smith caravan
set out: a sultry day for Denver, with the wall of mountains half hidden by clouds. Mr. and Mrs. Smith and
Virginia filled the front seat, Grandpa and Penny, Junior
and Napoleum crowded the back, and the trailer bobbed
along behind, well packed and covered with a tarpaulin.

Junior wriggled round and knelt on the seat to watch
that trailer, for it carried those of his treasures that he
had been allowed to bring: his box of tiny cars, red,
yellow, blue, and green; roadsters, coupes, sedans. These
he had felt it impossible to abandon to the stored trunks.
This summer his life's whole interest was divided between
the cars and Napoleum.

Penny had a special interest in the trailer, too. A
certain canvas-wrapped parcel rammed into one end
held a secret that belonged to her and Grandpa. But
Penny did not look around at it.

Virginia sat sulkily silent, Mrs. Smith wearily relaxed,
Grandpa eagerly straining forward. But Penny was as
still as an image. She was afraid to breathe or to shift
her eyes, lest something should change the scheme of
things and take from her this summer. Summer was a
piece of heaven which might be hers to live fully, no
matter what horrors of charts and clicking teeth were to
follow. 'When I'm an old, old woman,' she was telling
herself, 'I can look back and recollect it. The hills, and a
family. If only nothing don't happen to spile it.'

Mr. Smith had tinkered the car with loving care; he
had greased it; he had oiled it; he had consulted his many
booklets, propping them up so that he should not soil
them. The car responded by spinning along cheerfully
through the town and onto a highway that bent back
and forth across the mountainside, each loop laid above
the last — something like rickrack braid, Mrs. Smith said.

For an hour the car clucked along thus contentedly,
letting out its own cracked bleat at every turn in that
crooked road. And then it began suddenly to protest
with loud smackings.

Mrs. Smith jumped. Grandpa leaned forward, hand

cupped behind ear, and mutely inquired of the engine. Mr. Smith drove doggedly. The smack continued.

'And it's settin' in to rain!' said Grandpa.

'Oh, it's raining a'ready!' shouted Junior, bouncing up and down, to the inconvenience of his seatmates. 'I just love it to rain and me in where I don't get wet.'

'*If* you don't get wet!' Virginia glowered back at him by way of the driver's mirror.

They did. The windshield was hastily closed. The windows were screwed shut, rebelling noisily, for they had been warped out of line by some past wreck. And still drops splashed plumply on heads and spattered off. Mr. Smith peered upward, jerked his eyes back as the engine smacked more viciously.

'I kind of hoped that top would last out the summer, after I painted it. It claimed on the label that the stuff was waterproof.'

The sky emptied upon the world, as it can do in a canyon, in blinding sheets of rain that hissed on the pavement and rebounded in spray. Large spots darkened on the ceiling and small streams trickled from the centers. Gleefully Junior drew his sweater over his head. Grimly Virginia turned up her collar and took off her brand-new hat. Anxiously Mrs. Smith craned backward.

'I hope to goodness you tucked in the tarpaulin tight enough so our bedding won't get wet, Henry.'

Mr. Smith could spare her no answer. The engine was exploding more loudly than ever, and laboring like a runner out of breath. He jiggled the lever on the wheel to give it more gasoline. He creaked into low gear. He stepped on the accelerator. The car labored, it crept, it halted.

Glancing anxiously into the mirror, Mr. Smith coaxed the car to the edge of the pavement and let it stop. He scrubbed his forehead with his handkerchief: a damp ball of handkerchief, for a leak had directed its stream into his khaki pocket.

'Well!' he said limply.

'It ain't a spark plug, Son?'

Mr. Smith shook his head.

'It's getting dark, Dad, do you realize that?' fretted Virginia, stiffening back against the seat as a new stream smote her on the nose. Behind her, Penny wrapped her coat around Junior and smiled down palely, out of her anxiety. He sparkled up at her, eyes overbright and lips parched, the only one of the six who was entirely happy and carefree.

Mr. Smith pressed the starter, jiggled the choke, coaxed the car to limp on through the hissing rain.

Dusk had fallen, hastened by the storm clouds that overhung them in a low wet roof, when they coughed and smacked and snorted into a village. Mrs. Smith leaned forward and probed the thickening dark.

'We can't possibly camp out, such a night as this, with everything we've got wet,' she said. 'But I don't see a sign of an auto camp.'

'Two cabins are going to take quite a bite out of our pocketbook,' Mr. Smith muttered.

'They's a row of them little houses,' said Penny, pointing.

'Sure enough,' Grandpa crowed, 'there's your auto camp all hunky-dory, Son. Down betwixt the road and the crick.'

Thankfully they crawled to the nearest cabin, its logs dark with rain and its roof streaming. A face appeared at the window; a man stood in the doorway. 'Want a cabin? Well, drive in under this next shelter, pardner, and I'll be right over with the key.'

'My heavens!' — Virginia got out and made a dash for the door as soon as it was open — 'What did I tell you? Oh, heavens!' In its frightened haste a chipmunk had run over her foot.

Penny scurried with Junior through the downpour. Mrs. Smith and Grandpa followed stiffly, Napoleum almost upsetting them in his haste to join the family. With a last reproachful shake of the head at the secretive blue hood of the car, Mr. Smith buttoned his coat tight and turned up his collar and attacked the knotted rope that criscrossed the tarpaulin on the trailer. It was a wet job, for the trailer stuck out of the shelter into the storm.

He came in presently, his patient arms piled high with the bedding, water streaming from his old hat.

'It's wet!' groaned Mrs. Smith, pouncing on the bedding.

'Oh, not hardly more than damp, Mamma! Not hardly more than damp.'

'Wet!' she contradicted firmly.

'I'll build a fire,' he promised, 'and we'll have it dried out in a jiffy.'

It became evident that the wood had just been brought in from the downpour. Moreover, there was no paper to start the kindling. Penny plunged through the rain after newspaper from the office-cabin.

Mrs. Smith felt Junior over with anxious hands ('If you'll put some sulphur in his shoes,' said Penny, 'he won't take no cold.') Mr. Smith crumpled newspaper in the rusty sheet-iron stove, laid on in a lattice the slivers of pine Grandpa's clever old hands had shaved off, reached into his khaki pocket for matches. Pfh! Futilely they scratched on the stove-lid.

'Wet!' he snorted. 'Wet as all outdoors.'

Again Penny, silent and eager, plunged through the rain. Again she returned, this time with the matches clasped close under her coat.

At last the little stove leaped with flame.

Tight-lipped, Mrs. Smith spread moist bedding on the few chairs around the fire. Mr. Smith kept lifting a stove-lid, thrusting in wood. Grandpa hobbled to and fro. Penny worked feverishly to help Mrs. Smith. She couldn't help feeling that the rain and the wet bedding were all her fault. Virginia stared out of the window into the deepening dusk, hands thrust into pockets, shoulders hunched high.

'Gosh, but I'm hungry,' she flung over a slim shoulder.

'Me too. *I* want *pop* roas'!' Junior chanted. '*I* want *pop* roas'!'

Mrs. Smith pressed her palms to her temples. 'Virginia,' she said, 'will you look after the supper this time? I'm just about all in.'

Virginia turned quickly, hiding remorse with reproach. 'Well, for heaven's sake, why didn't you let us know? We've told you and told you we don't want you to make a martyr of yourself, Mother. Where is the stuff?'

'In that black bread-box,' answered her mother, dropping into one of the quilt-draped chairs and waving a vague hand.

'Where?' Virginia asked.

'The big black bread-box,' Mr. Smith said. 'Ought to be able to see anything that big, Ginny. Where'd you set it, Paw? You must have carried it in.'

'No, I didn't, Son,' Grandpa disclaimed. 'Must be still out there.'

But he hobbled back with empty arms through the door Penny held wide for him.

'Got to get the flashlight. It's so dark I can't see hide nor hair of it. Where at did you stow it, Son?'

Mr. Smith stood staring down at the stove-hole, the lid upraised. Abruptly he clattered the lid into place, reached for the light, and went out.

He was back in a moment, his arms empty, too.

'I just remembered,' he confessed: 'I set that dang thing on the running-board while I was packing, and I didn't ever put it in at all. Likely it slid off at the first bump. Of all the dang idiots —!'

'My very best steel knives were in it,' Mrs. Smith said grimly. 'The set your mother gave us at our kitchen shower, Henry. And dish towels and dish cloths and I don't know what all. And of course our supper.'

'I'm h-hungry!' howled Junior. 'I wanted some of that pop roas'.'

Mr. Smith pulled out his lean purse and shelled a few coins into his palm.

'We'll have to go and buy us some grub,' he said.

'Isn't this just a splendid beginning!' Virginia said scathingly. 'Folks, do let's have a little sense and go back to Denver tomorrow.'

VIII. ZIP

PENNY could not persuade even herself that the first night of their adventure was a comfortable one. Valiantly as the little stove roared and crackled, it succeeded better in bringing out damp smells of wood and wool than in driving out the chill. And the dangling electric bulb laid a pitiless finger on the unlovely clutter.

Seeing Virginia frown at the oilcloth on the table, Penny scrubbed it fiercely. She scoured the frypan that hung behind the stove, too, and warmed a can of beans in it.

'They was a cake in the black box, wasn't they, Mamma?' Junior inquired dispiritedly, leaning his elbows on the table and studying his plate.

'Yes, I was going to start us off so well,' Mrs. Smith nodded wanly, between sips of tea.

'Pot roast would have tasted prime, night like this,' Grandpa chirped, picking up a forkful of cold salmon.

'Best thing for us to do is to pile off to bed and get our sleep,' counseled Mr. Smith. 'I aim to get up bright and early and see if I can make out what's wrong with the car.'

'I'll wash up theseyere dishes,' offered Penny.

'Good heavens, can't we leave them till morning?'
Virginia protested. 'I'm simply too tired to move. And
we still have the beds to make. And I suppose a fire to
build in the other cabin.'

'I don't mind washing up,' Penny said, scraping plates
onto a dish for Napoleum. 'I ain't so awful tired.'

'I'll wipe, Penny,' Grandpa said. 'Do my j'ints good,
hanging round the stove.'

'Would it hurt if I took Napoleum for a little run,
Mis' Smith?' Penny asked, when the dishes were done.

'But don't get out of sight of the cabin, child,' Mrs.
Smith assented.

The nearest store wasn't out of sight of the cabin,
Penny knew. 'No, mom,' she promised, and hurried
away, Napoleum frolicking stiffly at her heels.

Back again, she fished a tiny paper box from her
pocket and poked it at Mrs. Smith.

'Aspirin!' Mrs. Smith exclaimed. 'Why, Penny!'

'That's the right kindy stuff, ain't it? I thought I
heard you-uns say ——'

'How much was it, kid?' asked Mr. Smith, reaching
for his flat wallet. 'That was sure thoughtful ——'

Penny tucked her hands into her pockets. 'Please tell
the Mister to leave me do it,' she appealed to Mrs.
Smith. 'I couldn't find you no present, that time to the
dime store.'

Even Penny was dazedly weary by the time she went
at the making of the beds in the two cabins.

'Don't let the quilts and things touch the floor,' Virginia said fastidiously.

'If there's any bedding that's really dry,' advised Mrs.
Smith, 'put it on next the sheets. If we don't all catch
our deaths ——'

'Oh, folks don't catch cold from damp bedding in Colorado,' Grandpa assured her briskly.

When the beds were ready, the rain-swollen windows refused to stir.

'My heavens!' puffed Virginia, as she tugged at them, 'how do they think people are going to sleep, sealed up like sardines in a can?'

Penny, sharing a cottage with Virginia and Junior, fell asleep at once, in spite of the closeness and crowding. She woke with her heart in her mouth when Napoleum padded round the room on clicking toenails and stood growling by the door. All night she slept and woke, slept and woke; woke finally in the grayish dawn with a furry-feeling mouth and heavy eyes.

The clothes that they had hung on chairs when they went to bed were chilly and damp.

'They feel like fishes,' Junior remarked, squirming into his underwear. 'They's clouds clean down over the mountunes!' he crowed a moment later, peering out, half dressed.

By this time smells of coffee and bacon were issuing from the other cabin, and Grandpa called them to breakfast.

The scene was little more cheerful than it had been the night before. Mrs. Smith wavered dizzily round the room, in spite of the aspirin; and Grandpa moved as if on rusty hinges. Mr. Smith came in after they had started eating, holding grease-blackened hands away from his clothes.

'Well, Son, find anything?'

'Vacuum tank!' said Mr. Smith. 'Line's pulled right loose, see? I just this minute made it out.'

'That ought to be easy fixed,' Grandpa cogitated. 'Mebbe with adhesive tape.'

'That's what I thought,' Mr. Smith agreed, interrupting himself with a large bite of bacon. 'That's just pre-cisely what I thought, Paw.'

Mr. Smith looked tired, under his day's growth of beard, but his eyes were as interested as if he were a professor discussing a scientific problem. He just naturally hankered after machines, Penny thought, and all these years he'd had to sit at a desk working over figures instead.

'Well, I certainly hope,' said Virginia, pushing her half-emptied plate away, 'that we'll turn around and go back to Denver, the minute you get the car fixed, Dad. You know Aunt Retta said she'd wait till today to find someone else to go into her apartment. If we telephoned ——'

'Oh, now, V'ginia!' Grandpa protested, his blue eyes rounded with alarm.

'The doctor said I ought to be in the mountunes!' shouted Junior, his voice rising to an hysterical squeal. 'I heard him through the door.'

'Aunt Retta's apartment has a sleeping-porch,' argued Virginia. 'That would make it about as good as the mountains for Junior, I should think. And a fat lot of fresh air we got last night.'

'Well, it might be best ——' Mrs. Smith started feebly. She had lain down on the spread-up bed, a wet cloth over her eyes.

Penny's heart slowed with fear. It was natural that Mrs. Smith should be discouraged when she felt so ill. Probably Aunt Retta's apartment beckoned her like a bright haven, just as the hills beckoned Penny. The difference was that Penny's haven had room for them all.

Silently she took the cloth from Mrs. Smith's eyes,

wet it anew, wrung it out, and replaced it. Then she went
doggedly at the work. She wanted to do it all herself,
for she still had the guilty feeling that everything was
her fault. Besides, the easier she could make it for Mrs.
Smith and Virginia, the more hope there would be ——

Hope dwindled as the day wore on. Penny took Junior
down beside the stream — milky from the refuse of the
mines along its course — and showed him how to skip
flat stones on the surface of a pool, while Napoleum
dashed barking around them. She kept an anxious eye
on the car shelter, where Mr. Smith worked steadily,
with Grandpa crouched stiffly beside him as consult-
ant. At any moment she expected to hear a call and to
learn that they were to turn back from the promised
land.

The hills — my help cometh from the Lord: the words
ran through Penny's mind over and over. It did seem
as if Someone was nearer, here in the hills: Someone strong
and kind. Even if Penny had never been taught about
Him, she had felt Him often enough; especially when
the sun shone on pine needles and made each littlest one
shine. And when the wind came toward you from far
off, and sighed away up high above you in the pines.

She thought that her doom had fallen from an unexpected quarter when a smart gray coupe came flying
up the hill and drew to a stop before the blue car and
Mr. Smith. The gray coupe was piled with noisy youth,
and from the driver's seat Zip Spencer shot out.

'Hi, Ginny!' he called, reaching back to press the horn
in raucous summons. 'H'are you, Mr. Smith?'

'Do some more stones that way, Penny!' Junior
ordered, tugging at her arm. 'What you looking at? —
Oh, gee, it's Ginny's gang!'

He raced back to the cabin and Penny followed him with slow feet. She lingered behind Grandpa and Mr. Smith and watched the greetings.

Virginia came to the door, darted out. But what a changed Virginia! Gone were the sullen down-droop of lips, the coldness of eyes.

'Hi yourself, Zip Spencer!' she called gaily. ''Lo there, Frannie and Hoot! 'Lo, Betty! What are you doing up here?'

'What are we doing? Behold a band of heroes and martyrs!' Zip declaimed, beating his green sweater with a dramatic hand. 'We braved the wind and clouds; we left our bright and happy city; and all to comfort you in your despair. Wasn't that what you had in mind when you told us what road you were taking?'

'It was not! And whose despair are you talking about?' Virginia mocked. 'Where's your good old pioneer blood, boy? We're off for the open spaces, and I bet you'd give something to be in our shoes. Nothing like it!' she added, flinging her arms wide. 'You poor fish, cooped up in an old town!'

'Poor fish!' Zip scoffed. 'You can't fool me, Ginny Smith. Why, you've heard her a million times, Betty, giving a lecture on how much she loves camping out. And I don't blame you, Ginny. Gosh! Cold and wet —— You look like a picked chicken already,' he added frankly. 'I'm betting you're back in town inside a week.'

'How much'll you bet?' Virginia challenged. 'How much'll you bet I won't stay all summer?'

Penny had moved as near as she dared, keeping out of sight behind a corner of the car shelter. This was like watching a play. How would it come out? Virginia

was so proud; proud and vain, too. Zip had chanced on
the surest way to flick her on the raw.

But Zip had another stroke.

'Oh, come off, Ginny,' he exhorted her. 'I say you
can't fool me. What'd you say if I told you there was
a job for you in Denver?'

Penny's heart flopped. The summer without Virginia
would lack a definite savor for Penny; but, more than
that, if Virginia voted for a return to Denver, now when
Mrs. Smith was ill and the car troublesome, her vote
might be enough to turn the party back. She peered out
at Virginia tensely.

Virginia was silent a moment, her face empty of expression. She cleared her throat.

'Might depend on the job,' she said.

'Well, of course there aren't a lot to choose from,'
Zip said, rather disgruntled. 'This is the Five-and-Ten.
I'm not too snooty to go on as soda-jerk myself, and I
got you a place as waitress at the lunch counter. Where
I can keep a fatherly eye on you, my good girl.'

There was another silence; confident on Zip's part,
breathless on Penny's, noncommittal on Virginia's.

'That sure makes a difference, what?' Zip observed.
'I had a hunch it was like that: Virginia loves the
mountains as long as there isn't any help for it.'

Virginia's eyes sparkled dangerously. 'That's all you
know about it, Zip Spencer,' she said. 'It was awfully
good of you to get me a job. Thanks a lot. But I'm
touring in the mountains this summer.'

IX. THE TOWN OF JANE

EARLY the next morning the Smith car started on.

The sky had cleared to a deep, rich blue. The fresh-washed trees and bushes sparkled in the sun. The spirits of the adventurers soared high — all but Virginia's.

As Penny flew around, washing dishes, folding bedding, helping Junior dress, she watched Virginia. Virginia had been so positive, yesterday, so suddenly and miraculously enthusiastic. Today she was more cool and withdrawn than ever. Penny felt even an increased resentment in her manner.

All day Penny puzzled about it. Zip's words, she thought, might be the key: 'Virginia liked the mountains just as long as there wasn't any help for it.' That was it: Virginia's pride had worked the change yesterday. She couldn't bear to have 'the gang' suppose that she was forced to do anything she didn't want to. Her only way out was to make them think she did want to.

Before her family she needn't keep up the pretense. As Penny told herself sagely, 'She cain't keep it up that way all the time or her face'd crack. She's got to kindy turn loose and rest herse'f.'

The rest of the Smiths bubbled with excitement, and

even the blue car seemed to feel the tingle of the mountain morning. It climbed an endless hill steadily, if noisily.

'Oh,' Virginia gritted, as it roared deafeningly upward in low gear while other and smaller cars spun past it in high. 'Even that little old Model T can pass us up.'

'Pretty is as pretty does,' her father said, not too appropriately, as he tooled the elegant blue length into a niche which had been scooped out of the cliff for a safe stopping-place. 'The old girl isn't doing so bad today. Not for her. But listen to her boil!'

They not only listened; they felt. She rumbled and gurgled and shook.

'I jiggle like I was the lid of a tea-kettle,' Junior giggled.

Mr. Smith clambered down to the stream, far below the road, and brought back a battered tin filled with water, unscrewed the dashing Greek athlete radiator cap with his handkerchief and stood back to avoid the geyser of oily water. When it had died down, he poured in his canful and climbed into the car.

'Can't blame her for boiling on a hill like this,' he excused the blue car, and they went on.

'Jest where we bound for, Son?'

'Well, I thought we might take a look at a ghost town up here a few miles below Central.'

'Ghos' town?' shrilled Junior. 'Is they ghos'es? Ghos'es in it?'

'It's the town itself that's a ghost,' Mr. Smith explained. 'The houses stand there, and the old stores and barns, and sometimes schoolhouse and church; but there isn't a speck of life. Or not hardly. Dead.'

'Where's the people went to?' Junior demanded. 'Didn't they want their houses no more, Papa?'

'They couldn't earn their board and keep any longer. They'd built their towns when there was gold, and by and by the gold was gone and there wasn't anything to do but move somewhere else.'

'The gold wasn't alluz gone,' Grandpa interrupted. 'Sometimes they'd got out the easy part, and was too lazy to go after the rest. Or else it cost too much — all the machinery they needed, and the men and everything. Say you get twenty dollars an ounce for your gold when it's all refined. And say it costs you twenty-one dollars to get that ounce out of the ground and refine it — well, it don't take no perfessor to see that you ain't a-goin' to get rich at mining.'

Mr. Smith rasped the gear shift to intermediate and to high as they dipped from the long hill, and everyone sat back and breathed more freely when the shuddering roar subsided. The car settled down to the cluck and chirp of the engine at its best.

'This little old town I'm aiming at was a placer mining camp, name of Jane,' Mr. Smith chuckled.

'You mean the town's named Jane?' Mrs. Smith asked incredulously.

'It would be,' said Virginia. 'We would stop at a ghost town named Jane. But at least we can have our mail addressed to Central City. Central City doesn't sound so bad, now they're opening up the old opera house in summer and folks are — well ——'

'Now the four hundred are making a new fashion of it, Virginia,' her father said dryly.

'Placer mining?' Grandpa was sitting forward, awaiting a chance to speak. 'Crick through the town, mebbe, Son? Man told me sumpn funny about this stretch along Clear Crick not so fur from here. White men worked at

it, long as gold come easy. When they got done with it,
bunch o' Chinamen went after it. Took out seven million
dollars worth in one mile.'

'Lots of gold all around this district,' Mr. Smith
assented, 'if it didn't cost so darned much to get it out.
They do say the strip of pavement between Denver and
Colorado Springs has got a million dollars in the sand
of it. Of course it would likely take two million to
get it out.— Now you-all be watching out for a side
road that leads off to the right. Partly overgrown now
— hasn't been used for so long.'

'Son!' Grandpa called presently, pointing a knobby,
shaking finger ahead. 'That looks likely, that road in
amongst the quakin' asp. You reckon it's the one?'

It looked like a wood-haulers' road, leading off through
a grove of aspens that shimmered on their pale stems
among the evergreen deeps. Mr. Smith, craning forward
over the wheel, coaxed the car up the jolting ascent.
It jerked and sidled between and under raking branches.
It came out after a few minutes upon a small hillside
clearing, where cabins slept in the sun.

Penny thrilled at the sight. Four-Mile Draw was more
isolated than this, but it had a similar setting. Among
such hills she had lived her life.

She was out as soon as the car had found a level
stopping-place. She breathed deep the smells of sun-
warmed pine, of wild sage, of chokecherry, still in blossom
here, though it had shown green fruit-beads lower on
the mountain. She gave a little run and jump, and then
walked stiffly, hoping no one had noticed. Galloping
cow! she scorned herself.

The clearing was a saucer, tilted at an angle among
the evergreens and aspens that pushed in, pushed in, to

take back the open space. A mountain brook bordered
its higher edge. Across it straggled a few log cabins, a
few larger buildings, whose flat fronts, extending above
their roofs like cap visors turned straight up, showed
that they had been stores or saloons. Evidently a broad
road had run between them, but grass and weeds and
flowers had long taken the road, as the trees were
trying to take the clearing. Squarish holes in the earth
and jumbles of débris were all that was left of most of
the houses.

Of the rest, some had partly fallen in; others had lost
their roofs; a few still stood foursquare and hatted with
waving grass. At the far end of the street one chimney
wore a feather of gray smoke. Its door had opened when
the car coughed to a stop and a black figure stood there
regarding them.

'Suppose we just go up and say how d'you do to this
lady,' Mr. Smith suggested. 'She's the one bit of life I
mentioned. Quite a character into the bargain.'

'Everyone hereabouts knows old Mis' Trent,' added
Penny.

'Use' to own big mines up near Central,' Mr. Smith
said, lowering his voice as they drew nearer her. 'Or
Mr. Trent did. Lost them all. Settled here, where she can
live on next to nothing and sort of keep an eye on some
of her old properties. Claims she'll have them back one
of these days. She's a little bit — you know!'

Mis' Trent stood with a knobby, black-gloved hand on
each side of the door frame and watched them unblink-
ingly from beneath a cape sunbonnet of a past style.
Her high-collared black waist was faded to green and her
black skirt dragged in heavy folds around her feet.

Mr. Smith and Grandpa touched their hats. 'How do

you do, Mis' Trent?' Mr. Smith greeted her. Everyone
called her that. 'Mrs.' Trent wouldn't have sounded
like her name.

'How do you do?' she croaked rustily. 'Are you set-
tling in Jane? Move in wherever you please. Going into
business, I suppose?'

'Business? Here?' stammered Mr. Smith.

Mis' Trent looked past him indifferently. Penny and
the others were stealing glances over her shoulders into
the room she guarded: a wretched place, the part of it
they could see — broken chairs, a stove propped up with
stones, a sagging bed.

'Are you the only person living here?' Mrs. Smith
asked.

Mis' Trent waved a nonchalant hand toward the other
end of the street.

'At the moment. Except for old Mr. Peters. But
they will return. They'll all come flocking back, fools
that they were to go away. The gold is here. My mines
are as rich as ever, the mines they've stolen from me.
And they'll all be back, every mother's son of them.'
Her voice had risen, and Junior dodged behind his
mother's skirts because Mis' Trent's eerie gray eyes
chanced to fasten on him.

'But — that Mr. Peters?' asked Penny, suddenly
bold. 'I thought — where at does he live?'

'In the farthest house,' Mis' Trent answered. 'With
the blue door. An ill-disposed man. I haven't spoken to
him these twenty years.'

'But that house with the blue door is all fallen to
pieces,' stuttered Virginia.

'Is it?' Mis' Trent asked calmly. 'Possibly. Possibly.
I do seem to recall that Mr. Peters left Jane recently.
They came and took him away.'

The Smith family made its farewells and retreated. Virginia went back to the car, contemplating the fuzzy pulls in the ankles of her silk stockings. The others poked about the sleeping town. Grandpa gathered treasures: old-fashioned square nails, a massive door-latch, a rusty cow-bell. Junior hung on to his mother as she peered into dim interiors through broken doors or through cracks in boarded windows. Mr. Smith ran appreciative hands over squared logs with axe marks still visible on their silvered surfaces.

Penny walked, sedately, when she could remember. One cabin after another she surveyed with care, and at length she approached Mr. and Mrs. Smith.

'I found one we could fix up awful easy,' she said, 'back yonder.'

They followed her along the grassy street to a log cabin that stood staunch and square, and boasted a shade tree besides. A great yellow pine stood guard at its corner, lifting its pompons of needles high above the grassy roof.

'But, child, it hasn't even got doors,' objected Mrs. Smith.

'They've been took off right lately,' said Penny. 'The inside's kep' too good for it to have stood open long. And we can easy borrow a pa'r of doors off'n another house.'

They looked doubtfully across the threshold before they followed her in.

'Ain't it nice?' she asked proudly. 'Floor ain't rotted bad. 'Course they ain't no glass in the windows, but you cain't hardly look for everything. Not for the rent we-uns'd pay.'

'That's pretty good, Mamma!' Mr. Smith ejaculated,

after a moment's astonished silence. He could scarcely
have looked more amazed if Napoleum had tried humor.
'Can't look for everything for the rent we'd pay! Well,
well, Penny, kid, I didn't know you had a joke anywhere
about you.'

Penny stood self-consciously on one foot.

'But it would leak — the roof,' pondered Mrs. Smith.
Disks of yellow light overlapped each other on the lit-
tered floor, signs of the cracks and holes above.

'It would be easy fixed,' Penny replied quickly. 'I
helped Unc' Jeff many's the time. And till we fixed it
solid, we could spread the tent on the ticklish places and
hold it down with rocks.'

'Of course there isn't any furniture,' Mrs. Smith tried
again.

'You don't get furnished apartments for this rent,'
Mr. Smith reminded her, still chuckling.

'And they's bunks in both rooms'— Penny's eyes
shone. 'And a table and chairs is awful easy made.
And we could cook in the fireplace. 'Tain't so often you
see a fireplace in a miner's cabin.'

'I declare if I ever thought to bring a broom,' Mrs.
Smith exclaimed.

Penny sprang to that emergency also. 'Me and Junior,
we can pick up a heap of twigs. We'll have us a middling
broom in two jerks of a lamb's tail.'

Penny seemed equal to all needs. She told them how
to cut spruce boughs and lay them in the bunks to serve
as springs and mattresses. She lugged pails of water from
the 'crick' and scrubbed the bunk boards with sand and
water and the twig broom. She swept out the big fireplace and reached up to brush down as much of the ac-
cumulation as possible.

'Hit's stopped up some way, seems like,' she reported. 'Maybe some of the rocks has fell down in.'

'I learned how to make a stove in Camp Fire,' Virginia suddenly offered, forgetting her sulks. 'An outdoor stove. Stone.— Oh, heavens, what has that dog found now?'

This day had been the crest of Napoleum's young life. Though still somewhat stiff in the mended leg, he had dashed about, jerked hither and thither by strange and delicious scents. He had clawed lightning-fast at solid patches of floor. He had lumbered after flashing chipmunks, and after squirrels that sat with twitching tails and angry chatterings far above his head while he sniffed the ground in bewilderment.

Now, he was doing his best to enlarge an opening formed by a broken board in a corner of the cabin. Penny plumped down beside him and thrust him away while she applied her eye to the hole.

'Oh, them little pretties!' she murmured.

Junior was there in an instant, and she moved aside to let him see.

'Oh, Penny, they can be mine, can't they? Penny, can they? Huh, Penny, can — ?'

Virginia peeked, too, but she drew back disgustedly. 'What *are* they? What horrible little pink things! Why, they haven't got a speck of hair!'

'No, of course not. Baby mice don't.'

'Mice!' Virginia sprang to her feet in horror. 'Mice! Oh, my heavens and earth! And anybody can tell by the smell that there've been chipmunks all over the place, and maybe ——'

'Skunks,' Penny informed her serenely, 'and them big fat fellows that sets up and whistles.'

'Would the gang ever laugh themselves sick!' snapped Virginia.

'I'll put a piece of tin across the hole,' Penny comforted her; 'and maybe Grandpa and the Mister can find boards around loose-like to fix up the weak spots tomorrow.'

'Slick's a whistle!' nodded Grandpa. His eyes were bright with anticipation, though his back crooked at a sharper angle than usual. Even in Colorado damp bedding had not proved so good for rheumatism. 'And we'll knock together a bench and a table, won't we, Son?'

Towel over hair, Mrs Smith swept and scrubbed. Mr. Smith and Grandpa pounded and nailed wherever they were allowed. Junior capered around in everyone's way, and Napoleum chased his charming new enemies until he had to lie down, panting and happy, flattened out in the middle of the floor where he could best be stepped on.

Virginia showed Penny how to make the outdoor stove. She even rummaged an old stove grate out of a rubbish heap. Penny tunneled a passage for a draft, set stones in a neat, firm rectangle, scoured the rusty grate with sand, and set it across the rectangle.

'That isn't bad, if I do say it!'— Virginia stepped back and surveyed it complacently. 'And I don't know but I can remember some of the recipes we used for outdoor feeds. Kabobs were awfully good. Only I don't suppose we have any veal or round steak. Camp omelet, though — Mother, have we canned milk?' she called. 'And eggs?'

They had; so with Penny's help she concocted an omelet. She fried the bacon in the skillet they had bought in the village to replace the one lost in the black box.

Removing the crisp slices to a plate, she emptied part of the drippings — into the fire, before Penny could stop her — and broke in the eggs and poured in the canned milk.

She wrapped the skillet handle awkwardly with paper to protect her already blistered fingers. She flinched and scowled when the smoke drifted acridly into her eyes. She slopped a quarter of her omelet over the edge of the pan when she was blinded by smoke and tears. But she stirred and stirred, nevertheless, until the mixture assumed a creamy smoothness.

By this time the whole family was sitting around watching her.

'Do get ready quick — quick!' she begged them. 'It's half spoiled if it gets cool.'

She scooped it out into the plates, and Junior importantly carried it to the family.

'I suppose the ashes are a newfangled seasoning, daughter?' Mr. Smith joked. 'It's perfectly all right with me,' he apologized, as Virginia stiffened resentfully. 'Pretty fair. Pretty *good*. I don't know that I ever ate any of your cooking before.'

'Ginny's cooked sumpn somebody can eat!' chanted Junior, his mouth full and oozing.

'You'll make a good cook yet, I shouldn't wonder,' Grandpa offered with peacemaking intent.

'It's the last thing on earth I want to make, you may be sure!' flared Virginia. 'A cook! Good heavens!'

Nevertheless, she brought the conversation around to her omelet several times that afternoon and listened to favorable comments with evident pleasure.

By night the cabin had changed. It would take more scrubbings to rid it entirely of mousy odors. The inhabitants must watch their step, too, for Grandpa and the Mister had only begun the work of repair and treacherous boards remained. Yet the place had a different look and feeling.

Penny had found some ancient can-lids, scoured them fairly bright in the sand, and used them in pairs for candle-holders. She bent one at right angles in the middle and nailed it up for a tiny shelf, with three nails pounded through the bottom to hold a candle. The other she nailed flat against the wall to protect the wood from the flame. Each of these crude sconces held its gleaming light. And over the springy spruce-bough mattresses in the bunks the neatly spread bedding added its suggestion of comfort.

'Seems kind of like the little old shack must be happy tonight,' mused Grandpa, 'holding a regular fam'ly again, after goodness knows how many years.'

'How did Penny come to know so many things to fix?' asked Junior, who had crawled into his mother's lap as she sat on one of the bunks.

Penny hesitated. 'Thisyere's the same kindy house I lived in,' she explained shamefacedly, 'with A'nt Sally and Unc' Jeff. In Four-Mile Draw.'

'What were they like, Penny, your aunt and uncle?' Virginia asked curiously.

'A'nt Sally and Unc' Jeff? Well, I don't rightly know,' Penny puzzled. 'They could shore lick hard. But they said they'd got to lick, 'cause I'd never had no fetching up.' She flushed.

'They was mean ol'— !' snorted Junior, sitting up and glaring.

'I reckon they thought they got to,' Penny said fairly. 'My folks ——'

But she closed her lips firmly on that. She couldn't
tell them — not even the Smiths — how A'nt Sally and
Unc' Jeff had scorned her father and mother.

'Penny Adams,' mused Mrs. Smith. 'What is Penny
short for?'

'Jest Penny, I reckon,' the girl said vaguely. 'They
always poked fun at it for a heathen kindy name.
They always said I was like a cur dog that couldn't
hardly amount to nothin'. Me and Napoleum, I reckon.'

Junior tumbled from his mother's lap and hurled himself upon Napoleum, who rolled over and waved all four
paws in air in friendly response.

'Napoleum does, too, amount to sumpn,' Junior cried
in falsetto, the exaggerated, hysterical tone of the child
who wants to focus attention on himself. 'And so does
Penny! So does my Penny!'

They all sat silent for a few moments. Mrs. Smith
rose to pin a piece of canvas over one of the window
openings when a cool little piny breeze sent a candle
flame flaring. The stillness deepened around them; the
wind sighed in the pine boughs and sawed one, violin
fashion, against the logs. Little creatures scurried across
the roof. A subdued chorus of squeaks came from the
deermouse's nest. A cricket tuned its fiddle in the empty
fireplace: cur-rick, currick.

'Let's go to bed!' Mrs. Smith said briskly.

Grandpa yawned and stretched. 'Suits me to a T. I
got plenty to do tomorrow.'

'I'd like to try some flapjacks for breakfast,' said
Virginia.

''Bother anybody if I get up around four and take a
turn with my fish rod?' asked Mr. Smith. 'Confound it,
if I didn't forget the bait!'

'I know where at they's almost always big white worms that do pretty good,' said Penny. 'I can get up early, too, and show the Mister.' Penny usually spoke to the Mister in this roundabout way, addressing her remarks to Mrs. Smith.

'Penny and me, we got sumpn to try out, too,' said Grandpa.

'Well, I think it's about time, Paw!' teased Mr. Smith. 'What've you and Penny got up your sleeves, anyhow? Or what have you got in that bundle you keep hiding away from the rest of us?'

X. UP THE CHIMNEY

PENNY awoke next morning with a 'Whoof!' of sleepy amazement. Napoleum had jumped up on her bunk and onto her stomach with a force that sent the breath from her body. Napoleum still supposed that he was a lap-dog.

Junior, waking in his bunk on the other side of the room, rolled over and laughed; Penny looked so funny, held firmly captive between Napoleum's forepaws, while the dog scrubbed her face with a purposeful tongue.

'Turn loose of me, you Napoleum!' ordered Penny, sitting up and blinking around her. 'Land sakes, if it ain't clear light! You go back to sleep, Junior: it's too early for you.'

She leaped from bed, pulled on her overalls and shirt, and ran the comb through her hair.

Mr. Smith and Grandpa were awaiting her in the cool crispness of morning. Grandpa was picking away at the ground with a broken spade.

'Jest rock,' he complained. 'Worms'd starve to death.'

'I opened the door a crack,' said Mr. Smith, 'and let the pup in, Penny. Did he wake you up?'

Penny nodded, grinning. 'I shut him up again.'

She set out straightway for the encroaching pine forest, the two men following. Looking keenly this way and that, she soon spied a rotting log and had pushed and kicked it over before they caught up with her. Its underside revealed some of the fat white grubs she had expected. Grandpa promptly baited his hook and dropped it into a tiny pool deep between the rocks of the rushing stream.

'Kind of drop it in and yank it out again,' he said softly. 'That's what they tell me. I never tried for no brook trout before.'

He and Mr. Smith made their way upstream, climbing over the boulders that rimmed it. Penny looked after them wistfully. Those were swell rods they had, she thought. But, after all, she had caught plenty of fish without any swell rod. She cut a pole, working deftly with her cumbersome old jackknife; then she took a length of line from her pocket and a treasured leader and hook, which she baited, and started after the others, wriggling the fat white grub tantalizingly across the shadowy water.

Flash! — a trout rose to the lure. Penny let him run with it till he was firmly hooked, herself stepping into the stream and stretching the pole at full arm's length as he dashed through the water. Then she swung him sharply upward, a curving slip of ruddy silver glinting in the morning light.

'There's anyways one,' she said contentedly, as she took it from the hook, killed it with an expert blow, and strung it on a forked stick. 'And I ain't lost my hook, neither.'

Up the stream to another pool she went, happy in the

keen, sweet smells of morning, the level shadows, the low, green light. Here a miniature cavern, shadowy under arched tree roots beneath the bank, was a place of gleams and glooms. The dark slip she had seen there made a leap for his victim, grew suspicious, and sulked back into his cave. Penny trailed the bait lightly across the surface for a minute, and went on, probing sheltered holes between boulders and still pools where the water rested before taking another leap.

Two more trout she strung on her stick. Until now she had kept well behind the men. Now, she came up with Grandpa, snorting through his nose and tugging at his rod till it bent into a loop.

'Dang thing had to ketch on one of them bushes!' he muttered, as his eye fell on her.

Penny clambered lightly over the rocks — in the hills she was no cow, but a deer — untangled the line and freed the hook.

'How many'd you catch?' she asked.

'There ain't no fish in this crick,' Grandpa averred. 'You ain't found none, have you, Son?' he asked Mr. Smith, who peered between the bushes at them, alarmed by the thrashing of the branches.

'Not had so much as a nibble.'

Penny held out her forked stick timidly. 'I knowed about where at they'd be,' she explained. She had early learned that nothing could so rouse the wrath of Unc' Jeff as to have his 'wimminfolks' succeed where he had failed. Likely all menfolks were that way, she thought. 'But I ain't catched but theseyere. That least one would tickle Junior, maybe.'

Mr. Smith, shaking his head in surprise, nevertheless took from his pocket a folding ruler and measured the 'least one.'

'Sorry, Penny, but it isn't legal,' he declared regretfully. 'Lacks a good inch of seven.'

'Legal?' asked Penny. 'I didn't know. But the little fellow's dead. I always knock 'em on the head first off. I cain't bear to see 'em hurting. 'Twouldn't do nobody any good to throw him back would it?'

'Well, maybe not. But measure 'em before you swat 'em, after this, kid.

'The others are beauties,' he added enviously. 'Rainbow, isn't that one? And look at those speckled fellows. Now, if we can get three more, we'll have a breakfast fit for a king.'

But luck was gone for that day. They stumbled up and down, and caught their hooks between boulders; and Grandpa hooked his own hat and sent it sailing through the air.

'It's nigh onto six o'clock,' said Penny, squinting at the sun.

Grandpa leaned his rod against a tree and tugged his fat old watch from his pocket. 'Purty good guess, Penny. Quarter till six, pre-cisely. And I'm holler clean to the toes.'

Trudging back, they were greeted by lusty odors of frying bacon and boiling coffee. Mrs. Smith was busy over the outdoor fire, and Junior was capering about her. At sight of them, he ran and opened the cabin door. Napoleum shot out and hurtled upon Penny.

A little way from the cabin, Penny stopped and dressed the fish on a flat stone. In a trice they were spraddled flourily in the bacon pan and were adding their gift to the bouquet of breakfast smells. By the time the fishermen had washed, Mrs. Smith and Junior had served the bacon and fish and hominy heated in the can and well buttered. Virginia joined them, combing her hair as she came.

'I just woke up,' she explained. 'Slept like a log.'

Her mother glanced at her questioningly. Virginia usually took it for granted that she should come late to breakfast.

Grandpa sat on a box they had found for him, so that he need not fold and unfold his stiff old legs. He balanced his enamel plate on his knees, set his steaming coffee cup, golden with condensed milk, on the ground beside him, and made a vague, circular motion with his hand, taking in sunny grasses and pines, birds and butterflies and creaking grasshoppers.

'That there bird on the tiptop of the spruce — it puts me in mind of the angel on a Christmas tree,' he said. The bird caroled and fluted and trilled a rich and varied song, with three notes, poignantly sweet, at its close. 'It's all so — so kind of good,' Grandpa said solemnly. 'Everything is. Makes you want to say grace.'

'I don't remember saying grace, not for a blue moon, Paw,' Mr. Smith responded, rather embarrassed. 'But you go as far as you please.'

Grandpa bobbed his head and mumbled something. Penny watched him, wide-eyed, as Junior did. She couldn't make out a word, but she had heard blessing asked at the Home, and she fancied the idea. Like enough God could hear him, she thought.

The morning was still, so that even the quaking asps only shivered a little, and the evergreens stood watching them, thrusting their pointed tips into the sky, which was just deepening from its early morning pallor to the rich blue of the high altitude.

The morning was cool, too. The butter had been so

hard that it lay lightly on the bread, in flakes. Mrs. Smith impaled the slices on sticks they had cut the night before, and toasted them till the butter melted. The thin strips of trout were of a delicate whiteness and of a delicious flavor.

'Ain't they nothing more?' asked Junior, his mouth crammed with the last mouthful of his heaping plate.

'My heavens!' Virginia ejaculated. 'Mother, do you see he's eaten even his hominy?'

Up at the other end of the town they could see old Mis' Trent picking up sticks, breaking dead twigs from the spruces, pottering round, pottering round, face always turned toward her new neighbors.

'I bet she ain't got nothing to eat but sourdough and beans,' Penny said wisely. 'I bet she's hankering after your good victuals.'

Virginia gazed curiously at the distant figure in its rusty black. 'I never would have thought of calling hominy and bacon and coffee — and a sliver of fish — such an extra good breakfast,' she said. 'But it wasn't half bad. I could eat more, myself.'

'May be we could have the poor old soul over to dinner some day,' said Mrs. Smith.

'It would be awful clever of you,' Penny said doubtfully. 'Only she'd never stir a step if she suspicioned you was sorry for her. Once she and her mister used solid gold plates when they had company to supper.'

'Gold plates! — Well,' said Mrs. Smith, dragging her startled eyes away from Mis' Trent and reaching to collect the plates and wipe them with a crust for the patiently begging Napoleum — 'Well, a campfire meal is fun, once in a while. But supposing it rains? Penny, are you going to find out what's stopping up our chimney?'

'Yes, mom, I'll go up on the roof right now.'

'I'll wash the dishes, Mother. I suppose you have something else you can be doing,' Virginia offered. 'How do you manage to heat dishwater for these greasy things?'

Mr. Smith set down his third cup of coffee and stared. 'I say!' he declared. 'Did I hear my daughter offer to wash dishes? Of her own free will?'

Virginia colored angrily and disclaimed any helpful intention. If she washed dishes, it was because she wanted to! 'There's no use my even trying to keep my hands decent now,' she snapped. 'And it's so chilly the hot water'll feel good.'

Everyone was busy. Mr. Smith and Grandpa went happily to work at floor and roof. Mrs. Smith tacked up flour-sack curtains at the window openings. Junior crawled under the cabin to investigate the nest of deer-mice: soft gray creatures, when they attained their fur, with underparts exquisitely white. Penny mounted the logs where they criscrossed at the corner of the cabin, and, testing the roof-logs first, swung herself up on the grassy slope. Presently she was down again.

'The rocks is good and solid,' she reported. 'But they's sumpn stuffin' up the chimley. I cain't make out what.'

She stooped into the fireplace and reached up the capacious chimney-throat. Her arms encountered a square wooden bulk. She grasped it and felt over it.

'It's some kindy box!' she called over her shoulder to Mr. and Mrs. Smith and Grandpa, who had stopped their work to circle the hearth. Her voice came hollowly.

'Wait a minute, Penny! Don't bust nothin'!' warned Grandpa.

But Penny had already pulled at the box with such vigor as to loosen the rusted staples which had held it to iron rods in the masonry. It came banging down to the hearth so suddenly that she barely dodged in time, cracking her head sharply against the stonework.

If gold pieces or bank notes or other rich plunder had leaped into anyone's mind, it emptied out as quickly. The old box broke in falling and revealed books; a dozen books — nothing more.

'What in tunket?' inquired Grandpa.

'Someone's stuck it up there for safekeeping, see?' guessed Mr. Smith. 'I'd like to know how long ago.'

'Is they any pitchers in the books?' demanded Junior, who had dashed in to investigate the crash.

'Lined with zinc, the box was,' Grandpa commended. 'Kep' the books in purty good shape.'

They had a musty smell, and yellow spots on the warped covers, yellow stains on the leaves. Yet most of them remained whole and legible.

'"David Copperfield,"' read Virginia, moving the volumes carefully with a finger wet from the dishpan. '"Bleak House." "Tennyson's Poems." "Uncle Tom's Cabin." Shucks. Everybody's read those.'

'You read all theseyere?' Penny asked, in awe.

'Everybody's read them,' Virginia repeated firmly.

It was warm by noon, so they built their fire outdoors again.

Virginia tried a new recipe, with canned corn and tomatoes. For a while after the meal was ready, she was too tired and hot to eat. She sat watching the circle of plates to see that everyone was properly appreciative of her fancy cookery. But presently she, too, was partaking with zest.

After lunch Mrs. Smith spread the army blankets under the pine tree and they all gathered there. Penny took out her old mouth-organ, cuddled it in her hands, played softly so as to disturb no one. At the first notes, Napoleum came pattering around the cabin and stationed himself before her. Up went his muzzle: 'Ow-wow-wow!' he wailed.

'Does he like it or does he don't?' shrieked Junior, dancing around them and laughing.

'That's more than I can say!' said Grandpa, wiping the tears of laughter from his cheeks.

With some difficulty, because her own mouth writhed into laughing, too, Penny played 'Old Zip Coon,' 'Turkey in the Straw,' and 'Dixie,' while Napoleum sang and the family laughed. But presently Virginia fluttered the leaves of one of the old books a trifle impatiently.

'How would it be to read out loud?' Mr. Smith ventured, looking up at the blue sky between half-closed lids.

'Well, we could try a chapter and see how it went,' Virginia assented, with a glance at the mouth-organ. 'Goodness knows there isn't much else to do.'

Penny put her mouth-organ away, and Virginia read.

The treetop bird sang and others joined it, though more languidly as the day grew warmer. Chipmunks, small and swift, made darting sallies after breakfast crumbs, provoking Napoleum to pursuit. Their larger cousins, the painted chipmunks, waddled out after them. A marmot issued from his hole under the next cabin, whistled shrilly, and ducked back.

Grandpa stretched out where the sun could strike his aching knees. Mrs. Smith pillowed her head on her arms like a little girl and stared at the shine of the pine needles. Junior lay curled up beside Napoleum, listening with wonder-wide eyes that drooped and widened, drooped and widened, until at last boy and dog slept together. Penny lay on her stomach, reaching out to pick dandelions, growing there in golden luxuriance, and curl the ends with the tip of her tongue. She had never been quite so happy before.

'That wasn't so bad,' Virginia commented, closing the book on a spray of wild geranium for a marker. 'Awfully slow, of course. But it isn't as if we were rushed for time.'

'Slow as the Dickens,' Penny drawled solemnly, her eyes glinting.

'Slow as the Dickens!' chuckled Mr. Smith. 'There she goes with her jokes again. You get the point, Mamma? "David Copperfield," by Charles Dickens. Slow as the Dickens!'

'It was nice,' said Mrs. Smith, laughing politely. 'We could do it again tomorrow. A person doesn't seem to find time to read any more. And I don't know when we've ever done anything all together like this.'

'Wisht I knew what kind of bird that is — on the top of the tree again,' said Grandpa. 'Purtiest singer!'

'It's a kindy robin, I *think*,' Penny opined. 'Least-ways, it's got them same colors. Maybe brighter. Big black head and bill, when you see it close up. Body kindy hair-colored —— '

'Whose hair?' Mr. Smith said, grinning.

'My hair!' Penny grinned back. 'And black-and-white wings, real showy. Look at it!'

The singer flew, with a sharp black-and-white flicker of wings.

'I never saw a robin like that,' Virginia said doubt-fully.

'Well, I never knowed no names for 'em, exceptin'
sparrows and hawks and owls and robins. They's one
kindy robin that sings nice when it rains: nice and sad.
If you hark, you can hear that kind scolding away right
now. And then they's a ground robin. I seen one
scratching at the weeds while we was eating. Got a
black bib, like, and a long tail; and a kindy red breast.
And the funniest thing, it's got a red eye, like a stone
in a ring. Listen! That's one of 'em, making that
noise now.'

Ch-ch-ch-cherrink! the call sounded heartily. Grandpa shaded his eyes and looked for its source. 'Bet I
know that noisy feller without so much as laying eyes
on him. What was it we use' to call him back home? —
I got it! Chewink! Tunket, but it brings back old
times. Chewink, that's it. And would you listen to
that other one?'

An impudent mew came from a thicket near at hand.

'Catbird, sure's you're alive!' Grandpa rejoiced. Painfully he worked himself up from the ground. 'Wouldn't
it be kind of cozy and sociable to put up a feeding-tray
for 'em, so's we could watch 'em better?'

'High enough so the dogs and cats won't bother them,'
Virginia suggested, 'if there are any cats around here.
Our Camp Fire counselor told us a lot about that. Suet's
a regular feast for chickadees. Have you seen any chickadees?'

Even with the few tools he had, Grandpa had soon
erected a square of board, on a four-by-four, about
shoulder-high. The Smiths set the table with dry crusts
and fat meat, and their first feathered boarders approached it that very afternoon, though cautiously. A
chewink, alert and nervous, perched shyly on the edge

until one of the treetop singers hustled him out of the way. A pair of great birds volplaned down from the air and sent the singer himself into the bushes. Beautiful birds, they were, sooty black in front and deep blue on back and wings.

'Them's jays, sure as shooting,' said Grandpa. 'No mistaking them topknots.'

'They got white specktickles on!' cried Junior.

'I used to hunt birds' eggs when I was a kid,' Mr. Smith remembered. 'Had quite a collection.'

'It's fun just to find the nests,' Virginia said, out of her Camp Fire training, 'and leave the eggs to hatch.'

'Lets us!' squealed Junior. 'Say, lets us!'

While their elders sat still and scanned trees and bushes at a distance, Penny and Virginia and Junior beat through the underbrush, annoying a gray squirrel till it followed them on its sky highway, scolding in two keys at once.

Penny was first to make a find. She sent a bird flying up from a loosely woven nest in the fork of a tree just above her head.

'What *was* it?' asked Virginia, coming up breathlessly. 'It was striped like a chipmunk.'

'It's the wife of that kindy robin that sings so nice,' said Penny.

Mrs. Smith had good fortune, too. She pointed to a rust-red tin can nailed on its side to the roof-beam of the nearest cabin. Watching for a little while, they saw a small brown bird dart nervously in and jerk back to look outside.

'It's brown-checked,' said Virginia.

'It's got Saint Vitus's dance,' chuckled Mr. Smith.

'It's a house wren,' Mrs. Smith told them. 'I know that one, at least.'

XI. GOLD IN THE RUNNING BROOKS

'ONLY trouble with the bird tray,' Mrs. Smith said on the second day, 'is that the Smith family eats everything in sight; don't leave crumbs enough to keep a bird alive. I never saw anything like it. We've got to make a list and go up to Central after supplies, Papa.'

She looked anxiously at Mr. Smith and he looked anxiously at her.

'A careful list, Mamma. We've got to spread that money awful thin if it's to last the summer.'

Penny cleared her throat. 'That bacon you-uns buy is mighty tasty,' she observed.

They looked at her and waited.

'But it ain't so filling. It's jest a kindy whiff of taste.'

'So what?' urged Virginia.

'You can get a slab of bacon a sight cheaper and slice it yourse'f. And salt pork ain't bad, cooked with greens and suchlike. Or with beans.'

'I used to get the slab bacon, myself,' Mrs. Smith recalled. 'When we were first married, Papa. I've been too busy to bother, here lately.'

'I bet I could slice it thin enough for you,' Mr. Smith said boyishly.

'But you said greens, Penny. Where would we get greens?'

Penny waved an inclusive hand. 'They's still dandelions that ain't too old. And they's dock. And other kinds that A'nt Sally used to cook up. Lamb's-quarters and mustard and like that. Lickin' good, some of 'em.'

'Beans are a good idea, too,' Mrs. Smith said thoughtfully.

Penny stood on one foot and scratched her knee with the other toe. 'Did you-uns ever take note,' she hesitated, 'how the swellin'est victuals is the cheapest? Fillin'est, too. Like beans. And corn meal.'

Laughing, Mrs. Smith got pencil and paper and started a list: 'Slab bacon, salt pork, navy beans ———'

'Them speckledy brown ones is cheaper,' Penny observed, spelling out the words over Mrs. Smith's shoulder.

'— pinto beans,' Mrs. Smith substituted, 'corn meal.'

'If it's the swellin'est we're after,' said Virginia, with a flicker of a smile, 'what about rice?'

Mrs. Smith put down rice.

'What about dried apples?' asked Grandpa.

'And dried prunes and apricots,' nodded Mrs. Smith. 'And canned milk. It don't swell, but I suppose we've got to have it. That's one thing that worries me. Junior ought to have milk. — Got an idea about something else, Penny?'

Penny was standing on one foot again and again rubbing her knee with a thoughtful toe. But she shook her head.

'I reckon dandelion greens would go right good with that hunk of ham you got left over,' she said. 'You want to he'p Penny gather some, Junior? Hoecake wouldn't set bad, neither. Ham and greens and hoecake.'

'Hoecake?'

Penny stared. 'Don't you-uns never make hoecake? They's no trick to hoecake and pone and such as that.'

That noon it rained so heavily that the cooking had to be done indoors.

'They ain't a thing to hang the kettle on,' Penny regretted, carefully examining the wall of the fireplace.

'I reckon I kin rig up sumpn to hold it,' said Grandpa; and he did.

The rain beat in at the open windows, and occasionally someone dodged a small stream that descended from the roof. The fire roared and crackled, and savory whiffs of ham mingled with the fragrance of pitchy pine. In the ashes at one side, potatoes were roasting; on the other side, Penny was baking her hoecake on a sheet of scoured tin — a shingle she had found.

Napoleum lay stretched before the fire, nose on paws, eyes watchful. He was in the age-old dog attitude of delight mingled with suspicion. When a rich vein of pitch hissed sharply or a spark snapped out, he leaped to his feet and sought shelter behind one of his people.

Junior, quiet for once, sat on the floor in a trance of enjoyment, the fire picking out vivid lights in his eyes, his hands clasped about his knees.

'Isn't it funny about a fireplace fire?' — Virginia spoke dreamily. 'It's like the heart of a room. It makes everything come alive.'

'And a brook is like the heart of outdoors,' agreed Mrs. Smith.

'Hearty folks, we are,' chuckled Mr. Smith.

When the meal was ready, Grandpa sat on the edge of a bunk, but the others made a circle on the floor around the fire.

'Son,' said Grandpa, setting his emptied plate carefully beside him and leaning back contentedly, big hands clasped across lean stomach, 'we've got to get busy and knock together them benches and the table.'

'And windows, Paw,' Mr. Smith added. 'Little bit dark when the windows have to be covered to keep out the rain.'

'I like it dark!' squealed Junior, hugging himself. 'I love it dark in daytime.'

'If you-uns would grease brown paper real good,' Penny suggested, 'and tack it onto the frame, it'd let in a heap of light.'

'I could make frames so't they'd swing open in fair weather,' said Grandpa, revolving his thoughts and his thumbs together, 'if only I had hinges.'

'Couldn't you use kindy leather strops?' asked Penny.

'I never see sech a young un fer contrivances!' cried Grandpa.

Everyone beamed at Penny, and Penny intently pursued a last microscopic shred of dandelion around her enamelware plate, and then jumped up to open the door for Napoleum, who was asking to get out.

'Whyn't we learn Napoleum to open doors his own self?' queried Junior.

'It wouldn't be a bad idea, at that,' Mr. Smith agreed, stretching his arms wide in delicious satisfaction. 'I bet we could train him to carry in wood and fill the woodbox, too. If we had any wood and any woodbox.'

'We've got to get to work at that, Son,' Grandpa told him. 'There's all the wood you could ask or want, jest fer pickin' it up and draggin' it in.'

It was raining too hard for outdoor tasks. Mrs. Smith and Penny washed the dishes, and Grandpa experimented with bacon grease and brown wrapping paper. Junior had found a page of cartoons on the wall in a far corner of the cabin and teased his sister to read them to him.

'"Harper's" had a queer brand of humor in 1860,' Virginia commented disgustedly.

The cabin was completely papered with old newspapers and pages of aged magazines. One wall contained several chapters of a serial story, pasted on in proper order: large sheets, with an installment complete on one page. Virginia had climbed on the bunks and dragged in a wooden box to stand on, to read the upper rows. She had followed it to the right-hand corner, close to the floor, only to find 'More anon' at the end.

Penny, the dishes wiped, took out her mouth-organ and coaxed some sobbing, crying tunes out of it; and again Napoleum, who had come damply in again, stationed himself before her and turned up his nose and howled.

'Great Caesar's ghost!' roared Mr. Smith. 'Quit that and open the door, Napoleum. Open the door!'

Napoleum stared at the pointing finger with intense brown eyes and jumped hopefully to lick it. Mr. Smith seized him by the collar and dragged him to the door, Napoleum hanging back until he had almost backed out of his collar. So began his education, Junior leaving even the funnies of 1860 to look on.

'Why, did you ever!' Mrs. Smith ejaculated, as she opened the door to throw out the dishwater. 'The sky's as blue as anything!'

The storm had passed suddenly, as mountain storms do, leaving the world miraculously fresh again, with a million diamonds glinting in the sun.

'Ain't it about time me and you showed the rest of 'em

what we brought along up here, Penny?' asked Grandpa, as the sweet wet air flowed into the cabin and coaxed them all outdoors.

Penny darted away to the blue car, which they had parked under a fragment of roof near the cabin, and to the trailer standing beside it. She staggered back with the large, canvas-wrapped parcel. Breathlessly letting it down on the grass, she squatted beside it to unknot the cord. The family gathered close.

'Rusty old pans!' Virginia protested, when the canvas was laid back. 'Why would you make such a fuss over rusty old pans?'

Mr. Smith lifted one, tilted it thoughtfully. 'Gold pans, Paw?'

'Gold pans?' echoed Mrs. Smith. 'What for, Father?'

'Are they the kind it shows in the pictures, where the old miners use them to get gold out of the streams?' asked Virginia, coming nearer.

'Yeah, but we wouldn't make much of a go of it, I'm afraid, Paw,' Mr. Smith said reluctantly. 'There's a trick to it. There's things you need to know.'

'Sure there is.' Grandpa hooked his thumbs into the armholes of his vest and chuckled. 'Sure there is! And that's where me and Penny comes in. Where'd you think we was gallivantin' to, all them afternoons we was gone?'

'You were so everlastingly close-mouthed about it ——'

'Well, first off we went to the liberry and learnt all we could about placer minin' and pannin' the streams. 'N' then we went down to the Platte and watched the men pannin' there.'

It had been one of the picturesque sights of the depression, the gathering of men along the banks of the river, panning in the fashion of the lusty pioneers. Even where the waters ran through the heart of the city, with tall buildings rising dark on each side, they panned, oblivious to the onlookers who leaned over the bridge railings and cheered them on.

'And *then*,' Grandpa went on, 'we found us a free class, under the unemployment booro, and we learnt some more. Penny did. I vum if it didn't run in one ear and out the other, as fur's I was concerned.'

'Unc' Jeff used to prospeck up and down the cricks,' Penny explained. 'I knowed how to slosh one of them pans around pretty good already.'

'You mean you get *gold* with one of those dishpan effects?' Virginia asked, eyeing them with new respect.

'When can we try it?' asked Mrs. Smith. 'And where?'

'Now,' said Grandpa. 'And we might as well try right in this here little crick.'

Crouching at its edge, Penny scooped out some earth from the overhang of the bank, carefully dipped in water, and then cradled and sloshed, cradled and sloshed, while the others bent around her, scarcely drawing breath.

She sent the floating sand and gravel out over the edge of the pan, dipped in more water, cradled it again, and drained off the water with care. The Smiths crowded so close that their heads bumped above the pan.

'Gosh!' sighed Virginia, 'there isn't any gold, is there?'

Penny nodded. 'Yes, mom!' she said proudly. 'Got color first whack. Looky!' She nodded toward the edge of the fine dark sand in the bottom of the pan. Palely bright gleamed the thinnest hair-edge of flour gold.

'And looky!' Penny urged again. She set down the pan, took out a pin that was run through the shoulder strap of her overalls, and with it picked out a rough grain of gold. 'Nugget!' she explained.

'How much is it worth?' Virginia demanded.

'Oh — a few cents,' Grandpa guessed. 'Dime, mebbe.'

'Why, I thought a nugget —— Why, *that's* nothing!'

'Well, look, Virginia,' her father remonstrated, 'these days it's something when you can pick even dimes out of the water.'

XII. 'IMAGINARY'

WHILE the shadows lengthened and the air cooled, the Smiths kept at their fascinating new occupation. One panning led to another and another and another. They were drunk with the allure of plucking gold from the sand and unconscious of fatigue or hunger.

Junior was the only one who did not take a hand with the gold pans. He gathered wild flowers. Some of them he crowded into a milk bottle and set proudly in the cabin; others he left in wilting handfuls on the ground while he gathered brighter and bigger ones. He tried to carry on his father's training of Napoleum, till they both grew tired of it and ran together through Jane's grassy spaces, Junior shouting and Napoleum barking, for the sheer fun of it, till the boy fell down in a breathless, laughing heap, and the dog nipped at him and kissed him and cut joyous, yelping circles around him.

'But, gee, I'm awful hungry!' he informed his mother reproachfully at last, prancing over to the stream and squatting down beside her. 'Ain't we ever going to have any supper?'

'Oh — supper!' Mrs. Smith looked with startled eyes from Junior to the brightness which the sun had

left in the sky when it dipped behind the hills. Reluctantly she rinsed her hands and went back to the cabin,
leaving the others crouched on the bank, completely
absorbed.

'But, Penny, what do you do when you've got all
this black sand with the little bit of gold in it?' asked
Virginia, putting back her hair with a muddy hand.

Virginia was asking Penny for information; asking
with respect. Penny straightened her shoulders and
looked directly at the questioner, instead of shooting a
glance through her lashes.

'Sometimes they catches the gold with quicksilver.
And then the old-timers puts the 'malgam through buck-
skin. Squeezes the quicksilver through and leaves mostly
gold behind, all turnt white like silver. Then they puts
it in a shovel, some of them, and burns off the rest of
the quicksilver.'

'And it's pure gold that's left?'

Penny nodded. 'Most takes the black sand to the
assayer, though, soon's they've gotten enough to make
more than an ounce of gold. He gets part for refining
it.'

Every day, after that, the Smith family went mining.
They made a sluice-box to use instead of the pans for
the first processes. The sluice-box was a sort of trough
of boards, placed so that water from the stream could
run down through it. It had cleats along the bottom,
and Penny and Grandpa had secreted a worn old rug in
the canvas bundle, to lay in the bottom of the trough
so that it might catch more of the fine gold. One person
would shovel in the earth and one would pick out large
stones with a pitchfork. The running water carried away
the lighter soil, leaving the heavy black sand and gold

lodged against the cleats and in the nap of the carpeting.

Slowly, slowly, the pay sand accumulated, till Mr. Smith forced the blue car up the winding way to Central City, and bought quicksilver, so that they might try amalgamating and retorting the gold for themselves.

'I wonder if you couldn't get a gallon of good fresh milk somewhere?' Mrs. Smith asked. 'I don't like Junior's not having milk to drink. He'll eat the canned milk on his oatmeal, for a wonder, but he can't drink it.'

'Do you reckon the Mister'd mind if I went along?' asked Penny.

'If Penny gets to go, I do, too! Don't I? Huh, don't I?' Junior demanded.

Mrs. Smith and Grandpa were engrossed with their panning and Virginia with gathering flowers for her new herbarium: blue and white columbine, painted mariposa, coral gilia, purple pentstemon. They did not care to ride up to Central.

But they were all on hand to greet the shoppers when they returned. The dwellers in Jane were like desert islanders welcoming a merchant ship: every purchase was interesting to them. Today revealed an extraordinary purchase indeed. When the blue car stopped, Junior leaped out, proudly dragging a bearded animal by a rope halter.

'Lookit, lookit, lookit!' he shrieked. 'Mother, lookit here! Grandpa! Ginny! Lookit!'

'Good heavens, a goat!' Virginia ejaculated.

'A — goat!' Mrs. Smith echoed feebly, gathering up her skirts as if for quick retreat. 'Will it butt, Papa?'

'It ain't that kindy goat,' Penny reassured her. 'This-yere's a nanny.'

Mr. Smith surveyed it proudly. 'Penny's idea. Got

it for practically nothing. And it's no common goat,
either.   It's a Schnizzlehorn or a Spanglebergenblitzen-
heimer or a Dachshund or something. I forget what.
Anyway, there's the gallon of milk you asked for,
Mamma, fresh as day after tomorrow.'

'And I git all I want of it!' squealed Junior, his reedy
voice evaporating on the top notes in his enthusiasm:
Junior, who had never been known to drink a whole
glass of milk without coaxing. 'I git *all* of it if I want,
and the rest of you take what's left.'

'Napoleum!' Grandpa ordered. 'You leave that goat
be!'

'Well,' Mrs. Smith submitted, 'I have heard that
goat's milk is fine for building a person up. Anything
that's going to be good for Junior —— But who's going
to do the milking?'

'Penny'll milk him, of course,' Junior responded
confidently.

But milking was an art Penny hadn't acquired. The
family took turns in persuading the absent-minded-look-
ing beast to surrender her white cream.

'She shore held back something fierce.' Penny mas-
saged her tired fingers resentfully. 'Maybe she won't
be so stingy, though, once she gets acquainted.'

Junior drank every drop they secured, tipping the tin
cup upside down over his face and smacking his lips.

Junior insisted that the goat be 'Christianed' at once.
After long thought he decided on Barkis as an appropri-
ate name, out of 'David Copperfield,' which they continued to read during the afternoon rest hour.

'We shore got to shut her up nights,' Penny warned
Mrs. Smith. 'They's always mountain lions around.'

The nearest cabin — the cabin where the wren lived

and the whistling marmot — made a good stable for
Barkis. It was well that she was within secure walls.
The second night her bleating wakened Penny from a
dreamless sleep, and, leaping to the window, she caught
one moonlight glimpse of a long, snaky-headed cougar
crouching on the stable roof.

Napoleum barked frantically around that cabin next
morning, and raced across Jane, nose to ground, track-
ing this new beast.

But about midday his clamor took on a different note.
He barked incessantly at some one spot below them in
the pine forest, keeping it up so long that Penny finally
went to see whether he had treed any dangerous creature.

'He's jest scolding at a rock!' she told Junior, who
tagged after her. Disgustedly she ran home again.

Napoleum soon followed them, but he whined and
looked up at Penny restlessly.

'Ain't you done with your foolishness?' she asked him.

He was not. All that day he barked and cried, and next
morning as soon as he was released, he ran down through
the pines again, with backward glances at Penny, who
stood watching him.

Slowly Penny followed. She didn't like his acting so.
A'nt Sally had always said it meant death when dogs
barked and howled without reason. Chills ran down
Penny's spine like a stream of ice water. Why should
Napoleum carry on so when there was nothing but a
speckledy rock to carry on about?

But this time she forced herself to go all the way.
And there, nestled against that boulder, were two small
creatures so nearly matching the lichen-mottled granite
as to be almost invisible.

Breathless with excitement, Penny hastened back to

the cabin, carrying the babies. She stumbled in at the door and woke Virginia to show her.

'My heavens!' Virginia exclaimed through a yawn, blinking her eyes to clear them. 'What funny, spotty things! What are they, Penny?'

Bodies no larger than Napoleum's were elevated on slim, stilt-like legs finished with small black hoofs. Flat sides were striped with light polka-dots, like a seven-stripe gopher's. Below their long, large ears, their big eyes, strange and opalescent, were fringed with long lashes that gave them a shy, childlike gaze.

'Baby deers,' said Penny, setting them on the floor, where they collapsed weakly. 'Twin ones. And starved most to death. I reckon that big brute I seen last night has et their ma.'

'Oh, what can we feed them?' Virginia asked, sitting on the floor beside them and stroking their shivering bodies.

'I'll borrow their breakfast off of Barkis,' said Penny.

Squatting on the floor again with a basin of warm milk beside her, she dipped her finger into the liquid and presented it to the fawns, which sucked and pulled greedily, holding tight with their fringe of little teeth.

Junior had wakened and lay staring, mouth and eyes wide, as if he thought himself in the midst of some enchanting dream. He swallowed once or twice and then managed to speak:

'What are them?'

Being told, he slipped from the bunk, padded across to them and took his turn at the feeding, giggling and wriggling as the babies tugged at his fingers.

When the rest of the family were up and dressed, Virginia and Penny appeared at their door, each girl holding a fawn.

'I never did see anything so hard to pick up and hold!' exclaimed Virginia, struggling to balance the unsubstantial body and the lengths of leg.

'What in tunket?' cried Grandpa.

He set to work at once making them collars of old leather, so that they could be tied without injury.

'But we got to turn them over to the Gov'ment,' he told the family wisely, 'or else get us a permit to raise 'em. Awful big fine if you take a deer without the Gov'ment says so.'

'We've sure got imaginary now!' Junior declared complacently, standing with his hands in his pockets and surveying Barkis and the fawns and Napoleum sniffing suspiciously at the newcomers.

'Imaginary?' Virginia inquired.

'Sure. A whole 'maginary.'

'Menagerie, Junior; menagerie.'

'What's the differnce? We got goats and birds and dogs and deers and chipmunks and squirrels.'

'And skunks,' added Grandpa. 'There's a family of the little spotted kind living under Barkis's stable, along with the marmot.'

'My grief!' mourned Mrs. Smith; 'then we're in for trouble.'

'No, mom,' Penny contradicted politely. 'Skunks is right good neighbors if they ain't no chickens round. Only we got to learn Napoleum to leave 'em be.'

Napoleum seemed to get the idea when Penny dragged him to the faintly odorous hole and warned him severely to leave its occupants alone. The skunk family led a peaceable existence next door throughout the summer. With other neighbors Napoleum was not so discreet. Penny had kept him shut in at night, lest his puppy spirits lead him into trouble with more dangerous animals. The Smiths' first visitors in Jane so distracted her mind that Napoleum ran free.

The Smiths were having their afternoon rest with 'David Copperfield' under the pine tree when the double hoot of a horn at the edge of their domain startled them. They turned to see Zip Spencer's gray coupe dashing along the grass-grown road.

'So this is Jane!' Zip condescended when he had greeted the older people. 'And some burg, I'll say!'

'Well, how on earth did you poor city waifs come to find our camp?' demanded Virginia, recovering from her surprise.

'Oh, when we'd moused around Central City awhile we went and asked the postmistress. She made us a map. Great doings up at Central, Ginny. They're putting on the "Merry Widow"— gay nineties and all that — in the old opera house; and if ever the old town was wide open!'

'A German band for the dances — and do those guys shake a mean drumstick!' added Hoot.

'We're going to have dinner at the old Teller House,' said Zip, 'and then go to the show, and then dance awhile. Get dolled up, Ginny, and come along.'

'Oh, *will* I?' Virginia cried. 'It'll be gorgeous, Zip. But did you bring the books I wrote you about sending?' she remembered to ask. 'There was a bird this morning —— And the little dictionary? And what about your job? How did you get off?'

'One at a time, ladies and gentle-men! The job's washed up. They wanted a nigger, and me, I'm free, white and eighteen. I told them they could have their old job and go roll their hoops. Your little old books are somewhere in the car, Ginny. I lifted them off the counter on my way out. The meanies gave me a good-bye present they didn't know about.'

'This is a cute camp, Mrs. Smith.' Betty looked about her curiously. 'But don't you absolutely die of lonesomeness, Ginny? How under the sun do you kill the time?'

'I haven't been really lonesome,' Virginia answered, her tone tinged with surprise when she put the fact into words. 'And, good heavens! there isn't half time enough for all we want to do! Besides, any time I do get fidgety I can go up with Dad and Granddad when they — attend to their mining interests,' she added airily. 'Gold mining, you know.'

She glanced quickly at her father, hoping he would not be too explicit in his remarks about his mining interests. But he only drew down the corners of his mouth drolly, and winked the eye farthest from the visitors.

'Producing well, Mr. Smith?' Zip asked, chewing a grass end with the air of one man of the world addressing another. His manner showed a subtle change.

'Can't complain,' said Mr. Smith.

'You mean you really like it here, Ginny?' Betty asked incredulously.

'It's sure agreeing with her,' Hoot admired.

'Oh, yes,' assented Betty. 'How many pounds *have* you gained? But it doesn't hurt, Ginny, if you just stop right now.'

'Well, she doesn't look like she had pernicious anemia, the way she did last winter,' Zip commended her. 'But you better scram, Ginny; we want to get up there in time to take a table at the Teller.'

Virginia beckoned Mrs. Smith and Penny furtively into the other room and closed the door.

'Good heavens — *stockings!*' she hissed desperately.

Mrs. Smith had been wearing cotton, and ankle socks had proved a practical economy with Penny's overalls from the first; but Virginia had not submitted to the indignity until she had roughed or snagged most of her silk stockings on the shrubs and weeds that grabbed at them with spiteful fingers at every step.

Mrs. Smith made an exasperated mouth. 'You thought it was impossible for you to wear anything but silk,' she couldn't help reminding her.

Working silently, they set their suitcases on the bunks and laid out all the stockings in the establishment.

'Here's a pair of mine that're good as new,' Mrs. Smith offered.

'And thick as a board,' Virginia groaned. 'They've got to be chiffon, Mother. Surely you can see I couldn't wear anything but chiffon tonight.'

'Here's the only chiffon ones I've got, and one of them has a sewed-up run on the instep,' her mother went on.

'Doesn't this one of mine match them?' Virginia whispered hopefully. 'It's all right except for a hole in the toe.'

'I'll darn that while you dress yourse'f,' Penny said, running to the sewing-box on the shelf.

'They don't *quite* match,' Virginia decided, holding them close to the window and squinting at them earnestly.

'Not a soul is going to notice, especially at night,' her mother assured her. 'It's lucky you brought one dress-up dress, Virginia.'

'We can put you all up overnight,' Mrs. Smith told them when they were packing themselves into the car, 'if you don't mind roughing it. Better telephone your families from Central, so they won't worry.'

After the young people had gone, Mr. Smith and Grandpa and Penny set up a tent for the boys and made spruce-bough beds for them, and Mrs. Smith hurriedly washed and stretched the Japanese tablecloth and the rainbow napkins of fringed crepe.

A long time after the family had retired, Penny was wakened by stifled giggles from Virginia and Betty, as they crowded into one bunk. Penny knew it was late, for the Great Dipper, which she could see through the open window, was turning itself upside down.

The other girls were still soundly sleeping when Penny dressed and stole softly out into the other room, where the bunks were already spread up and Mrs. Smith was making things tidy for breakfast.

In the weeks since their first fishing trip, Penny had scouted through the hills and found the deep, choice pools that the trout loved. Mr. Smith had invested in a few flies, too. The three rarely came home from their ventures empty-handed. This morning the men returned, jubilant, at half past six, each with a darkly gleaming burden; and an hour later the fragrance of frying trout wakened even the reluctant guests.

The zestful air of the mountain morning sparkled in at the open door and casements of the cabin. The table was vivid in its blue and yellow and vermilion cloth; and Penny had gathered a mass of varicolored gilia for a centerpiece. She watched eagerly for Virginia's look of pleasure at sight of the inviting room.

The look of pleasure came, but it was quickly swept away by a frown and a flush. Coldly Virginia looked at Penny's feet. Penny was standing in her favorite crane pose, and her feet were bare.

She was learning, painfully, that big girls do not go

barefoot; not even in the house; not even before breakfast. Penny always had; A'nt Sally always had. Today, of all days, she had forgotten, in the hurry of helping with breakfast and gathering the loveliest possible flowers and calling Napoleum, vainly, over and over. And Mrs. Smith had not noticed her omission.

Penny slipped away into the other room, jerked on her anklets and oxfords, eyes burning with humiliation, and slid into her place.

'I sure wisht we had comp'ny for brecklefiss every day,' sighed Junior, taking a heaping teaspoonful of jam.

For everyday meals, that jam was doled out in tantalizing portions. Penny had found a few early raspberries, and Mrs. Smith had made them into preserves so good that they had to be guarded on a high shelf.

But the breakfasters had barely whiffed the full nutty fragrance of their hot buttered corn pone, had barely savored the flaky white sweetness of well-browned trout, when they were startlingly interrupted.

'I-yi-yi-yi!' A shrill crescendo traversed the town of Jane and shot toward the cabin, where it went circling round and round, the pain-stricken yelping of a dog.

After a paralyzed minute, everyone rushed to the door, Penny in the lead and Junior ducking between people and under their arms to see.

It was Napoleum, his tail tucked between his legs, and the legs crossing each other like a camp stool's in their haste. Such a Napoleum, a racing pincushion, his head a-bristle with gleaming points.

Penny seized a piece of canvas, and, drawing a deep breath, caught him in full flight.

'Had a match with a porcupine, huh?' asked Zip. 'How do you get them out?'

'Where did you get him, Ginny?' asked Hoot, leaning over the quivering creature. 'Pity if you have to shoot him. Slick Airedale, isn't he? Good show dog, shouldn't wonder. Got papers on him?'

Even in this anxious moment the words penetrated to Penny's mind. *Napoleum* a show dog? She glanced up questioningly.

Grandpa hobbled from the car with a pair of tweezers. 'I reckon we'll jest have to pull 'em out one at a time, Penny, girl,' he sympathized. ''Fraid we'll have to brace his jaws open first. Even an awful good-natured dog'll snap when he's being hurt so bad.'

Zip was glancing toward the cabin door. 'What say we go back to that swell breakfast?' he queried. 'It's a crime to let such fish get cold.'

Penny surprised a quick glance of annoyance from Virginia. It really seemed as if Virginia's eyes were more coldly displeased than when they had chilled Penny's bare feet. But she recalled a hostess's duties and answered courteously.

'We may as well. I don't suppose there's a thing we can do to help, is there, Granddad? — Poor old Napoleum!' she murmured, lowering her voice as she turned to follow her guests, 'it was dumb of you, but I'm sorry.'

There in the morning sunshine Grandpa tugged at the instruments of torture.

'So, old fellow, so!' he crooned. 'Alluz *was* scaret you'd meet up with a porkypine. They've worked in purty far already, Penny. I don't know if we kin —— You know they've got little spines, like, that turns away from the point. That's why it's so tarnation hard to pull 'em backwards.'

Penny nodded. She knew all too well. She held the

beloved brown-and-black body in arms that ached with tension, and the tears ran down her face.

Grandpa sat back on his heels and rubbed his nose reflectively with the back of his wrist. 'What you reckon, Son?' he asked, peering over his spectacles at Mr. Smith, who stood watching with furrowed brow.

Mr. Smith tightened his lips. 'You won't get them out, Paw,' he said regretfully. 'And they work in ——'

'Into the critter's vitals,' Grandpa nodded. 'Penny, girl, we'll try a while longer, but I'm scaret we'll have to borry a rifle.'

Penny clutched Napoleum in an embrace that brought a yelp from the dog.

'I cain't leave him die!' she muttered hoarsely. 'I cain't. He's the onliest thing in all the world that's mine.'

XIII. VINEGAR

DOWN the grassy street of Jane sailed a gaunt shadow, head thrust forward in its black sunbonnet and nodding as it drew near.

'That's what I supposed. Porcupine,' said Mis' Trent.

As if the old woman had been coming to see them every day, Penny looked up at her through streaming tears. 'They cain't — *shoot* him,' she appealed. 'Poor old Napoleum!'

Napoleum rolled agonized eyes at Penny and flicked her hand with a feeble tongue.

'Tk tk tk! I never heard such a ridiculous name.'

'They say they'll have to shoot him, Mis' Trent. My Napoleum.'

'Absurd.' Mis' Trent disposed of the idea briskly. 'Have you any cider vinegar in your larder, Mrs. Smith?'

'Cider vinegar? What would cider vinegar — ?'

'Keep the abominable things from breaking off when you tweezer them. Softens them, I suppose, so that they aren't so brittle. I went after my cider jug as soon as I heard the commotion, but it was unfortunately empty. I have neglected to replenish it,' she said, with dignity, 'because I have found the acid injurious to my health.'

'Vinegar? You really mean it? Mamma, we haven't a drop, have we?'

No, the Smiths hadn't a drop.

'I'll drive up to Central and get some, right straight,' said Mr. Smith, glad to be doing something, and glad of any chance of relief for Napoleum.

He chugged away in the blue car, tooting conscientiously at every empty turn. Penny and Grandpa and Junior crouched round the victim, and Mis' Trent sat on the outdoor stove gravely, like mourners on a tombstone. Mrs. Smith returned to the cabin to attend to the wants of the breakfasters, who drifted outdoors soon after, when the fish and pone and jam and coffee had all been consumed.

'Mis' Trent, she says we can save him, V'ginia!' Penny told her, lifting wet eyes. 'The Mister's went for cider vinegar.'

'That's keen,' said Hoot. 'Shame to lose a dog like that. Be worth real money when he's got his growth.'

'Hoot, you make me tired,' Virginia flared. 'As if money was the only thing in the world. Junior would have cried his eyes out if we'd had to shoot Napoleum. And so would Penny.'

'He's the smartest dog in the whole world,' Junior boasted. 'You say to him, "Open the door, Napoleum!" and he opens it. And you say, "Shut the door, Napoleum!" and he shuts it. Mostly.'

'You said how he was an Air — Air — ?' faltered Penny.

'Airedale,' Virginia told her, looking at her in some surprise.

But Penny was thinking: 'He's *some*thing, Napoleum is. He's something that folks respect and pay money for, even if he is homely and whiskery and black-and-brown. We thought he was only a cur, but look what he's turning out to be! Maybe I could turn into something myse'f. You can't always tell by the looks.' That is what Penny was thinking.

'Well, Ginny'— Zip interrupted himself with a half-covered yawn —'I guess we'll have to be breezing along. Gang's putting on a scavenger hunt tonight. Come along, can't you?'

Eyes thoughtfully bright, Virginia considered the invitation. (Penny somehow liked it that Virginia had put on overalls this morning, instead of dressing up: clean overalls and a clean shirt, though both unironed. She looked like a russet-brown boy, slim but round, her nose peeling from sunburn.) She shook her head after a moment.

'I don't feel so much like going to town,' she refused. 'Last night was heaps of fun, and it'll last me a good while. Summer's going so fast I hate to waste any of the time I could have up here. But thanks a lot, all the same.'

Zip reached into the car and fished out three small books from the broad top of the seat. 'When do you mean to come home, where you belong?' he demanded, handing them to her.

'Oh, thanks, Zip.' Virginia took them with the tips of her fingers. He *swiped* them, Penny thought disgustedly: plain swiped. 'We haven't discussed it much. But of course there's school, the first of September, if Junior's well enough. And winter's mostly early, up here.'

'Isn't it swell to think your own school days are over?'

Zip asked idly, standing with the car door open. 'Going to hunt a job, Ginny?'

'Well — there's Quenton U., of course. I might decide to use my scholarship if I hadn't anything better to do. Jobs aren't lying around loose.'

'Oh, think again!' Zip advised, tossing back his curly mane. 'What's the big idea, Ginny? Quenton's great stuff if you've got plenty of money. But it's no cinch if you're going there to study.'

'And I wouldn't be interested in anything but cinches?'

'You're not interested in what you used to be,' Zip grumbled. 'Go into a trance over some kind of sparrow and don't even hear what a fellow's saying. I can't make you out, Ginny.'

'Oh, she'll be all right when she gets back to Denver,' Betty assured him.

'You nuts ever coming?' Hoot called impatiently.

'Good-bye, Mrs. Smith! Thanks for the swell eats! We'll be seeing you, Ginny!'

The little gray coupe roared away.

A few minutes later the blue car snorted into Jane, and Mr. Smith leaped out, a jug of vinegar in his hand.

Following Mis' Trent's orders, he saturated his automobile sponge with the liquid, and sponged the dog until the quills were drenched. Napoleum whimpered at the added bite of the acid, and turned his eyes away as if the operation would hurt less if he could not see the surgeons. Grandpa soon took the stick from between the dog's jaws, for Napoleum's gentleness was proof even against pain, and he made no attempt to snap at the helping hands.

'You sponge him every half hour, or thereabouts,' advised Mis' Trent, 'and wait several hours before you take the tweezers again. The theory is that the vinegar softens the spiny little protuberances so that they can be pulled out without tearing the flesh or breaking off themselves.'

'Well, Virginia,' her mother said suddenly, when Napoleum and his friends were resting between applications. 'We haven't heard a word about your good time. It's been pretty lonesome for you up here, I know. Was last night a lot of fun?'

'Fun?' Virginia looked up from where she was crouching at Napoleum's side. 'Why — yes, it was stacks of fun. The "Merry Widow" was slick, and they'd renewed the old decorations in the opera house so that you could imagine you were back fifty years. Even the chairs, old handmade wooden ones.'

'I attended the opening,' dreamily observed old Mis' Trent, who sat so still that the others had almost forgotten her. 'March, 1878, it was. I wore my first really décollété gown.'

'Oh, what was it like, Mis' Trent?' Virginia asked. 'Do you remember?'

'Certainly I remember. It was white paddy soy, with tarlatan looped over it in panels, and clusters of pale blue ribbons. And my shoes were high blue kid, laced up on the outside. It was a gorgeous assemblage, and the music was of the finest.' She lapsed into a meditative silence.

'Afterward,' Virginia went on, 'they had old square dances that were simply too weird, besides plenty of regular modern ones. I felt as if I could dance forever. But — good heavens! — getting to bed so early certainly does spoil a person. I was so sleepy I simply staggered, before the kids were anywhere near ready to come away. Those kids —!'

'Pretty peppy young uns, ain't they?' Grandpa remarked.

'But they — they've sort of gone stale. Dumb,' Virginia pondered. 'Of course they're grand kids, in a way, but I didn't realize how one-track they are. It's clothes and dances and shows and cars, and that's all. Goodness knows I like all that, too, but ——'

It was a peaceful morning, now that the little gray car had roared away. The fawns ventured close to the quietly suffering Napoleum, standing side by side and gazing unwinkingly with their long-lashed, opalescent eyes, as if invincibly attracted and perplexed by their traditional enemy. A pair of robins chattered and scolded in the bushes where Penny had found their nest, full of hungry baby beaks.

This was Sunday, and Grandpa and Mr. Smith did not pan on Sundays. They donned clean shirts and overalls, shaved with unusual care and warm water, and took their day of rest.

Grandpa had wistfully suggested that they might hold church and Sunday School, but no one had taken the proposition seriously.

'Why should we shut ourselves up in four walls when we can — well, when we can think about those things right out in the world God has made?' Mr. Smith asked, with unusual eloquence.

Grandpa shook his old head, with its thin hair wetly parted and combed. 'Folks talk a lot about worshiping God in his great outdoors,' he commented wisely, 'and it sounds purty fine. But I jest do wonder how many of their thoughts rise any higher than the water of the trout pool.'

Penny liked to watch him sitting under their pine tree

on those Sunday mornings, with his Bible open on his knees. The black leather binding of the book was worn brown and its edges were ragged; the leaves were frayed and many of them loosened. It seemed a proper part of the picture, as the old man read a while and for a while sat gazing off to the hills that rose above and around them. His thin, bluish lips moved as if forming well-loved words, and lines of patient waiting circled his mouth and creased his gentle brow.

Today the talk turned back to Central City.

'Society people from Denver,' Virginia said, 'flocks of them. And the Teller House was simply jammed. Goodness, but they charge enough to stop there during festival time. Zip and Hoot had to pay plenty for that dinner, too.'

'When they opened,' Mis' Trent interjected, 'the charge was five dollars a person. In 1872, that was. My father and mother attended, and they told me about it: a notable feast, that first dinner.'

'We had ours in the cutest little court,' said Virginia.

'Court?' queried Mis' Trent. 'Oh — doubtless it was the old conservatory. Teller House had a conservatory, yes, indeed. There was little Central City didn't have, though a mining camp in the heart of the Rockies. Doubtless you saw the President Grant suite.'

'Oh, yes, with the biggest old heavy furniture, and stiff lace curtains, and all that.'

'The toilet set,' Mis' Trent remembered, 'was Royal Minton, and really exquisite. — They laid a pavement of solid silver bricks across from the road to the hotel door, for President Grant to walk over. Twelve thousand dollars' worth of silver.'

'Those were the good old days,' Mr. Smith regretted.

'Everything alive and stirring, and millionaires made every month.'

'Unmade every week, too,' Grandpa added.

'And now the rows of empty stores make you feel funny,' said Virginia, 'with their windows boarded up. Some society people are buying houses there, though, and fixing them up with old-style furniture for their summer homes.'

'They's one house I — I always kindy like,' said Penny. 'A white house with stone steps and an iron gate like.'

'Beautiful houses in Central City. Beautiful!' Mis' Trent spoke severely, rousing herself again from the dreams in which she seemed held fast.

Again and again Grandpa had saturated Napoleum with the vinegar, until the sweet air reeked with sourness. As the sun mounted high above them, Grandpa took the tweezers again.

'I'm going to feel a sight more like tacklin' the Sunday dinner if this poor beast's resting easy,' he said.

'And Penny found us watercress for a salad.' So Junior strengthened the claims of the meal.

'Mis' Trent, we'd count it neighborly if you'd stay to dinner with us,' Mrs. Smith invited.

'Oh, thank you, no. I never accept invitations,' refused Mis' Trent, rising hastily from the camp stove.

She could not go, however, till the final operation was completed. Napoleum was patiently enduring the extraction, still rolling his melancholy brown gaze as far as possible from his surgeons.

The vinegar had done its work: the quills were far more pliable and released their hold less bitingly.

'Twenty-five — *and* — twenty-six!' Grandpa counted

triumphantly, holding the last quill above his head.
'Hooray!'

Mis' Trent patted the dog's whiskery head. 'If you'd
only learn the lesson, poor doggie,' she said. 'Good-bye!'

'Dinner is all ready and waiting.' Mrs. Smith artfully
left the door swinging wide, so that the odor of potatoes
fried with onions drifted out, and a brown crisp smell of
baked beans. 'We'd consider it an honor if you'd join us,
Mis' Trent,' she urged.

The fragrance of frying onions is an invitation it is
practically impossible to resist at an altitude of eight
thousand feet. Mis' Trent hesitated, sniffed again, and
was lost.

She looked more human without her somber sunbonnet, which she took off, after a vacillating moment, and
hung on a peg. More human, but not more beautiful:
her gray hair was strained back so tightly that it showed
the scalp between the strands; and it was twisted into a
walnut-sized knob.

Sitting down at the table, she unconsciously stroked,
with hands like bundles of twigs, the gay Japanese print
tablecloth.

'Pretty,' she murmured. 'I had satin ones, once; and
linen damask thick as a board. But it was a long time
ago. It was forever and ever ago.'

'Nice thing about this kind,' said Mrs. Smith, 'is that
it does without ironing.'

The lack of an iron had seemed serious at first, but they
had soon found that they could stretch shirts and dresses
and overalls carefully and wear them as they came from
the line.

'They smell wonderful, they really do,' Virginia acknowledged—'the unironed clothes. They're all fresh-

airy and sunshiny. But there are some things that need ironing. I want Dad to get a gasoline iron if we ever take out enough gold.'

'Gold!' Mis' Trent was kindled by that bright word. 'Are you getting much?'

'Well, not to say much,' Grandpa admitted. 'But we're taking out mebbe a dollar and a half a day, all of us working a few hours at it every day. And we're getting by on that. Fish, you know; and Penny, here, she's showed us lots of wild stuff for greens, and ——'

'A dollar and a half a day' — Mis' Trent blew it away on the breath of her scorn. 'Our Melody Mine brought us a half million a month. But I know a place where you'll certainly pan more than a dollar and a half a day.'

She caught herself, bit her lip, and seemed to deliberate. Then her face cleared, and she nodded. 'Yes, I'll show you. Why not?' She started to rise, resting her hands on the table.

'Let's wait till after we've eaten, Mis' Trent,' suggested Mrs. Smith.

Mrs. Smith didn't 'take no stock in it,' Penny thought to herself, gripping her hands in her lap and studying Mis' Trent's face. Penny wasn't so certain. Mis' Trent might have a screw loose, but she knew these hills. She knew gold, too.

'You are right. It is a half day's excursion, by the nearest foot trail,' Mis' Trent agreed. Contentedly she settled down to her baked beans with their strippings of crisp brown salt pork, her savory potatoes and onions, casting meanwhile an anticipatory eye at the big bowl of tapioca custard gemmed with raspberry preserve.

'I feel a sight better having the poor old lady friendly,' Grandpa observed, when she had taken her way back to the cabin at the end of the street. 'Neighbors, so. But I don't suppose there's anything in what she said about knowing a better place to pan.'

'Not likely,' Mr. Smith assented. 'You can see that gold's the thing she's off on.'

Penny glanced at him through her lashes. 'You tell the Mister,' she coaxed Mrs. Smith —'please you tell him it won't do a lick of harm to go see if she asks us again.'

Mis' Trent did ask them again the next day, and Mr. Smith accepted the invitation.

'Wild-goose chase, more than likely,' he told Mrs. Smith, 'but we can call it a picnic. It won't take any half day, going in the car.'

It wasn't easy to urge Mis' Trent into the blue car. Her eyes flickered uneasily when the door was opened for her and she made a sidling motion of flight.

Grandpa was already established in the back seat with Junior between his knees. 'Sure, Mis' Trent,' he coaxed 'if an old man like me isn't scaret of the contraption, a young lady like you's going to be game for it.'

Grandpa and Mis' Trent were already on friendly terms, but their attitude toward one another gave the rest of the town, Smith and Adams, some amusement. There may have been two years' difference in their ages; but to Mis' Trent Grandpa was 'the old gentleman' well preserved for his years; and to Grandpa she was 'that poor old thing with one foot in the grave.'

'No horse was ever too spirited for me in my youthful days,' Mis' Trent said, with dignity. 'As for fear, none of my race has known the meaning of the word.' She climbed in, shuddering slightly, and sat poised on the edge of the seat beside Grandpa.

The place where she directed them was the site of a famous old 'diggings'— a lode from which millions had been taken in the early days. Its old mine buildings, even its shaft timbers, were gone.

'There!' proclaimed Mis' Trent, moving across the rough ground in her voluminous skirt like a ship on a choppy sea. 'Mr. Trent always said that if anyone had sense enough he could gopher down — that was his word — gopher down around this old lode, and take out plenty of gold yet. If he wasn't afraid of strenuous labor.'

Mr. Smith and Penny and Grandpa exchanged sober glances. Penny broke the silence. 'Then why ain't you had it done, Mis' Trent?' she asked politely.

Mis' Trent lifted a haughty chin above the greenish, threadbare collar. 'I can't be troubled with small workings,' she rebuked them.

'But haven't you told any of your friends?' Mr. Smith inquired.

'Friends? I have no friends,' she said.

'Reckon we-uns could — could gopher down a little bit and try it, like you said?' Penny suggested.

There was plenty of time. The blue car had made the trip in a half hour, and Mrs. Smith had prepared a picnic lunch. The men had brought pick and shovel, too, and Mr. Smith set to work with a will, while Grandpa picked persistently at the rocky soil, stopping to mop his brow with a large bandanna.

After an hour of their digging, Penny sneaked a panful of dirt and trudged to the nearest stream to wash it. It proved far richer in 'color' than the gravel in Jane. Not, perhaps, so wonderful as Mis' Trent believed, in her grand dreams, but good pay dirt. Penny trotted back, beaming, bent under her load.

'Where you been, Penny?' demanded Junior, racing to meet her with Napoleum at his heels. 'Why didn't you take me along? What you got the pan for?'

Grandpa, resting on his spade, screwed around to watch her approach.

'You been panning it, Penny, girl?'

She nodded, and lugged the pan up to where the men were digging. Triumphantly she set it down and straightened to look at them.

Mis' Trent bent her black bonnet above it and poked a gloved finger into the wet sand. 'Rich dirt,' she said calmly.

'How would we git leave to work it?' quavered Grandpa. 'Who you suppose it belongs to?'

'Feel perfectly free to go ahead. You're welcome to all you can take out.' Mis' Trent waved a nonchalant hand at the landscape.

'But who does it belong to, Mis' Trent?' insisted Mr. Smith. 'The owner wouldn't be so ——'

'Whom would you suppose?' Mis' Trent's eyes widened with surprise. 'The owner, of course, is I.'

CAUTIOUS inquiry in Central City convinced the
Smiths that the old Pipin' Jenny lode really belonged
to Mis' Trent. It was one of her properties that had
not been sold for taxes.

'But that's only because nobody thinks it's worth
anything. I think we'd better keep it dark that we're
getting anything out,' said Mr. Smith.

'Then we shore ought to do our own retorting. Anyway, we dassent take much gold up to Central,' Penny
observed. 'They'd begin to wonder where we was getting
it, and then they'd go poking around to find out.'

'We'll keep it hid till we can go down to Denver with
it,' Mr. Smith agreed. 'Better hold on to it awhile,
anyway, with all the talk there is about gold going up.'

'Don't you say a word, Junior Smith!' his mother
warned automatically.

The Smiths met an obstacle when they tried to persuade their neighbor to take payment for the use of the
ground. She was offended at the offer of anything so
trivial. Penny solved that difficulty. Penny had learned a
surprising amount about human nature in the years when
she had had to 'look sharp' to avoid Unc' Jeff's rawhide.

She went to Mis' Trent alone. She wanted to explain to her, she said, about the Smiths. They were poor folks, yes; but terribly proud. A lady like Mis' Trent, who'd always had plenty, could hardly understand how folks felt when they'd never had anything. The Smiths would think they were on charity if they were to take even that little bit of gold off from anybody. It would save their pride, and it needn't hurt Mis' Trent's feelings, either, if she'd let them mine it on shares.

Thus it was settled. The Smiths were happy in this new opportunity, and Mis' Trent, once more the Lady Bountiful, beamed with new graciousness on the household of her beneficiaries. She had sugar in her tea and bacon for her breakfast, besides, the Smiths advancing part of their scanty store of money 'to bind the bargain.'

Those July days were busy ones for the inhabitants of Jane. Every morning the men went early to the Pipin' Jenny and spent the forenoon there. Their spare time they used in fashioning the rough tables and benches that completed the cabin furniture and the casement windows with their translucent panes of oiled paper, and in making the roof rainproof and the floor safe.

Another of Penny's contributions was a timepiece. Both Mr. Smith and Grandpa had let their watches run down again and again. Virginia's pretty trinket did not stand the jolts and the high altitude. Mis' Trent had long ignored the passage of the hours.

'Too bad we haven't a sundial,' said Virginia. 'There's hardly a day when the sun doesn't shine.'

Penny blinked at her seriously. 'I don't know nothing — anything — about them dials. But we can easy nail us up a board in under the roof where we can squint at it out the window; and then we can make chalk marks

where the roof shadows hits it at six and seven and eight
and such as that. And if we was to put one on the other
side for afternoon, we'd be pretty nigh fixed, even when
the menfolks' watches does quit.'

With no time-clocks to punch and no cars to catch,
Penny's timekeepers proved adequate and in key with
the sunny tempo of the days and weeks, even though they
did grow gradually slower with the changing course of
the sun.

The family spent little time inside the cabin's wall,
except when the swift, clean showers drove them there
for an hour or two each day. Mrs. Smith panned the
creek whenever an hour hung heavy on her hands.
Mr. Smith and Junior were attaining results in training
Napoleum.

Besides Napoleum, Junior had the twin fawns to play
with. The neighboring ranger sent in the Smiths' application to the game warden and he gave them permission
to keep the young creatures. There was endless fascination in watching them run through the village, rising
above barriers like puffs of down, with effortless leaps
straight into the air. Only at night were they shut up,
in the cabin with Barkis.

As for Virginia, she was collecting flowers with growing interest. The reaches of Jane were embroidered
with their bright colors, and excursions into the woods
continually rewarded her with new specimens — gentians,
moccasin flowers, alpine columbines. She tried to excuse her enthusiasm, as if she were ashamed of it. If
she should use her scholarship to go to Quenton, she
defended herself, she rather wanted to take botany: it
wouldn't be such a bore as most courses. And if she
were to take botany, the herbarium would come in handy.

She usually ended by saying that she couldn't imagine herself really going to the stupid old university, but it was just as well to provide against emergencies.

She had made good use of the books Zip had brought her, though she said she felt like a jailbird when she thought how they had been obtained. Now she plunged into a more technical study of botany, stirred to fresh efforts by a surprising gift from Mis' Trent.

The family had already noticed that the hodgepodge of Mis' Trent's cabin was like a Swiss Family Robinson bag, except that it never, by any chance, produced everyday conveniences. Its exotic treasures, however, were many. Now she thrust into Virginia's hands a fine French microscope in a rosewood case and a botanical key that she had used at the select female academy she had attended as a young lady.

During one of the almost daily mountain showers, Virginia was spreading her newly gathered specimens artistically between layers of newspapers. She had pulled some of the yellowed old papers from the cabin walls to use for the purpose. They were too old and brittle to absorb the moisture as fresh ones would have done, but the Smiths were doing without the luxury of the daily news.

When she had weighted flowers and papers with stones, Virginia turned to her microscope and key. The microscope had revealed unguessed beauties to them all: the delicate fashionings of stamens and pistils, the fairy carving of seed capsules. But the key presented problems in its strange words: hirsute, gibbous, palmate, and countless others as unfamiliar. A dictionary was one thing that Mis' Trent failed to produce.

'Oh, jiminy Christmas!' Virginia cried passionately.

'I can't see why I didn't learn *any*thing in twelve years of school. It seems as if I didn't know straight up.'

Penny had been kneeling on a bench and peering at the pages of an 'Atlantic' that had just been laid bare by the pulling off of a newspaper. She turned an amazed and woeful face on Virginia.

'*You* don't?' she faltered. 'Then what about *me?*'

She turned back to the yellowed page along which her finger had been traveling, but too late to hide the downward jerk of her trembling lips.

'Why, Penny!' Virginia stared wonderingly. 'Why — Penny.'

'You don't know nothing about it — you so smart and lucky and pretty-looking —— Not to have no kindy folks, nor no kindy fetching up — and then not to know nothing, either.'

'But what's the matter, Penny? I mean, what's the matter now?'

'It's thisyere reading,' Penny explained in an angry voice. 'You'd say it off easy as nothing. And me, I cain't get the drift of it no more than as if it was thisyere Latin they talk about. And I do hone to. Oh, Great Jawns, V'ginia, seems like I *got* to know things.'

Virginia sat very still, her finger unconsciously pressing down on the mystic phrase, 'umbel with widely divaricate rays.'

'Why, Penny,' she repeated helplessly. And then, in a softer tone than Penny had ever heard from her, 'As bright as you are, Pen, it's going to be just fun for you to learn stuff. I tell you, Penny, we'll — we'll have a school.'

Penny shot a questioning glance over her shoulder.

'Yes, a school. I'll spend an hour a day teaching you.

We've got such loads of time. And we can teach Junior, too. He hardly learned a thing in school, anyhow, and this whooping cough has lost him what he did have. Maybe we could get you far enough along so you wouldn't have to go into quite such a low grade when Mrs. Henley — if Mrs. Henley takes you again in the fall.'

Penny disregarded the Mrs. Henley part of Virginia's words. She was trying with all her might to forget Mrs. Henley.

'You — mean it?' Penny asked at last in a muffled voice. 'It'd be a turrible chore to learn me anything.'

'Of course I mean it, honey,' said Virginia.

The face Penny turned toward that endearment was tear-stained, but it was nevertheless a face transfigured.

'They's — golly poppings, they's even a schoolhouse,' she said, after a moment.

They had seen the schoolhouse on the first day, but now they explored it thoroughly. It was a tumbledown old shack, with a small square cupola above the entrance. Of its furnishings remained only three double desks and the teacher's table and a blackboard. The rest had doubtless been broken up for firewood.

The blackboard was scrawled over with countless names of people and towns, and the dates ranged from 1900 to 1933 — showing that the first date had marked the end of its usefulness. 'Fools' names, like fools' faces, Alluz seen in public places,' Grandpa quoted, when they took him to see their find. But faintly discernible beneath these names were sums and spelling in childish chirography. And Virginia traced out the triumphant words:

> 'No more lessons, no more books,
> No more teachers' sassy looks!'

The doggerel seemed prophetic. For thirty-three years there had been neither books nor lessons, teachers nor pupils, within these four walls.

The floor was deep-littered with dirt and leaves and rubbish. The girls spent a busy day sweeping it out and scrubbing seats and desks and blackboard. At ten o'clock, five mornings of the week, Junior pompously rang the rusty cow-bell, and he and Penny took their places on opposite sides of the room, while Virginia seated herself with dignity at the teacher's desk.

'We couldn't ever get Junior to stick to it if we didn't make it into a game,' she explained self-consciously.

In truth, she found it fun herself. There was romance about it. She sat in the shadow of long ago, where barefoot boys and little girls in pigtails and pinafores had ciphered and made pothooks with squeaky slate-pencils. Behind this very table, so Mrs. Smith said, had sat a teacher with her hair rolled into a pompadour over a wire sausage, and wearing a collar with points that jabbed her under the ears, and skirts down to her toes, and an elegant Grecian bend in her hourglass figure.

Besides the romance of the past, the present held beauty. The sunlight laid bars of dusty gold light across the air; the wind sighed high in the spruces; an occasional butterfly flitted in and out — a swallowtail, yellow and black, a rust-red Monarch, or a speck of throbbing azure; and in the sunny stillness outside Barkis's bell went clanking here and there.

Virginia had Penny read aloud from 'Uncle Tom's Cabin.' She used it as a general textbook, besides, not only correcting Penny's pronunciation (with considerable uncertainty at times), but giving her spelling and writing lessons based upon it, on big lined pencil tablets bought at Central City.

To start with, Junior was very cocky, because he could read and write almost as well as Penny. For a while each day he worked hard to keep pace with her; but his zeal would soon wane, and he would wriggle around in his seat and coax Napoleum through the open door, or watch the fawns, standing and stretching their long necks to look in, all graceful awkwardness and innocence. Or he would hide a lizard in his desk and try to harness it with string. Yet he did well enough.

Virginia made numbers bearable to him by using an old ladder that they dragged over beside the schoolhouse. On the rounds she chalked 2 — 4 — 6 — 8 — and so on, and Junior ran along them, trying to keep his balance while he chanted a number with each step, until he could erase them and still remember. The twos mastered, he went on to the threes and fours. Virginia found Penny solemnly pacing that ladder and murmuring the numbers, too, so she turned it over and gave her the upper multiplication tables. For the first time, Virginia herself thoroughly memorized the sevens.

The teacher was teaching herself some unexpected branches. She had moved her botanical equipment into the schoolhouse and worked at it while her 'classes' were studying; but botany was not the only subject in which she progressed.

Penny, quite confident of Virginia's knowledge, asked her embarrassing questions: about the geography and history of Uncle Tom's period; about slavery and the Civil War; about Harriet Beecher Stowe. Virginia had always been satisfied with her own fund of information, but these definite queries made her feel woolly and uncertain. She waylaid her father and mother and got what she could from them — in private — and raked together from her helterskelter school days every scrap she could recall.

Nature study was added to the curriculum. Mr. Smith, grown increasingly fond of the birds that came to their feeding-tray, begged from a grocer in Central a large poster bird chart, published as advertising, and Virginia hung it beside her desk. Soon even Junior could name all the birds shown there, and to his delight many of their own visitors were of the number.

Among them were the three kinds of 'robins,' as Penny had called them: the real robin (which wasn't a real robin, either, the chart said, but a thrush), the chewink or towhee, with its ruby eye and black bib, and the big-billed one with the primadonna song. It was like happening on a fifty-cent piece in the road, to learn that the sweet singer was a black-headed grosbeak.

'You feel so friendly like, oncet you know a body's name,' said Penny.

XV. BUT WHAT NEXT?

JULY slipped into August. Warm summer mornings were washed clean and cool by the swift rains of afternoon. Evenings hummed with the contented fiddling of insects; and young grosbeaks plaintively called through the twilight, like baby ghosts 'crying,' Junior said, 'for their mammas.' Chickadees, heard singly throughout the summer, now flocked into the clearing, whispering and lilting their prophecies of autumn.

The men worked eagerly at the Pipin' Jenny. 'And believe me,' said Mr. Smith, flexing his tanned right arm, 'I can put in a lot more time at it now without feeling like something the cat's dragged in. Walt French says he never saw a fellow change so fast as I've done. Almost lost the old bookkeeper stoop already.'

Walt French, the ranger, stopped often at Jane. It was he who had put through the Smiths' application to the game warden and gained them the right to keep the fawns. Dum and Dee — for so they had been named — were growing as little fawns should. They were an unwarrantable expense, as no one could deny, consuming quantities of canned milk and mash. Yet no one could suggest giving them up: their baby faces and plush noses were so endearing.

Besides, Penny, in some inexplicable way, found a Central City grocer who was loaded down with wormy corn meal, and a part of their problem was cheaply solved. His raisins had gone wormy, too, and the chickadees turned extra somersaults around the Smith feeding-tray. Raisins were favorite tidbits of theirs, and worms only added to the charm.

Virginia was concentrating on her herbarium. She was analyzing the difficult composites now, the many species of goldenrod, the sunflowers and daisies and asters, that take the place of the early summer flowers. She used every moment when her two classes were studying, for the one hundred and fifty specimens she had classified were but a tantalizingly small part of those she had gathered.

Together, Virginia and Penny had manufactured a sign for the schoolhouse and hung it above the door:

JANE

School District No. 1

Virginia Smith — Principal

In the first place they had lettered it:

THE GHOST TOWN SCHOOL

That sign had not stayed. Mis' Trent, sailing over to visit, had stood with one black elbow cupped in a black glove and studied it bleakly. Then she had tapped at the door and entered.

'I thought better of you, Virginia Smith!' she snorted. 'Ghost town, indeed! Are you like the silly tourists and authors that miscall the town of Jane and blacken

her name through the length and breadth of the land?
Central City — Nevadaville — Black Hawk: ghost
towns, indeed! The fools!' She shook a ragged black
forefinger at the girl and waited, with rapidly blinking
lids, for her reply. Virginia sat abashed.

'Ghost towns? Why, any year — any day — you'll
see people crowding back again, and mills opening, and
the air buzzing and beating with stamps and rumbling
with ore-cars. You mark my words!' Her tone dropped
abruptly from the oratorical. 'You'll change the sign,
won't you, Virginia?'

Virginia did, and thereafter Mis' Trent visited the
school several times. In place of the black sunbonnet
she wore a beaded bonnet, evidently as a mark of respect. It sat on top of her head, scooped out in the back
to make place for the walnut of gray hair. Junior could
scarcely drag his eyes away from its sprays of grass or
feathers, worn to stubs, and the glitter of its jet sequins.
The confection was tied under her ear with ribbons that
had been frayed to skeins of silk thread through the
years.

The jet winked and twinkled and the sprays quivered
as she listened noddingly to recitations. The Third
Grade read:

> 'It was an old, old, old, old lady
> And a boy that was half past three ——'

Third Grade, of course, was Junior, who occupied a seat on
the left-hand side of the room. The Fifth Grade, in a seat
on the right, read a passage from 'Uncle Tom's Cabin.'

'Would our visitor tell us,' Virginia suggested, and
altered her sentence tactfully —'Mis' Trent, do you
remember anything your father and mother told you
about the Civil War times?'

Mis' Trent rose. 'I remember clearly the years of the
following decade,' she said, standing very erect and
looking around the room as if it were filled with children,
all hanging on her words. 'My father had had one of
the first pianos carted up into Central City: a great
square rosewood piano, hand-carved. We had a singing
master and a dancing master and a piano teacher. And
our families held social affairs, my dear children, that
would have graced the cultural metropolises of the East.
Needless to say, we had our own stables and our own
carriages, and the people of consequence entertained
lavishly, as became ladies and gentlemen. And then ——'

A phoebe that had nested in the rafters swooped
down through the bars of dusty yellow light. Mis'
Trent's brow puckered and she looked about her almost
in fright, as if the walls had suddenly emptied out their
throng of pigtailed girls and boys with bowl-shaped
haircuts. She passed an uncertain hand over her eyes,
under the tilted old bonnet.

'And then,' she repeated, 'and then —— But they'll
come back. You'll see them all come back.' She sat
down.

Penny was proud of her fifth-grade standing. 'But I
ain't going to feel so biggity when I go into that sixth
grade, come fall. Those little old boys and girls — golly
poppings, V'ginia, they ain't going to be more'n eleven
years old. And nobody believes I ain't fourteen yet.
Oh, V'ginia, I'd jest work myse'f black in the face if
you'd keep on learning me, come fall.'

'But I don't know where you —— I don't know where
any of us are going to be, Penny. I might even go to
Quenton, after all. I'm not planning to, of course. I'd
have to get some sort of work to earn my board and room.

And I always vowed I wouldn't go to college if I had to
work my way through. Half the good of college is its
social advantages,' she said. She spoke vehemently, as
if strongly reminding herself of a fact. 'And think of
Betty and Hoot and maybe Zip, all there at Quenton,
too, and in those gorgeous big fraternity houses. I
couldn't stand that.' She didn't have to remind herself
of this fact.

'Social?' Penny asked interestedly. 'I always thought
college was more for book-larning, V'ginia?'

'Learning; only you'd better say education,' Virginia
corrected her automatically. 'Well, books do *count*.
They count quite a lot,' she conceded thoughtfully.

Penny's mind had returned to her own problem. She
was intently screwing the point of her lead-pencil around
in a tiny hole in the desk. That hole had been dug by
some schoolboy of the past, a grandfather now, perhaps.

'You reckon I got to go back to that old Home?' she
faltered, lifting a pansy-brown gaze to Virginia's face.

Virginia was mounting a pressed button snakeroot,
pasting strips of gummed paper over its stem to fasten
it to the cardboard. She, too, was intent on the work
of her hands. 'Penny, I don't — don't know,' she said,
without lifting her eyes. 'If we go back to Denver and
Dad doesn't get work, why — well, honey, it's going to
be hard sledding for the Smiths, and I don't see how we
could ——'

'If we go back to Denver.' It was a question that
must soon be answered. School was scheduled to open
the first week in September.

'I ain't healthy enough to go back to that old school,
maybe,' Junior suggested. 'I got glams and a temper,
the doctor said so.'

But Junior's 'glams' were almost invisible now, and the patchy fever flush on his thin cheeks had given way to a plump brown tan.

'You're nothing but a little fraud,' scoffed his mother, tousling him thankfully. 'You've got no excuse for staying out of school now — not in any way, shape, form, or manner, Henry Smith, Junior.'

Junior took a mighty swallow of goat's milk. His white-rimmed smile showed two teeth missing. 'Well,' he conceded, 'I don't mind. I bet I kin lick them old city kids, this year. And I want to show 'em that my warts are gone.'

'But they aren't gone!' Virginia objected.

'They're going to be. Penny rubbed 'em with a split bean and buried the bean and said things,' Junior explained.

Penny reddened. 'I told you *maybe*,' she reminded Junior. The sure old spells were beginning to lose their power for Penny.

They were at supper, sitting at a picnic table they had made for outdoor eating. The evening was soft, but the sky was already chilling its blue and lighting the horizon with a cool primrose behind the pines. The days were growing shorter, and that fact fell like a shadow across Penny's heart. No longer did they hear the husky cascade of song from the willow thrush where the brook ran deep in the woods. The chickadees and the jays had taken possession of the hills, with a few other wayfarers, nuthatches, and yellow-throats and an occasional strayed magpie.

Penny twisted her hands in her lap and sat silent. Napoleum whined softly and reared up to lick at her face. Penny sniffed.

'It's a fine evening. Sort of feel of autumn in the air,'
Grandpa tried, and took a hasty mouthful of corn-meal
mush to hide his mistake.

'They — they do say there ain't many more jobs in
Denver than they was last spring,' Penny said desperately.

The family looked at her with startled eyes.

'Why bring that up?' inquired Virginia.

Penny gulped. 'I mean — why cain't we keep on like
we are? We're getting along so good, and all. And if
V'ginia wanted to go to college, why, I'd learn — teach
— Junior every last thing she's learned me, and ——'

'But, Penny, you have to remember Mrs. Henley,'
Mrs. Smith reminded her gently. 'You mustn't run the
risk of losing such a chance as that. Well-to-do folks
like the Henleys ——'

'They ain't home from Europe yet,' Penny hastened
to put in, her eyes dilating with dread.

'I cain't see why I didn't think about a garden,' she
began again, when the silence still held unbroken. 'We
could have had all the garden sass we needed if we'd
planted it jest as soon as the moon was right. Even corn.
They's one kind gets good before frost, even up so high.'

Grandpa cleared his throat. 'But you can't never tell
how soon winter's going to set in, Penny, girl,' he said.
'Any time, oncet September's come, you kin look for
snow. Couldn't work the Pipin' Jenny. Get snowed in.
Wouldn't do, Penny, girl.'

'Well, then — Central City!' Penny popped it out
desperately.

'What do you mean, "Well, then, Central City?"'

'I bet Grandpa and the Mister could get work in a
garage. They're so handy-like. And you could buy you

a house. Why, Great Jawns, the Mister could buy him
a house for fifty dollars.'

'A house for fifty dollars?' gasped Mrs. Smith.

Virginia confirmed the statement. 'Really, Mother,
that's so. Not such bad houses, either.'

'I've heard they go awfully cheap. Tax sales,' added
Mr. Smith. 'Rows and rows of them stood there empty
for years. Windows boarded up and everything.'

'You'd — you'd have to make tracks, though,' Penny
went on, glancing with quick hope from one to the other.
Their faces were incredulous, but at least they were
listening. ''Cause business shore is picking up, and they's
going to be a rush for good houses.'

'That's right, too,' Mr. Smith nodded. 'They do say
business is chirking up some. Lots of talk about higher
prices for gold. President Roosevelt's shaking things
up. And once you get higher prices for gold, there's
going to be a lot of difference in the mining camps.'

'D'you reckon we really could get us work, Son?'
Grandpa quavered.

'I just wonder'— Mrs. Smith absently tossed Napoleum her choicest mouthful of trout —'I never have seen
a beauty shop in Central. But good gracious! we
couldn't go around buying houses, no matter how cheap
they were. And I suppose we'd have to have a few chairs
and beds. What would you suggest that we use for
money?'

XVI. CENTRAL CITY

'AND we'd have to keep enough of a reserve so that we could eat for a few weeks, in case you had to stop work at the lode,' Mrs. Smith continued reasonably.

'We could live on goat's milk,' Junior suggested, 'and trouts and greens. I like milk and trouts and greens all right.'

'It wouldn't be any worse to starve in Central City than in Denver,' Virginia added brightly.

Mr. Smith glanced at Grandpa, who jerked his head affirmatively.

'We've been keeping it for a sort of surprise, Mamma,' Mr. Smith said boyishly. 'But we've been taking out a bit more than we said — out of the Pipin' Jenny. You know we've been carrying part of our pay sand up to Central every week or so: just about what we'd been getting from around here, so nobody'd get curious. But we've been retorting the rest and stacking it away till we could take it down to Denver. And at the present price of gold, what do you guess we've got on hand, Mamma?'

Mamma wordlessly shook her head and Penny's heart hung midway of a beat.

'Well, near as we can reckon it — and we weighed it carefully — we've got two hundred and thirty ——'

'A good plump two hundred and thirty,' insisted Grandpa.

'Dollars?' Mamma asked feebly.

'Why, we can buy a house!' Virginia exclaimed.

'Gee whizz, gee whizz, we're going to live in Central City!' shrieked Junior.

'Great Jawns!' Penny murmured reverently.

They sat there while the darkness deepened round them. This was an hour of day that Penny had always loved and feared. As a little girl she had run away from the squalor and the scolding of the shack and found refuge on the twilight hillside. There she had sat on the prickly ground, hands clasped around bare knees and all of her silently aching for something she did not know.

At such times she had watched and wondered vaguely at the change that came over the earth when darkness fell. Birds flew into the underbrush with a rush of wings and twittered softly and were still. And — all in a moment — the trees stood hushed and dark. It was as if they gathered their cloaks around them and drew away from the human child. It was as if they resented her presence.

More then than at any other time she had longed for a dog or a cat: for anything at all to love and be loved by. A'nt Sally had hated animals; even the baby skunk and the chipmunks and the squirrel that Penny had tamed, A'nt Sally had driven away. Dirty varmints, she called them.

Darkness was different now. Her family surrounded her. She had shut Barkis and Dum and Dee safe and cozy in their stable. Napoleum laid his muzzle on her

knees and adored her with melancholy brown eyes. The trees might draw aside their robes if they wished: Penny had her own warm place in the world.

The Smiths sat and talked until they could no longer see one another; until the birds were still; until Junior laid his cheek on the table and slept. They made plans, and Penny was in all the plans. Her six months would be up the last of October, but if the Smiths had any luck at all, they would ask to keep her for another six months, or at least until the Henleys returned.

'We take her out — like a liberry book,' Junior observed, just before he surrendered to sleep. 'I wisht we could have her for keeps, Mamma. Can't we have her for keeps?'

Next day they set out for Central City as soon as lunch was over. Mr. Smith and Grandpa had put in their usual hours at the Pipin' Jenny. 'It'll git us a loaf of bread and a pound of beefsteak,' Grandpa said, when Junior whined over the delay, 'and mebbe overalls all round, too.'

The mining towns of Black Hawk, Mountain City, Central City, and Nevadaville had sprung up after Gregory's rich gold strike, back in 1859. For years they had lived fast and hard: gay, bright, dangerous lives. For years again Black Hawk and Central City had remained half awake, most of their houses boarded up at the windows and most of their stores staring on the street with blind eyes.

Mountain City had vanished. Nevadaville's hill still held an abandoned church and schoolhouse; still held its main street, with gaps like missing teeth in its double row of rickety leaning business buldings; still held a hundred houses. For years the only public building kept in repair was the Masonic Hall, where meetings were regularly held. For years the town's only inhabitant was one old man.

Now placer miners had set up their sluice-boxes, their jig-boxes, their rockers, in the gulch that lay at Nevadaville's feet. Now the boards had been wrenched off a few of the house windows, wisps of smoke from the chimneys told of miners camping out within their long-deserted walls. Now two or three rusty automobiles clung to the side-hill streets.

In Central City the somnolent streets were stirring, though still sleepily.

The Smiths parked the blue car in the drowsy main thoroughfare, which someone was sprinkling with a hose to lay the dust. They climbed the stairs opposite the Teller House and found themselves in the newspaper office.

It was one of the best places to get information. Editor and office had been there sixty years or more. The worn linoleum, the dark wallpaper, dimly gilt; the pinned-up handbills of fifty years ago; the black walnut desks; the gnomelike figure of the editor, meticulously garbed; — all these were of another day. There were two bits of vivid present life: the radio, just then calling out the stock reports from cities beyond the wall of the Rockies; and the keen eyes that peered from beneath the editor's skull-cap.

Yes, Mr. Reed could give them a list of houses that were to be sold for taxes; and the keys, too. And he would advise them to make a choice quickly.

'You're going to see great things in Central City,' he told them, swinging his sunken small body around in his creaking swivel chair. 'Ghost town! Bah! They make me sick with their chatter of ghost towns. Central never was dead. And now —!'

Central City is crammed into the gulch, street laid above street, 'so you can spit down the chimley of the house next under,' Penny said inelegantly. Shelf streets, with only one row of houses each; shored up with retaining walls of stone or log.

'Thisyere's the house I always did take to,' Penny breathed wistfully as they came to a prim building set in a yard hollowed out of the side hill.

'It really is nice,' Mrs. Smith assented. 'If it was repainted — but even with that white paint peeling like it is, there's something about the shape and style.'

'It's New England Colonial,' pronounced Virginia — 'those fluted corner columns, and the green shutters.'

'That little half-round kindy window up over the front door,' hesitated Penny, 'it makes me feel funny to look at it. And theseyere steps that go up into the yard. I wonder —— Do you reckon I use' to stop and set here when I was a young one? Out walking, maybe?'

The steps were of stone, and guarded at their foot by a gate. The gate was rusted and it hung by one hinge, but its traceries of iron were beautifully simple. The yard, too, was shabby; it had burned out until it was only a tangle of tawny grass; but a pair of spruce trees and some cottonwoods gave grateful shadow from the blaze of the sun.

Mrs. Smith started on reluctantly. 'This one is around seventy-five dollars,' she said. 'We'd better look at the cheaper ones first.'

They liked a long low brown house that backed up against a rocky cliff. 'I'd have a mountune in my own back yard!' shrilled Junior. 'I want it, Mamma! I say I want this one.'

The price was only thirty dollars. Grandpa shrewdly

estimated that it would take several times that sum to make it safe.

They liked a great yellow house that sat on the highest street and looked abroad over the hillsides pocked with mine dumps. Swallows had evidently built in the high retaining wall. They flew around the visitors, sweeping and swerving only a few inches from their faces. Beautiful birds they were, iridescent with peacock blue and green and purple.

'I want this house,' Junior decided. 'This is the house I want, Mamma. I could catch me a bird and keep it in a cage.'

'I could have whole house-parties,' Virginia chimed in enthusiastically — 'If we had furniture for such a hotel,' she added, crestfallen.

'It would cost like the dickens to keep it warm, once winter set in,' Penny said timidly.

Grandpa best liked a house whose owner had apparently loved it with devotion.

'It don't hardly seem possible a body could buy all that scrollwork under the eaves and round the porch fer no twenty-five dollars,' Grandpa protested, 'to say nothing of the house it's fastened onto. By gum, if it ain't neat and tasty!'

The 'womenfolks' traded amused glances. There was ornament wherever ornament could be: squares of red and blue and yellow glass bordering the urn of flowers in frosted glass on the front door; wooden curlicues heading the porch posts; bay windows; a cupola.

'But, Paw, it's built pretty flimsy,' Mr. Smith warned when they entered it, and Grandpa assented and went on with the rest, though he looked back lingeringly at the cupola.

In the end, they returned to the New England house. It had been loved, too; that was clear. You could tell by the way the garden had been built up. Those square yards of ground had had to be manufactured, a six-foot wall built and filled in with soil carried from afar. Bushes, trees, hollyhocks, grass, must have been petted and coaxed like delicate children. The walled-in stone steps, too, had a look of retreat, as if precious things had been guarded there.

'I think a little boy lived here,' Junior said astutely, 'and played underneath the bushes where the grass is wore off.'

'I don't remember seeing any little boy,' Penny pondered.

A pleasant surprise greeted them when they turned the key in the lock and stepped inside. A stale, unaired odor met them, but the interior was not in the state of dilapidation that some of the houses had revealed. Nor was it entirely bare. A heavy sideboard stood in the room with the sunny bay window, a rolltop desk in the room across the hall.

'What you look so funny for, Penny?' Junior demanded, running at her and butting her in the stomach to attract her attention. 'What do you, Penny? Huh?'

Penny had paused on the threshold and was frowning at the desk. 'I — don't know,' she murmured. 'I reckon I — jest like it.'

She was not alone in her feeling. Grandpa and Mr. Smith teetered testingly on floors and stairs and opened and shut windows. Virginia found a stoop-shouldered room with a dormer that sheltered a broad window-seat. 'Wouldn't it look darling with little looped Swiss curtains, Penny?' she cried. 'And we could probably pick

up some furniture cheap and paint it.' Mrs. Smith exclaimed over the built-in cupboards and the convenient
shelves and went from one sunny window to another.

Junior jubilantly slid down the walnut rail of the staircase and squealed with rapture over the back yard. The
back yard ran uphill so steeply that a boardwalk like a
bridge reached straight across from an upstairs door to
the back of the yard, and the garden lay in terraces below
it. To add to Junior's delight, the sidewalk that climbed
from the street in front of them to the street behind them
was not a walk at all, but a flight of wooden steps, hun-
dreds of them, gone gray with age and crazily crooked.
And there was a playhouse near the back door, a trig,
strongly built little structure, large enough for all the
Smiths to stand upright in. What play that yard promised a little boy!

As for Penny and Napoleum, they trotted in and out,
almost equally speechless. Napoleum hung out his
tongue placidly and gave no sign of disapproval; and
Penny glowed, from the ruddy crest of her top wave of
hair, through each of her sparse golden freckles and her
red-brown eyes.

'Like it, Penny?' Mr. Smith asked, when he had put
the same question to each of the others. 'Penny's got
as much right to vote as anybody. You realize,' he asked,
frowning in surprise at the thought, 'that if it hadn't
been for Penny —— ? Well, anyhow, you like it all
right, Penny?'

Penny nodded, still wordless.

'We'll come back tomorrow morning, the first thing,
and buy up the tax title,' Mr. Smith decided. 'Could do
it right now, only the treasurer shuts up shop too early.'

Throughout the Janeward drive, throughout the night,

Penny was churned by two emotions. Her heart would lift at the thought that she was to live — well, at any rate a little longer — with the Smiths, and in a house of dreams, too. Then her heart would plunge down at the fear that someone else might come to a decision at the crucial moment; that someone else might reach the treasurer five minutes, a minute, thirty seconds, before Mr. Smith. It simply could not be that such a treasure of a house should be theirs for seventy-five dollars.

But it was; and when the Central school opened on the sixth of September, the Smiths and Penny and Napoleum were settled in the New England house, and Barkis was tethered in the terraced back yard, and Dum and Dee leaped lightly among the rocks.

Mis' Trent had watched their preparations for moving with slight comment, but with settled gloom. Mrs. Smith had asked her to come and live with them that winter and a frosty gleam of pleasure had flickered in her eyes. But she had shaken her head.

'I am too thoroughly habituated to the solitude,' she thanked them. 'City life disturbs me.'

She gave Virginia the fine microscope, and dragged out of a shed storeroom an old French music-box, shaped like a modern cabinet phonograph or radio, and decorated with delicately wrought paintings of satin shepherdesses and fluffy silken sheep. This she insisted on giving the Smith family.

Only the fun of planning for their new home could have robbed their going of pain for themselves. Even as it was, they treasured those last days in the sunny stillnesses of Jane. Penny sought the woods and lay on her stomach in the elastic bed of pine and spruce needles (layer after layer of them shed there during long years), and breathed deep of their sun-warmed sweetness. Or she flopped over on her back and stared up through the trees, only wriggling a little when ants strolled over her.

Fireweed splashed its bright magenta everywhere, and asters lifted a blue mist, and clematis, gone to seed, smoked white. Chickadees, in still greater numbers, called and whispered; jays, steadily increasing in number, shrieked raucously.

Afternoons were so softly warm that the family still gathered in the shade and read, until the thousandth page of 'David Copperfield' was turned, and the book was finished. But mornings were so sparkling cool that the men went to the Pipin' Jenny with added zest, and the girls and Mrs. Smith worked busily at new tasks.

They gathered the last of the chokecherries and pincherries. Chokecherries were unusually fine this year, their clusters full and black like miniature grapes. When they found bushes of especially sweet one, they kept sampling one bunch after another till their throats were puckery and their teeth stained purple.

The cabin was puckery sweet, too, with the boiling of them.

'It's too strong if you make it all chokecherry,' Penny warned. 'Nor it don't jell nice. Apples makes it lickin' good.'

The frosty blue clusters of Oregon grape grew on low, holly-like plants. Their blue skin disclosed a startling blood-red pulp, sour to the tongue but making a delicious jelly, as did the fairy-like pincherries. Deep purple, garnet, ruby, the jellies stood on the Smith shelves, mostly in pint jars, since good money must be paid for containers.

Virginia and Penny gathered white fir needles, too, to

fill pillows for Christmas gifts. Virginia started gathering the shiny dry needles of pine and spruce. Penny watched her for a while, and disappeared. Presently she came back with a branch of another sort of evergreen: gray-blue-green, its thick waxy needles curved upward.

'Smell of it!' said Penny. It was richly pungent.

'Feel of it!' It was sticky to the touch.

'Thisyere kind keeps its smell heaps longer than them,' Penny declared, motioning toward Virginia's piles of pine and spruce.

Virginia studied the cones on Penny's branch. They were like velvet, lavender and green. 'It's white fir, I do believe,' she decided. 'What they call balsam.'

The girls stripped the new tips from the scattering fir trees near them till their fingers were black with pitch.

'Hop pillows is nice, too,' said Penny. 'They make you sleep.'

So they gathered hops. Penny knew where the vines spread mantles of fine-cut leaves over whole hillsides and hung swaying draperies from the bushes. The fruits were cone-shaped, pale green and fluffy. The girls filled flour sacks with the queerly good-smelling things. By the time the family was ready to depart, the trailer was loaded with the goods they had gained in the hills.

The trailer was loaded and the cabin and the schoolhouse were nailed shut. The Smiths might come another summer. Who knew?

'I won't permit any intruder to make free of your summer home,' Mis' Trent promised them, glancing at the shotgun that hung above her door. 'Jane' — she added the surprising postscript casually — 'belongs to me — if it hasn't been sold for taxes.'

'We come to Jane empty and we go away full,' Grandpa said soberly. 'Got a summer home and a winter home, all clear. And when had the Smiths owned proppity?'

XVII. PLANS

CENTRAL CITY was astir with that special feeling of bustle and importance that comes with the first day of school. Its source was in the children. Most of them had something new to wear: squeaky cords for the more prosperous boys; crisp plaid ginghams for their sisters; fresh hair-cuts. Most of them had something new to carry: long pencils, sharpened only once; corpulent tablets of bluish-gray pencil paper. Most of them had new schoolrooms, new desks, new teachers. All of them had a new year, with all sorts of new possibilities and a new start.

Penny went with Junior and soon found herself established in the sixth grade, as she had hoped. But, as she had not dared to hope, there were other sixth-graders as old as she, children who had come in from the hills. To her still greater comfort, there was a boy who was not only as old as she, but larger. Besides all that, Virginia thought that Penny could make two grades in one if the two of them worked hard after school hours. Virginia had decided to stay at home this fall and she would have plenty of time for coaching Penny.

Mr. Smith and Grandpa set out at once to make a

tour of mines and garages with work in view. When they
clumped tiredly in on the evening of the first day of
school, dinner was already waiting.

Dusk fell early in that town hemmed in by hills.
The lights were shining. Savory smells from the kitchen
filled the dining-room. Junior was sitting cross-legged on
the floor in front of the French music-box, which tinkled
its melodies in frosty drops of sweetness. When Grandpa
and Mr. Smith drew back their chairs and Mrs. Smith
carried in the bowls of brown stew, the music-box was
tinkling out 'Home, Sweet Home.'

'It looks more like home already than that Denver
apartment ever did.' Mr. Smith moistened his lips
expectantly as the oniony, meaty, hot savor reached
him.

The kitchen chairs had been lacquered with a quick-
drying Chinese red. The dingy old table was to undergo
the same treatment. There was nothing else in the room
except the music-box. Hot stew can do a great deal,
however, to make a house a home.

'It does seem cozy,' Grandpa agreed. He bowed his
head, and his voice was not noticeably less cheerful
than usual when he murmured, 'Dear Lord, Bless this
food to our use and us in Thy service, Amen.' You had
always the feeling that Grandpa was really talking to
the Lord, and that he was really thankful. Yet tonight
the cheerful voice had a tiredness about it.

Mrs. Smith glanced inquiringly from him to Mr. Smith.

'I don't suppose either of you found anything,' she
said with determined sprightliness —'yet.'

'Well, Mamma, you'd be surprised.' Mr. Smith
beamed at her over a spoonful of stew. 'At the garage
across from the hotel — the other hotel, not the Teller

House — they took my name and said they'd give me a try when they had anything. And at one of the mines they're going to take me on for a little job of bookkeeping. Not next month, either. No, sir, right now! And if I don't work up enough to keep us going, by the time snow flies, I'll eat my hat. How about you, Paw?'

'Same old story,' Grandpa confessed, crumbing crackers into his bowl. ''Guess I got to get used to it. They ain't no place in this world for an old man.'

'You didn't run across anything, then?' Mr. Smith said it matter-of-factly, fishing for a succulent forkful of beef. 'Well, I must say that takes a load off my shoulders, Paw.'

'A load — what was it you said, Son?' Grandpa quavered.

'Well, I got to thinking, and it looks to me as if you and I have got our hands plenty full as it is: anyway, as long as the weather stays open. We ought to get out all the pay dirt we can, up at the Pipin' Jenny; and we ought to get a permit and cut and haul every stick of wood we'll need to burn this winter. And the girls here have more little jobs for us than you can shake a stick at. I got sort of jittery when I thought of you taking a steady job anywhere. And on top of it all, a crazy notion struck me — something you'd sure have to boss, Paw, if it was to amount to anything.'

Grandpa's face creased with expectancy. Mr. Smith leaned forward while Penny took his bowl to the kitchen for another helping.

'I got the idea from a piece in the paper,' he began. 'And I bet we could sell it easy when we got it done, see?'

They all waited curiously. Penny, bringing a full

bowl of stew, splashed a scallop of it onto his shoulder.

''Sall right,' he reassured her genially. 'Couldn't blame a little thing like you. Lucky to have on overalls, I am.— Well, the scheme's this: a house car that we could put onto a second-hand chassis — and you can pick up a Ford chassis for ten dollars— and cruise around everywhere, without having to set up tents or go to the expense of hotels or auto camps. Live in your own cabin and roll it around where you please. Cheaper than rent or taxes.'

'Well, but ——' Mrs. Smith interjected.

'Just a minute, Mamma. You want to see how this fellow in this piece in the paper has got it planned out. Slick! Besides that,' he expanded, 'I've some little ideas of my own that aren't so slouchy.'

'But wouldn't the lumber and everything cost a lot?' Mrs. Smith expostulated. 'And then it's only about a fifty-fifty chance that you'd find a buyer. Do eat your supper before it gets cold.'

'Cost a lot?' asked Mr. Smith, obediently tucking a morsel of carrot into his mouth and forgetting it. 'That's the joke of it, Mamma! Of course you've noticed the little playhouse in the back yard.'

Mrs. Smith nodded.

'I've been out there with my rule. And that playhouse can be used almost bodily, see? Almost bodily.' He sat back triumphantly and chewed the parked carrot.

'Well,' conceded Mrs. Smith.

'You reckon we could look over them plans tonight, Son?' Grandpa demanded.

'But, Father,' Mrs. Smith interrupted, 'I wonder if you could do something for me first? I hate to bother you, but ——'

Grandpa nodded decisively, his face twisting into smiles.

Penny stole an appreciative glance at the elder Smiths. That house car — it would give Grandpa a holiday sense of something extra special to do, blotting out his sense of uselessness. And Mrs. Smith was giving more and more thought to the old man, now that she had normal leisure. She had asked many little favors of him lately, and the asking had chirked up Grandpa's drooping lines.

'I'm Johnny-on-the-spot, Daughter,' he said. 'Name your poison.'

'Could you make me a nice neat little sign to hang out by the gate?' she asked. 'Something about Beauty Shop, Latest Denver Methods.'

'What about your equipment?' Mr. Smith inquired.

'Can't we drive down to Denver and bring out the things we left stored there?'

'Cost us a couple dollars for gas, but I guess we can. All go along and make a day of it.'

'Penny, you do look so happy this fall,' said Virginia, looking across at Penny, who was helping Junior butter his bread. Penny held the whole slice on the palm of her hand and spread it with earnest sweeps of the knife, but for once Virginia did not correct her. 'You're just absolutely *shiny*, Pen.'

'My nose, you mean?' Penny smiled bashfully. 'Only trouble is, seems 'sif everything's going too smooth. Too awful nice and easy.'

'Sitting on painted kitchen chairs,' Virginia countered, 'and living in an unfurnished house with bare floors? And you with one decent dress to your name, and your shoes going through at the toes!'

'But — Great Jawns! we don't need a blessed thing

we ain't got. Not really *need*,' Penny murmured, catching her breath. 'And it scares me. It shore does. I feel like something bad was coming.'

It was only a few days later that something bad came.

The supper table had become a jolly place. Virginia and Penny delved in the free cookbooks they had collected from advertisers, and held a constant contest as to who could provide the best and cheapest meals. Appetites were so good that the occasional failures of the cooks, or their too severe economies, were eaten with small complaint. Spirits ran high, and Mr. Smith cracked his kind, stale jokes contentedly.

Tonight, however, he was constrained, and so was Mrs. Smith.

'I'm going to take a Campfire group in the Methodist Church,' Virginia announced. 'Little girls about twelve.'

Only a ripple of interest followed the announcement.

'Miss Jones says I'm doing swell in my English,' Penny contributed; and won but an abstracted smile.

'Mother, there's going to be an exhibit at the Town Hall, the last of this month. Everybody's talking about it. All you hear these days is bank bandits and exhibit. Mrs. Sands, next door, asked if we wouldn't enter something.'

'What kind of things do they want?'

'Oh, anything we've made. Needlework. Bread. Cake. Quilts. Jelly. It's a kind of fair.'

'Gee whizz, Mom, I forgot to tell you,' Junior interrupted. 'The school nurse was in our room today and she weighed all us kids and I ain't underweight a speck!'

'Mother! Has something gone wrong?' Virginia asked in alarm, when even Junior's report passed with mild attention. 'Someone hasn't found out about the Pipin' Jenny?'

Mr. Smith glanced at Mrs. Smith. He took a letter from his pocket and pulled it from its envelope without looking at anyone again. He cleared his throat.

'It's from the matron at the Home, Penny,' he said. 'She writes that Mrs. Henley's home from Europe and hot foot to get you back again, and — and she wants to know right off what we can do.'

'Oh, Papa! Oh, gee, Papa! We ain't going to send Penny back, are we? And Napoleum? Penny don't want that nasty old lady to get her. Oh, gee, Mamma! Can't we have Penny for keeps?'

All eyes were turned on Mr. and Mrs. Smith: turned in question, in hope, in anguish. Mrs. Smith laid a gentle arm across Penny's shoulders, suddenly drooping.

'Penny, dear, I — only wish we could — have you for keeps. But when I think of all Mrs. Henley could do for you — and we couldn't possibly — why, it doesn't seem as if we have any right. But, Papa, don't you think we might write Miss Fleming and ask her for another six months? We weren't expecting the Henleys to get back so soon. It does seem as if they might give us another six months.'

'We'll write her,' Mr. Smith agreed heartily.

XVIII. THE SIDEBOARD

SEPTEMBER and October were magic months in Central City. The early frosts and snows did not come; day followed day, crisp and clear, the beginning of a 'freak winter,' the mildest in the memory of old-timers.

Where the mines had not destroyed the very earth, the hills blazed with quaking aspen; the tiny, round leaves, set crosswise on delicate stems, quivered at every breath and made a shimmer of dazzling color against the rich blue of the sky. Penny and Virginia and Junior, with Napoleum at their heels, climbed the heights and broke off branches of yellow and vermilion and russet, to rob the house of its bareness. Mis' Trent had told them that the branches would hold their leaves all winter if the broken ends were thrust at once into equal parts of glycerine and water.

These expeditions were kept well within sight of town, for the bank bandits' gunshots were still echoing uneasily through the hills. The robbers had held up the bank at Fremont, ruthlessly seizing women for protection against shots, wounding, killing, and coming off with scant plunder after all their violence.

Moreover, they were thought to be 'hiding out' not

far away. Federal agents were scouring the numberless ravines of the high country, but it was slow work, and clues were slight. Evidently a new gang, only two members of it had been described at all, together with a car in which some of them had escaped.

The car was a green Studebaker sedan with a shattered headlight and Iowa license plates, and it had never been seen after the day of the robbery. That is, it had been seen so many times and in so many places at once that the authorities had come to the conclusion that it had not been seen at all.

So children skittered past even the boarded-up houses on the outskirts of town, and Virginia called Junior back when he went ten feet from her side.

There was enough to engage the attention without going far afield. Penny, for instance, was forever wondering, as they looked down upon the town, where it was that she and her parents had lived. Perhaps they had lived in several of these houses, moving from one to another, as 'poor white trash' so often do, to escape the rent. She wouldn't have minded — oh, not at all! — the thought that her father and mother had been poor people. She wouldn't have minded the thought of their living in one of the clean, bare cabins that trailed along the edges of town.

But even A'nt Sally, with her snuff and her bare feet and her slovenly housekeeping, had called the John Adamses ornery. So Penny scanned with fearful fascination the shacks with rags wadded into broken windows and paper blown against fences. Probably her mother couldn't help it, though; probably she hadn't had even so much bringing up as Penny herself. Anyway, Penny felt nearer to her family when she was in Central City.

It was another reason why she wished with all her heart to stay.

For the first time, too, she had a room of her own — or a half room. Virginia had shared it with her as a matter of course, and its furnishing had been a grand adventure. The furnishing of the whole house was an adventure. Every penny was counted, and everyone who had a plan submitted it to a family council, where the cost was weighed and the proposition accepted or rejected.

Mr. Smith had brought up in the trailer the dresser and bedstead they had stored, together with Mrs. Smith's favorite sewing chair and sewing machine and some treasured pieces of china. The girls had bought two cot beds for their room. Among the stored goods they had found a set of cretonne curtains from the old beauty shop, and out of the rich-hued stuff they had fashioned spreads and a cover and flounce for their box dressing-table. Grandpa was going to make them a dressing-stool as soon as he could get around to it.

The parlor was still empty, but the whole family was dropping pennies, nickels, dimes, into a tea can with a slit in the lid. Virginia ran the kitchen one week and Penny the next, and if they managed to squeeze through on less than ten dollars, the margin could go to the tea can. Mrs. Smith's beauty fees went there, too.

Penny had ransacked the second-hand store and found a promising easy-chair for three dollars. Grandpa was sure he could strengthen the frame as solid as new, and there was enough of the cretonne left to cover it. The first purchase from that same storekeeper, though, was a living-room table for fifty cents. It was rickety and battered, 'but easy fixed,' Grandpa had concluded.

The only lack was time. 'I've got two things I want to do for every minute there is to do them in,' Virginia grumbled. 'Things I really *want* to do!'

Grandpa and Mr. Smith were in a like state. The fine weather had let them work daily at the Pipin' Jenny, so that Mr. Smith was genuinely glad that the garage had found him no odd jobs. The bookkeeping he could manage easily in the evenings. He and Grandpa filled their spare time with repairing furniture for the house and planning all details of the house car. For them the house car was like paper dolls for a pair of little girls or an erector set for little boys.

They had added niceties of their own devising to the original specifications. It was to be a marvelous affair, with two sets of double-decker berths. Curtains would separate the tiny bedrooms —'but no tinier than these here Pullmans,' Grandpa defended them — and when the berths were swung up on their hinges and hooked into place, a table would spring from the floor, and storage chests would serve as benches. There was even a small icebox, and a cupboard for dishes and supplies, and a sink, and little windows with ruffled curtains.

The actual making of all these wonders had to be postponed, however; there were too many things that needed doing at once. Grandpa had made the swinging sign for Mrs. Smith, and she had fitted up the room where the rolltop desk stood as her shop, and was beginning to win customers. One of the summer people — staying while the mild weather held — came in for a shampoo and a finger wave; came in again, and sent some of her friends.

'I believe I could do manicures,' declared Virginia. 'I know I could; and I think I could put on some of the frills that would make people think they were getting their money's worth.'

The manicure table drew a few customers, the hair-dressing and facial departments more. The wind and light dry air made business for a beauty shop, drying out hair and cuticle and tanning faces and hands to a leathery brown.

Mrs. Sands, the woman next door, came in hesitantly for a hot oil shampoo and a permanent wave.

'I don't suppose you'd believe it,' she confessed, explaining her awkwardness in adjusting herself in the chair, 'but this is the first time I've so much as had any-body wash my hair for me — not since I was knee high to a grasshopper.'

'Where have you lived?' asked Mrs. Smith, combing deftly.

Mrs. Sands shrugged. 'Right here, ever since I was married and settled down. Right next door; same house the whole thirty years.'

Penny had come in from school and stood watching Mrs. Smith's swift hands.

'About time I gave you an oil shampoo, too, Penny,' said Mrs. Smith, looking at the copper mane tossed by the incessant wind.

'She does have the loveliest hair!' Mrs. Sands admired. She narrowed her eyes, pinching her lips to a reflective ridge. 'You don't so often see hair just that color. You can't hardly say whether it's more red than gold or more gold than red. And having the eyes match it that way. I've seen somebody else with that combination, but I can't remember who.'

Penny was wondering whether maybe Mrs. Sands might have seen her mother. She must have, in such a

small town, even if they didn't 'run with the same kind
of folks.' A'nt Sally had said her mother was a carrot-
top, too, with red-headed eyes like Penny's. Penny often
wondered whether her mother had hated it as badly as
she; for every one person that fancied red hair, it seemed,
there were two or three to call you Carrots and whittle
their fingers at you.

She would have liked to ask Mrs. Sands if she remembered a miner's wife — A'nt Sally said Penny's father
worked in the mines — with red hair, back in 1924, and
her little red-headed girl. But suppose Mrs. Sands should
recall someone scraping along the street in bedroom
slippers, with holes in her heels and the red hair half
combed? Penny couldn't risk it, so she only smiled shyly
and backed out of the room.

Virginia was calling her: 'Hoo-hoo! Penny!' Virginia
had been to the post office, and Penny looked apprehen-
sively to see whether there was another letter from the
Home. No, there was only one piece of mail, and it was
for Virginia, from her aunt, who lived near the university
in Quenton.

The two girls sat cross-legged on the floor in the empty
parlor while Virginia read the letter aloud. Aunt Caroline
hadn't heard whether or not her niece was going to use
her scholarship; she had looked for her in vain as the
students came in and classes began. She wished there
was anything she could do to help, but they were so
crowded as it was, and so hard up —— She didn't suppose
Virginia would care to help with dishes and cooking and
such things, anyway.

'She probably remembers what a brat I always was
about housework,' commented Virginia. 'She visited us
one summer; and I was usually somewhere else when it

came time to do dishes. I remember my conscience was
perfectly clear about it as long as I wasn't actually
there. And poor Mother coming home all worn out,
and dinner to get, and the dishes to wash — ! Gosh, but
can't kids be selfish!'

She returned to the letter. Aunt Caroline always
had two or three girls from the university to work for
their board and a few dollars a month. She's already
engaged them for this fall, of course, but it happened that
both of them were to be graduated at the end of the
quarter, and then she'd have to arrange for others — One
trouble, though, was that she had no extra room, and she
could scarcely pay enough to make it worth their while
to rent lodging, with times as they were.

'Aunt Caroline runs a sort of student boarding-house,'
Virginia explained, dropping the letter in her lap. 'It's
not half bad, either: a sort of pretty house and big shady
yard with lots of shrubbery. She's rather a peach even
to think of me, the way I've acted when she's visited us.
But, good heavens! imagine me waiting on tables in
white aprons, and washing dishes till my hands are all
soaked pulpy. I've always looked down so on girls like
that.'

'Looked down on?' Penny hugged her knees and
regarded Virginia. She did not quite understand, but
neither did she much question this adored one. 'But,
V'ginia, you mean the onliest reason you cain't go —
to college, I mean — would be because your auntie
hasn't got room enough in her house?'

Virginia nodded, folding the letter. 'That is, if I
wanted to work my way, that would be the only reason.
Only, Penny; not onliest.'

'Only. Yes, mom. Seems like a body could have a
tent, even, in that big back yard of hern.'

Virginia sprang up, shaking her head and shivering. 'Brrr! It gets cold, up there in Quenton in winter, Pen. Besides, I just can't feature myself ——' She giggled at the idea of herself in a tent. 'Do you smell the beans browning, Penny? I tried putting in two slices of onion the way it said in the "Register-Hall." Don't they smell divine? They might even make Grandpa forget that Economy Cake I baked yesterday.'

But the talk came back to Aunt Caroline that evening. Supper was over. The dishes were washed. Even dishwashing had become a family affair and a social occasion, since they had come to the New England house. One washed, one wiped, one put away, one read aloud; Mr. Smith and Grandpa tinkered anything that needed tinkering, while they listened.

Afterward they gathered in the dining-room and kept on reading a while if they had reached an exciting point; or wrote letters; or did homework. Tonight Mr. Smith was figuring out a new gadget for the house car. Grandpa had spread newspapers carefully on the floor and was lacquering the battered table, 'to start our parlor soot,' he said. Mrs. Smith was mending; she always had plenty of mending to do.

'You wouldn't want to help your Aunt Caroline, Virginia? Next quarter, of course?' Mrs. Smith asked, folding a pair of mended socks into a compact bundle and adding it to the pile of bundles on the table.

'Well ——'

'But if there ain't no room?' queried Grandpa.

Penny looked up from Junior and his spelling.

'I — kindy thought of something,' she said diffidently. 'About the house car the Mister and Grandpa's planning on.'

Mrs. Smith furrowed a questioning brow.

'If Virginia was to drive it to thisyere Quenton,' Penny explained, 'what would hinder her parking it in her auntie's back yard? Having it for her room, like? If the Mister was to put thisyere strawboard inside the wall, any little old stove would keep it warm.'

Grandpa smote horny palm with horny fist. 'Penny, you sure have got a headpiece on you. I don't see why it wouldn't work out slick as a whistle.'

'She'd have to have another girl with her,' Mrs. Smith cogitated, gazing through Penny with far-seeing eyes. 'But that wouldn't be hard. There's Dot Hooper, Virginia, would jump at the chance if she could make part of her expenses. Likely your Aunt Caroline would use you both, the way she said, next quarter.'

'Good heavens!' Virginia protested, her face flushed and mutinous, 'why does everyone take it for granted I'm so keen to go to that old university? And as for washing dishes till all hours and making a show of myself living in a house car —— Especially with Betty and Hoot and all the rest up there in frat houses ——'

'Seems like it would look awful cute, a little green house that way, with ruffledy curtains and all,' Penny said.

'Everybody'd think you were a smart little trick — if you carried it off with a high hand, as if you wanted to,' Mr. Smith said shrewdly.

'Can't I go along, Ginny?' begged Junior, who had his autos out again and was running them over Napoleum's unresisting back. 'Say, can't I go along and live in the teeny-weeny house? They's a school for little boys at Quenton, isn't they? Say, isn't they?'

Penny contemplated Virginia soberly. If it were she,

Penny, how glorious a chance she would think it! To sleep in the cunning little house, and study at the cunning little table, and go to the wonderful university with other young people, and learn everything in the whole world!

Virginia stirred restlessly under Penny's gaze. 'It was an awfully clever idea to pop into your head like that, Pen,' she admitted.

'You folks realize how many idees has popped into Penny's head?' marveled Grandpa. He stared at Penny with a candid wonder. 'You'd never think she'd be so smart, just to look at her.'

'She's always thinking up something to help us out of a hole,' Virginia acknowledged. 'Too bad she couldn't figure out something wonderful for herself, too.'

'All theseyere things — they've done me jest as good a turn as anybody,' faltered Penny. Jest look. Here I am, instead of with that Mis' Henley.' She shivered. ''Course, I know good and well you'll maybe have to leave me go back to her. But I've anyway had the whole summer.'

'I'd give anything, Penny ——' Mrs. Smith broke the thread and her sentence with a jerk.

'Now, if you'd only find a secret drawer in that roll-top desk you're staring at, Penny,' Virginia teased, 'and a thousand dollars in banknotes ——'

'Then we'd get Penny for keeps,' chanted Junior. 'We'd get her for keeps, for keeps, for keeps.'

Penny's eyes left the desk, which she could see through the beauty-shop door, and slowly circled the dining-room till they came to rest on the heavy oak sideboard. She moistened her lips, frowning.

'Secret draw',' she repeated. 'Secret ——'

While they all watched her, sensing something strange,

she got up from her chair and walked over to the side-board, moving as if asleep. For a moment she paused before it, uncertain. Then she dropped down on the floor and turned the key in the end door.

The door swung open, revealing a pile of bowls that the Smiths had brought up from the ten-cent store in Denver. Penny's hands went groping over the neat wood paneling behind them. She pressed something, and there was a visible movement of the paneling which brought the older Smiths tensely forward, and Junior thumping around to Penny on his mended knees, his mouth ajar.

Penny set the stack of bowls on the floor. The panel swung open like a narrow door, showing a recess behind.

'They ain't nothing in it!' cried Junior. 'They ain't a single thing in it.'

'But how did Penny know there was a secret panel there?' Virginia demanded.

XIX. THE ORNERY ADAMSES

'AIN'T they nothing in it a-*tall?*' cried Junior, pushing between Penny and his sister and climbing over Penny's knees into the compartment.

'There's something funny in it, if you ask me,' Grandpa replied, stooping painfully to look.

'Because if Penny didn't know the place mighty well, she wouldn't have remembered that panel, see?' added Mr. Smith.

Penny twisted around to look at them with wide, shining eyes. 'You don't mean — ? Do you reckon maybe — ?'

'We'll ask Mrs. Sands,' Mrs. Smith said briskly. 'She's lived right here so long.'

'I'll get her. What for? What you going to ask her? What you want to ——' Junior backed out crabwise and was scuttling to the door as he queried, nor did he pause for reply. In an incredibly short time he returned, dragging Mrs. Sands, puzzled and breathless.

'I hope we didn't put you to any bother.' Mrs. Smith rose and pushed forward a chair. 'But we were all so excited we let Junior go off half-cocked. Did anybody by the name of Adams ever live on this street, Mrs. Sands?'

Mrs. Sands sank down on the chair and caressed her unfamiliar wave. 'Adams? Oh, yes, indeed.' Her eyes sought Penny. 'That's it!' she cried. 'It was Mrs. Adams I was thinking of today. With the red-gold hair and the eyes to match. As nice neighbors as you'd need to have, Mr. and Mrs. Adams were. Mr. and Mrs. John Adams. On this street, did you say? Why, Mrs. Smith, they lived in this very house.'

Mrs. Smith quieted the rising jangle of questions and comments with a motion of the hand. 'It must have been awfully pretty, once, when the yard was kept up.'

'The Adamses kept it up nice,' Mrs. Sands assented. 'They were the nicest folks, once you got next to them. People here in Central did have the notion at first that they were a little — well, a little stand-offish. But they weren't. Not really. They were good plain folks, even if they were well educated. Goodness, I hadn't much more than got acquainted with them when they died. Just like that. Pneumonia carries people off quick in this altitude. I never was just easy in my mind about the little girl ——'

'There was a little girl, then?' Mrs. Smith asked, out of a breathless silence.

'Oh, yes, a darling, solemn little thing. And I always wondered if someone oughtn't to have investigated a little more. About the Adamses that took her. The old man had worked for Mr. Adams some, and he claimed to be kin; and he was the only one who did claim to be. But if he was kin — well, I suppose everybody has some pretty queer relations.'

'It does seem like somebody could have looked into it,' Grandpa glowered.

Mrs. Sands looked at him in some astonishment. 'I

was sick myself,' she said defensively. 'You see it was a
flu epidemic, with lots of it running into pneumonia.
And by the time I'd got back into the land of the living,
you might say, little Penelope was gone and ——'

'Pen-el-o-pe.' Penny tasted the syllables with silent
lips.

'Penelope!' Virginia exclaimed. 'Penelope Adams!
Why, then there isn't one bit of doubt. It's our Penny!'

Mrs. Sands sat back in her chair and dropped her hands
on her knees.

'Well, if I haven't been as blind as a bat!' she cried.
'Of course she's little Penelope Adams! And growing up
into the spit and image of her mother.' She sniffed, and
widened her eyes in a futile effort to clear them of moisture. 'Wouldn't your father and mother be happy if
they could see how nice you're turning out!'

'They weren't — weren't no 'count?' stammered
Penny. 'They lived *here?*' She touched the floor beside
her, and unconsciously her hand caressed the boards as
they patted.

'No account? Mr. and Mrs. Adams?' Mrs. Sands
retorted indignantly. 'They weren't well off, and I
guess your father lost everything he had in a mine that
didn't pan out. But they were as nice as you could hope
to see. And they fixed up this house and furnished it so
nice and tasty. Good gracious, the little old playhouse
Mr. Smith's going to use for his house car, your father
had the carpenter make that for you, Penelope. But you
never got so you played in it much, because you'd always
rather be around where your mother was working.
They set great store by you.

'I remember plain as anything seeing you sitting on
the steps behind the iron gate waiting for your father to

come home. Your mother'd doll you up in a pongee dress with blue smocking, and comb your hair with a wet comb, so it would go into soft waves. And if you weren't the picture of a sweet little girl —— Doted on you, they did, more because you were the only one, so, and they with no close kin, I guess, on either side. It seemed awful kind of hard ——'

But Penny could stand no more. She put her face down in Virginia's lap and cried with long, shuddering sobs.

Everyone sat silent. Grandpa finally shifted his feet on the bare floor and got up. 'Have to — have to have some sandpaper,' he muttered, and hobbled through the door.

'Honey, child,' coaxed Virginia, 'don't feel so bad.'

Penelope wriggled her shoulders. 'I — I don't feel bad,' she murmured thickly. Anyway, not half so bad as I feel good.'

Mrs. Sands blew her nose and got up. 'I can hardly wait to hear how she got away from those old Adamses,' she said. 'But I'll be running home now, before Mr. Sands has a searching party after me. Penny, you come over tomorrow and we'll have another talkfest. I'll rake up every single thing I can remember about your folks. And if only I can lay my hands on it, I do believe I've got a snapshot of the three of you.'

Life was made over new for Penny. 'You've turnt out to be an Airedale,' she told Napoleum, 'and I've turnt out to be Pen-el-o-pe Adams. I reckon a whole lot of cur dogs and ornery kids has got good enough blood to amount to something. But we got to live up to it. Reckon my father and mother would jest die to hear me talking like pore whites. I got to watch them cain'ts and ain'ts jest like a hawk.'

Mrs. Sands was as good as her word. She rummaged through boxes of dusty old pictures until at last she came upon the one she sought. It showed Penelope perched on her father's shoulder, her mother standing close beside them.

Penny studied the snapshot hungrily.

'My mother don't appear to be hardly growed up,' she said.

Mrs. Sands laughed comfortably, training her glasses over Penny's shoulder onto the picture. 'Fashions were funny, eight-nine years ago,' she explained. 'Looks like they were made for giant children: no ladies among us for a while. Skirts came creeping up towards our knees and belts — well, belts went creeping down to meet them. And of course we all had to wear those short-skirted, shapeless duds, no matter how we were built. But your mother looked right well in anything. She was a fine figure of a young woman. And you're going to be just such another, or I miss my guess.'

'She — she wasn't great big like me?' Penny asked earnestly. She drank in all these comments as a thirsty plant drinks in water. The bigness that had been such a burden to her — why, some folks thought it was 'fine.' The carroty hair and 'red-headed eyes'— Mrs. Sands admired them. 'She shore couldn't have been as big as me?' Penny repeated.

'You wait till you catch up with your own bigness, Penelope!' Mrs. Sands said sagely. 'All fast-growing girls are kind of awkward when they're thirteen. Your mother was fully as large: fine and upstanding. What you'd call statuesque, maybe. Your father was a big man, too. And how his eyes could snap!'

'Did they — did they have carpets on their floor?' Penny blurted out.

She wanted every detail Mrs. Sands could recall about them: the pictures on their walls; Penny's little clothes, and how her mother embroidered them; the way the table was set.

'Why do you reckon A'nt Sally talked like they was pore white trash?' she asked soberly.

The Smiths and Mrs. Sands discussed that question vehemently. They came to the conclusion, neither to be proved nor disproved, that the old people had been moved by some deep and bitter jealousy that had relieved itself by belittling the parents to the child as well as by bringing the child down from her natural level.

'When I'm growed up,' said Penny, 'I'm going to track it down and find out if they was really blood kin at all — A'nt Sally and Unc' Jeff.'

The precious snapshot she pinned on the wall above her bed. Scarcely had she done so when it disappeared.

Penny turned the room upside down. It had few nooks where even a snapshot could lurk unseen, with the floors still bare and the dressing-table and beds the only furnishings.

'I don't see how it could be anywhere in the room, possibly,' Virginia protested, when Penny unmade both beds for the second time.

'Then it must have blowed out the window,' Penny grieved.

Thereupon she and Junior and Virginia hunted the yard through — terraces, rocks, and all. Penny sifted every drift of dead leaves through her fingers, but to no avail.

Yet bitter though the loss was, the picture had given Penny something that could not be taken from her: a warm sense of family. She was Penelope Adams, and no longer ashamed of her forebears.

The new self-respect showed in her manner. She didn't
slide out of Zip's presence when next he came to see Virginia. She didn't even melt away into a corner when
Virginia brought him into the dining-room where the
family was gathered.

Zip's little gray car had lost its first jauntiness. Its
motor labored, and it chirped and creaked. Zip was
jaunty enough. He swung into the room as usual, sweeping back his blond mane with one hand while he lifted the
other in salute. Yet even about Zip there hung a slightly
different air: the questioning look of a little boy whose
world hasn't been running quite according to his plans,
perhaps.

No, Zip was not working at present, though he had
some profitable connections in view. No, he was not in
school. University didn't get you anywhere, these days,
unless you were going in for teaching or one of the professions. And didn't Mr. Smith think teaching and the
other professions were pretty slow stuff, with things the
way they were now?

'There's a dance down at Black Hawk tonight, with
that German band of theirs,' he said to Virginia. 'They're
perfectly respectable dances, Mrs. Smith.'

'But I'm not so keen about them,' Virginia demurred.

'Well, then,' he grumbled, 'I suppose we can just spin
around a while. If you'd rather.'

'Lemme go, too!' begged Junior, who had been parading his automobiles up and down with insistent honkings,
in a vain attempt to draw Zip's attention.

'Would you mind if Junior and Penny rode in the
rumble seat?' Virginia proposed.

'Well. Whatever you like,' Zip assented coolly.

In ten minutes the little gray car roared off into the

shattered evening stillness, carrying the five of them —
Napoleum in the rumble seat between Penny and Junior.
Through the town, past the German band, parading up
and down the streets with a blare of brass and flamboyant
advertising banners, onto a dark woods road, where they
swooped up and down with loud bangings. Napoleum
lifted high his muzzle, glorying in speed and wild, engaging smells. Penny clutched and gasped.

The road was like a roller coaster. Up one hill Zip
would send the car, climbing lightly. At the top it would
balance breathlessly before its downward swoop. Up
and down and up, fearfully and wonderfully.

As an added spice for the reckless, it was a ridge road,
falling away to a ditch on each side. Penny could not
hope that Zip would continue to avoid the ditches. She
shut her eyes.

She opened them just as the car dashed up another hill.
Well to the middle of the road Zip had swung, for traffic
was light. But just as they sped toward the summit and
could see over the crest, the lights of another car blazed
into their eyes — rushing straight upon them, as near
the middle of the road as they!

Penny braced herself for the shattering crash. It did
not come. Zip, his shoulders tense, whirled the wheel
and swerved sharply toward the right. Whirled it again
and swerved away from the ditch even as his right wheels
began to slip on the brink. One long, ripping jar, and the
little gray car was scooting down the hill again.

Penny could scarcely believe it when she found them
swaying to a stop at the foot of the incline, still right side
up. As one person, the five turned to look back. There
was nothing to see but blank darkness.

Zip groped in his car for a flashlight, tumbled out, and
raced up the hill, the others stumbling after him.

'Oh, Penny!' Virginia murmured, gripping her arm. 'Isn't this awful?'

Penny's eyes strained ahead through the dark as she ran. What would Zip's flashlight uncover when they topped the hill? Gruesome tangled wreckage? Flames? She stopped on the summit. The flashlight picked out the other car, tilted into the ditch, but on its four wheels. Its left side was smashed in and its fender crumpled. The driver was swearing stoutly. Zip only laughed, and stopped to comb his hair leisurely.

'You were as near the middle of the road as I was,' he pointed out, turning his light on the telltale tracks. 'You can see for yourself. Here, let's heave her out of the ditch.'

'But I wasn't driving sixty an hour!' snarled the man.

'Who says you weren't?' Zip countered. 'And who says I was?'

But when they had set the car in the road again, Virginia insisted on going home. 'I feel as if I'd been through an earthquake, Zip,' she said, 'and I don't think it's funny at all. Anyway, with these bank robbers still loose ——'

'Oh, they saw that green sedan in Oklahoma yesterday,' Zip told her.

'They saw it in Nevada at the same hour,' Virginia snapped. 'Zip, please do take us home.'

Zip sulkily drove back to the Smith house, sulkily jumped out and helped Penny and Junior from the rumble seat. Penny felt so wobbly, herself, that she went straight to bed. Only a few minutes later Virginia opened the door. She sat on the edge of Penny's bed and hurled her coat and beret onto her own.

'Really,' she stormed, 'wasn't that a nit-wit perform-

ance, Pen? Do you know what speed Zip was really
making? Seventy-five, and on a road like that. Could
have smashed us up, and the other man, easy as anything. I never want to step into his old car again as long
as I live.' She dragged off her blouse and emerged from
under it, mouth tight, eyes angry.

Penny sat up and hugged her knees. 'Then why do
you, V'ginia?'

'I don't intend to. Unless Zip should do a little growing up, all of a sudden. Isn't it funny how a few months
can grow us up? But it hasn't begun to work on Zip yet.'

'I've shore growed up a heap since April,' mused
Penny, cuddling back under the covers and watching
Virginia brush her shining black hair with indignant
strokes. 'You know, V'ginia, I ain't ——'

'I'm not,' Virginia corrected automatically.

'I'm not so terrible scaret of Mis' Henley as I was.
Scaret enough, but —— You know how kids puts pennies
and pins and things on railroad tracks?'

Virginia nodded. 'We used to lay pins on the street-
car tracks to make little knives of them. And cross two
for scissors.'

'Yes. Well, I used to think I'd be stomped out flat
like those pins if I had to live with the Henleys. I don't
know but the old Penny would have,' she said soberly.
'But Penelope Adams' — her eyes brightened — 'I
reckon Penelope Adams has got more backbone to her.'

The new courage was soon to be put to the test.

The week had been a perfect one. Even now, in late
October, the usual winter weather had not set in. Mar-
mots and chipmunks, who according to the calendar
should have been snugly settled in their burrows, were
still abroad in the mellow sunshine. It was as if winter —

as if all things — were being held back for the Smiths'
enjoyment and Penny's.

Mr. Smith and Grandpa had been able to work daily
at the Pipin' Jenny. They were taking greater care to
keep its location secret now, going and coming by different roads and at different hours, and panning the streams
conspicuously to throw the curious off the track. For
rumors that the United States was about to go off the
gold standard, sending up the price of the metal, were
waking general interest in workable deposits.

'Some mighty tough-looking customers keep giving
me the once-over every time I rattle into town,' Mr.
Smith complained. 'I don't like the cut of their jibs.
We'll have to look a little out, Paw.'

'There's one of 'em alluz puts me in mind of a skull
and crossbones,' said Grandpa, 'I don't know why.'

'That little slim one with the big top to his head,'
agreed Mr. Smith.

'What would they be after, Papa?' Mrs. Smith asked
nervously.

'Oh, they might be trying to find out where we're
working, so they could jump our claim if it looked good
to them.'

'They don't look like the kind that'd work for their
money, Son.'

'You're right, they don't. More likely they think
we're hiding some gold or going down to Denver with it.
You can bet they know we aren't depositing in the
Central bank.'

'Junior!' warned Mrs. Smith.

'Huh?'

'Don't you say one word about that gold. Not one
word!'

'Don't say one word about what gold?' Junior demanded. 'Huh, Mamma? What gold mustn't I say a word about?'

'My goodness!' Mrs. Smith laughed helplessly. 'Don't anybody say a word about anything to anyone. And, Papa, you be awfully, awfully careful. I don't think there's any use driving out after night the way you like to.'

'Oh, sure we're careful, Mamma,' he reassured her. 'Though I don't think there's any real reason to suppose those robbers are within a hundred miles of here. I saw in the paper yesterday how they saw a green Studebaker sedan without license plates in Montana headed west.'

The mild weather had also tempted summer dwellers to linger late in Central's hills, and the patronage of the beauty shop had actually increased a little instead of dwindling.

The plans for the house car were growing in finish and accuracy, too. Even Virginia studied them with interest. She thought she would write to Dot Hooper one of these days, she said, and ask her what she would think of the proposition of living together in their own apartment on wheels and washing dishes for their board: — supposing she should come to the point of considering it seriously herself, which wasn't likely, Virginia always added.

The big house was not lagging behind the other in its development. The fund in the tea can had swelled to the needed size, and the Smiths had proudly loaded the decrepit easy-chair into the trailer and brought it home from the second-hand store. With all of them working on it, it flowered into a quaint and comfortable piece of furniture. Next, Grandpa had put two new legs into an old straight chair he found in the playhouse, lacquered it

black, and moved it and the desk into the living-room —
the old empty parlor.

'I do believe, Father,' Mrs. Smith proposed, 'that you
could build a frame, and we could get some old automobile seat springs and rig up a sort of short davenport —
what do they call them?'

'Love seat?' Virginia asked. 'That's a slick idea.
And wouldn't it be classy to lacquer the floor black, and
wax it, and then make bright-colored braided rugs? —
Another thing I've been wondering, though: why under
the sun don't we get some of the things we need most, on
time? From Monkey-Ward or Sawbuck, you know?'

'Let's not,' her mother voted decisively. 'It's wonderful not to be dribbling out a little here and a little there
on things that are half worn out. I never knew what
comfort it could be. Let's stay on this cash basis, here
in Central.'

'Well' — Virginia admitted grudgingly — 'it does
seem nice and solid. And yet — why, we could easily
have rugs, and a whole set of overstuffed, and ——'

'We can't use the pa'lor this winter, anyhow,' Grandpa
put in cheerfully. 'The dining-room will be het nice and
cozy from the kitchen, and so will the shop, but the pa'lor
—— Likely by next winter, if we was to stay, we could
git us one of them heaters that looks like a overgrowed
talking-machine.'

'Monk's-cloth curtains will be cute in here,' Virginia
thought aloud. 'It *is* rather fun to have things come by
littles. Or you can make believe it's fun.'

'It's fun to have all that firewood stacked up in the
back yard,' Mrs. Smith chimed in. 'And jam and jelly
in the pantry.'

They had secured their permit from Walt French, the

ranger, and could cut down all the dead timber they pleased, plenty for a season's use.

'If we paid two bits a cord for it,' Penny now observed, 'we could peddle it for three bits. You got to pay, if you're aiming to sell it.'

'I won't do it, Penny Adams!' Virginia protested, with laughter flowing under her irritation. 'I draw the line at chopping wood and peddling it, even if you do propose it.'

'But me and Junior ——'

'I could train Barkis to pull a cart, like you said, Penny!' chortled Junior.

'I never did see sech a fam'ly,' said Grandpa. 'Sech a sight of irons in the fire.'

'I wonder why Penny don't play her mouth-organ and have Junior dance and Napoleum sing,' Mr. Smith teased. 'She might get quite a collection.'

Penny laughed sheepishly. She was especially happy that day because a package had come for her from a Denver kodak store. It was the first mail she had ever received. Opening it with puzzled and excited fumblings, she found a fine clear enlargement of the lost snapshot, simply framed.

'V'ginia,' Penny accused her adoringly. 'you done it yourse'f. And you scrabbling under them bushes hunting it as innocent as anything!'

But the next mail brought sorrow.

'Penny,' said Mr. Smith, coming out of the beauty shop, where he and Mrs. Smith had been talking in under-tones, 'Penny, it's bad news. It's bad news for all of us. I'd better read it aloud, with no ifs and ands, and get it over with. We've been having it in installments already, like a serial story.'

He looked at her gravely, and read:

MY DEAR MR. SMITH,

It is with genuine regret that I write you as I must, since Penny Adams is evidently happy and well in your care, and making reasonable progress educationally. I should be glad to let her stay another six months, as you request, but duty seems to prevent.

Mrs. Henley has always wished to undertake the rearing of the girl Penny, as you know. She is making urgent application for her now. And as you also know, she is a member of our board, and knows the conditions under which Penny is staying with you.

It seems that she has set her heart upon this particular girl. I think she intends a sort of intensive psychological experiment. And Mrs. Henley is a lady of great force of character. She usually attains her objective.

In the Henley home, Penny would receive every advantage, material and educational. I say, however, though with some hesitancy, that there is an element of affectionate understanding that might overweigh these more material advantages. If you were able definitely to undertake her adoption at this time, this element might balance the others, and in your favor.

But I do not feel that I can, in fairness to the young girl, allow such an opportunity to be lost to her when your own intentions remain so indefinite.

Therefore, I must ask you, at the behest of the board, to make a decision in one way or the other by the end of this month, October, arranging safe transportation back to the Home for Penny Adams, unless you can by that time make formal request for adoption.

With sincere good wishes
AMANDA FLEMING

XX. GOOD–BYE!

PENELOPE ADAMS tried to straighten her shoulders under the blow, but the old Penny looked up with the old slanting glance through coppery lashes. A beaten glance.

'And you wouldn't want to adopt me — take me for good,' she whispered. 'That would be too much.'

'Oh, Penny, it isn't that we don't want to.'

'You don't dast to? — You don't dast to.' Hopelessly she answered her own question, her lashes darkening with wetness. 'I'd — I'd live on 'most nothing at all. I'd do every speck of the chores, honest to Jawns.'

Her voice was spiritless, unexpectant. She had seen this a long way off. Every letter from the Home had brought it a step nearer, and with every step she had lost a little hope. She couldn't make them see that she'd rather have grade school with them than college and music lessons with Mrs. Henley. And didn't she belong to herself a little, so she could decide what mattered to her more than to anyone else?

'If it was ordinary times, Penny, like a few years ago ——' said Mr. Smith. 'But now I can't figure how we'd have the right. You deserve schooling, and a chance like Mr. and Mrs. Henley will give you. Your father and mother were educated folks and you've got a right to a chance.'

'I'd make my own chance,' Penny said passionately, 'and not ask nothing of nobody. Excepting only to live along with you.'

Mrs. Smith shook her head regretfully. 'Sometime you'll understand, child. You'll see that we couldn't take such a sure chance away from you. If you weren't bright and capable ——'

'I wisht I was as dumb as A'nt Sally said I was!' Penny cried.

Grandpa fitted his blunt finger-tips together and examined the joinings. 'You reckon with gold coming up — ? It's going to keep on coming up, too, now the President's put us off the gold standard. *Don't* you reckon — ?'

'But, Paw,' Mr. Smith reasoned gently, 'that may not mean anything to us except that we'll get along pretty fine this winter. We don't know how long the Pipin' Jenny'll keep pipin'. Or whether we can persuade Mis' Trent to let us buy it in for taxes and go on working it on shares. Or whether somebody's going to find out that it's worth something and buy it up from under us. Why, we don't even know but winter'll set in tomorrow and keep us from washing any more. It's all so unsettled. I'm like Mamma. I don't see how we have the moral right to lose Penny her opportunity. When it's your own family, they just have to take what comes, a streak of lean and a streak of fat; but Penny ——'

Penny wasn't anybody's own family. That was the trouble. She sat numb and cold, inside and out, while they talked it over.

'Tuesday's the thirty-first,' Mr. Smith said soberly, tilting back his chair to consult a small calendar on the wall. 'I'll write Miss Fleming and tell her Penny will be there Tuesday night. Keep her as long as we can. I suppose we'd better plan to drive down to Denver Tuesday. Take that gold of ours to the Mint and — take Penny to the bus.'

'I'll certainly be glad to get that gold out of the house,' Mrs. Smith said, with artificial interest, 'but I dread the trip down with it.'

'You still worrying about bank robbers, Mamma?' Mr. Smith chided indulgently. 'Take it from me, those robbers have got to California by this time. You can't take rumors too seriously.'

'But what about the men you thought were watching you?' Mrs. Smith persisted.

'Oh, at the worst a couple of pork-and-beaners like us, trying to horn in on any likely place we've found to pan.'

'Well, I'll be glad enough to get rid of the gold,' Mrs. Smith repeated.

'But that's on the Q.T., children,' Mr. Smith warned them. 'Junior, that was on the Q.T., remember.'

'What's on a cutie?' Junior asked vaguely. 'What *is* a cutie, Papa?'

Junior was drooping in a corner, his arms wrapped around Napoleum's neck. Napoleum sat with lolling tongue, amiable but bored.

'Don't tell any of your little friends ——'

'What about? — I don't want Napoleum to go away. I don't!' he burst out with genuine tears.

'You might as well — keep him,' said Penny. 'Mis' Henley, she wouldn't tech a dog with a ten-foot pole.'

Junior rose and flung himself upon her. 'I don't want you to go worse'n I don't want him to!' he cried.

She sat unresponsive under the storm of his affection.

'You could — I guess likely you could get that nasty old lady to like Napoleum.' Junior introduced the subject again, tactfully. The workings of his mind were visible: better keep Napoleum than nothing. 'Once she saw how smart he was, opening doors and sneezing and singing when you play the mouth-organ.'

Penny shook her head shortly. 'It don't matter. I reckon I'll go to bed.'

She wanted to creep away and hide out of sight. She took the enlargement of the kodak picture and hid it under her pillow. She had that, at least. Yesterday it had seemed a great deal. Today the only thing she could feel was that she had been shut away from the warm circle into which she had been fitting more closely every day. She had been shut out into the cold and dark.

This was Friday, and Tuesday would be the end. Each night, crying into her pillow, Penny told herself fiercely that she must not waste another of these precious days; not even another hour. Each morning found her encased in ice again, unable to rouse herself to enjoyment. All the hours were slipping through her hands without her even feeling them. 'I cain't act decent, even,' she thought helplessly.

She worked harder than ever. Not so hard at her lessons, because — well, what did it matter? But harder about the house. She wanted to show the Smiths how much she could do, and make them sorry now that it was too late. She washed dishes and swept and mopped with sullen energy.

'Don't you go wearing yourself to a frazzle, Penny,

girl,' Grandpa admonished. ''Better do up that burnt finger, too.'

'You mean a young kid like Penny turned out these dumplings?' Mr. Smith demanded. 'Light as a feather!'

But Mrs. Smith and Virginia seemed scarcely to notice her fury of industry. They were forever running 'over to Mrs. Sands's a minute.'

'Never the both of 'em home to once.' Penny's eyes stung and the lump grew heavier at the pit of her stomach. 'Seems like they might act like they cared. Cain't be they care like I do, or they couldn't never run off — theseyere last days.'

She wrapped herself in the old sulky-seeming silence. And sometimes that cloak wore ragged, as when, at dinner, Junior asked too eagerly: 'Penny, then is Napoleum honest to goodness my dog now? — And Barkis is my goat, ain't he, Papa?'

'Shore! Everything's yourn. Every last thing in this world,' snapped Penny, and rushed from the room.

She walked all over Central that afternoon when school was dismissed. She stood alone on the hill where brooded the old Catholic academy for young ladies. She gazed across to Quartz Hill, where millions of dollars in gold had been taken out, and where gold was being taken out today. She looked down on the winding shelf streets of the town.

She wanted to fill her mind full of it, so that she could go on for years and years with pictures of the place where her father and mother and she had lived together. She could see the New England house from this point. In it centered everything that had been hers: the real father and mother, the foster family, and even Napoleum.

She couldn't seem to fix it in her mind. Her thoughts and even her eyes slid over as a slick eraser slides over the paper. She trudged moodily home.

It was Monday, her last evening. Even on this last evening either Mrs. Smith or Virginia was always gone. Junior was so busy with his own affairs that he didn't ask for a story. It was the last straw for Penny when he pulled away from her, eyes bright, cheeks flushed. 'I got sumpn to do, Penny,' he stammered. 'I — I got to hurry.'

The next day started differently. Going out to the front yard to call Junior to breakfast, she found a disconsolate Napoleum tied to the front gate, and a contented Barkis, also tethered there, browsing on the parched grass. On the gate hung a large cardboard, the backs of two big pencil tablets shakily fastened together. Across them were printed with crayon:

VARY FINE AYerDALE DOG AND

goat FOUr SALE FOUr

100$

DOZE   TrIX

Penny turned in amazement to Junior, who stood back surveying his handiwork with anxious pride.

'Why, Junior, you wouldn't never go to sell Napoleum?'

He dashed at her impetuously, clasping her about the waist. 'I ruther have you, Penny!' he declared. 'I thought about it and I thought about it and I ruther have you than them. And a hundred dollars will be enough, won't it?'

Mrs. Smith and Virginia came out to see what was happening.

'But, Junior,' Mrs. Smith told him, sitting down on the step and gathering him into her lap, 'you know this is the day Penny's going. There'd be hardly time to sell them.'

'Why, *any*body'd want Napoleum,' Junior expostulated, pushing himself out of her arms in his excitement. 'Lemme lead them up and down the street, Mamma, and you'll see. I don't want any brekklefiss. Please, Mamma, let me!'

Penny was no hungrier than Junior. This meal reminded her of the dinner long ago in the Denver apartment, when Mrs. Smith had cooked pot roast — just so — and baked biscuit and upside-down cake, and Penny could scarcely find throat muscles to swallow with, because the feast was in honor of her leaving the Smiths.

This morning there was pancake pie — fluffy white cakes made with *two eggs*, piled up with butter and sugar between and jam melting radiantly on top, and cut down through in luscious triangles. There were sausage patties. There was orange juice. Since the Smiths had started buying everything for cash, table luxuries had become luxuries instead of necessities. And since the margins had gone into the tea can, necessities had in their turn become luxuries.— But again the food was as dry as sawdust to Penny.

'Lemme lead them up and down the street, Mamma,' Junior begged again, when the meal was over. 'I got to try, ain't I? Let me, Mamma!'

His mother reluctantly consented, and he hop-skipped away, the placard dangling from Barkis's neck.

'But what's the use of that, Mamma?' Mr. Smith protested. 'Nobody in Central'd pay ten dollars, even, for a dog; and Barkis went begging at five.'

'Oh, Papa, I know all that. But the poor little tyke will feel that he's done what he could.'

All this gave Penny a salt taste of tears that was almost worse than the bitterness of the past days. The tears overflowed when Virginia came downstairs and said with manufactured lightness:

'Penny, would you mind helping me with the beds?'

Mrs. Smith followed them up the stairs and stood in the doorway watching Penny. The beds were already made, and Penny's was almost hidden by the garments spread upon it.

An outfit of underwear in powder blue was folded across the foot. Penny recognized that underwear: it was Mrs. Smith's best set, scarcely worn. A golden brown dress was spread out beside it. By the dress lay a brown coat with a fur collar; and a brown beret; and brown oxfords and stockings; and brown fabric gloves.

'Penny, did you guess what we were doing, over at Mrs. Sands's?' Virginia demanded. 'We had to get her to help us, to get through in time. And we had to work over there, so you wouldn't catch on.'

'You better slip them on and see if they fit,' Mrs. Smith said, after a long minute when Penny stood blinking fast at the surprising finery. 'We had to measure by your blue dress.'

They did fit. Virginia stood the mirror on a bed and tilted it so that Penny could see as much as possible. Penny stared at the strange brown figure.

'How could you ever get such a heap done?' she muttered.

'We couldn't have, without Mrs. Sands. She worked like a Trojan. And — Penny, that dress was made out of one of your own mother's; and the coat was hers; we fitted it down and changed the style for you.'

Penny gazed at Mrs. Smith speechlessly.

'They sold almost everything out of the house, you see,' Virginia explained. 'But you know all that. Mrs. Sands got these of some neighbor who bought them and then couldn't use them. She's had them packed away in a trunk for years. We thought —— You do really like them, Pen?'

'You cain't — can't ever know how much.' Penny smoothed the lustrous brown silk with a reverent hand.

Junior was clumping dolefully up the stairs. 'They don't want no dogs and goats,' he admitted. 'They laughed.— Oh, gee, Penny, I never thought you was pretty. You do look beautiful. I won't mind marrying you when I'm grown up. That's what I'll do. Soon's I'm fourteen. And then that nasty old woman can't have you any more.'

'I wonder where Grandpa and Papa have got to,' Mrs. Smith interrupted. 'I suppose you might as well pack your things, Penny, though I hate to say it.'

'Great Jawns, what in?' Penny wondered suddenly, giggling through her tears at thought of the faded print dress with its missing sleeve which had been her luggage when she arrived at the Smith home.

Virginia brought a smart little suitcase from the closet and laid it on the bed. 'I want you to have this, Penny,' she said, 'to remember me by. I scratched off my initials and put yours on, the best I could.'

'Girls!' Grandpa's worried voice sounded from the foot of the stairs. 'That pesky car's had to go on the

blink just now of all times. We been tinkering her and
tinkering her, and this time we're stuck for fair.'

They all came to the head of the stairs and peered
down at him. He looked upward, his mouth helplessly
dropping open.

'Oh, gee, Penny can't go! Penny can't go!' squealed
Junior, capering around them in a war-dance of delight.

Mr. Smith appeared, wiping his hands on a cleaning
rag and lifting a grease-smeared face. 'She's got to go,
Junior, more's the pity,' he said. 'Today's the dead line.
We'll keep on working at the old car this morning. But
likely we'll have to put Penny on the stage — the bus:
there's one that leaves at two.'

The morning dragged. 'Once you're set to go, you
hanker to *go*, no matter how bad you hate it,' Penny
thought to herself.

At noon the two men came in and washed up de-
jectedly. They had failed to locate the trouble, and there
was no telling when they would succeed. Penny would
have to go down on the two-o'clock bus. Only so could
she reach the Home that night.

'And we gave our word she should,' Mr. Smith said
definitely. 'I wrote Miss Fleming and gave her my
word.'

They swallowed some more carefully prepared and
tasteless food, and Junior bustled over to tell Mrs. Sands,
and they all walked down to the drugstore where the
bus started.

Mr. Smith hurried ahead with the suitcase, to hold the
bus if necessary. Virginia walked with her arm around
Penny's waist; Virginia's small nose was pink. Mrs.
Sands brought up the rear with Mrs. Smith and Grandpa. Junior and Napoleum and Dum and Dee wove

around and through the group and managed to halt
them again and again. Dum and Dee, grown into beautiful young creatures with all their baby spots lost,
sprawled awkwardly when their polished black hoofs
struck the unfamiliar sidewalks. Their eight long slim
legs spraddled helplessly in eight directions.

Penny could scarcely laugh, even at them. She could
scarcely smile, even when she saw her reflection in the
window of an empty store and had sharp vision of the
contrast between Penny arriving and Penny departing.
This tall little girl, all in brown, with her glint of coppery
hair and her look of decent grooming — could she be
the scarecrow of the woolly locks and the red-and-black
mask?

But — she was departing! The Smiths were letting
her go. That thought rose to the surface and pushed
everything else under. It was all she could remember
when she was finally huddled in the broad back seat of
the old town car that was the stage-coach of today.
She huddled there, holding desperately to her self-con-
trol, thrusting back the bitterness lest it spoil the good-
byes entirely.

The driver, late already, delayed his starting during
unbearably long minutes. Junior clambered onto the
running-board and put up his face to be kissed, forgetting his grief in the excitement of the moment and the
importance of staying out of school a day; remembering
it again and puckering his face grotesquely. The family
and Mrs. Sands waved and waved and came to the window to give final messages:

'Be sure to write once a week. Be sure, Penny!'

'Penny, we want you to spend a week with us as soon
as she'll let you.'

'Keep a bandage on that burned finger, Penny.'

'See if she won't let you come up for Christmas vacation!'

'Penny, girl, you keep a stiff upper lip. Mind you do, and everything'll work out for the best. "All things work together for good."' Strange how Grandpa's own lip was twitching. 'Things does, Penny.'

Penny waved and waved until the smile seemed frozen on her mouth and her hand went jerking of itself. But at last the driver dashed out of the drugstore, wiping his mouth, leaped into his place and kicked the starter, leaped out and cranked, leaped in again; all in a grim hurry, as if he were the only prompt soul in Central, and all his passengers — Penny, thus far — had kept him waiting for hours.

They were away.

'It's all over,' Penny said in her heart. The towering shelf streets that twisted along on each side of her blurred and danced in the autumn sunshine. 'It's all over and done with. Oh, why didn't I enjoy every last bit of it twice as much while I had it?'

XXI. TRIAL BY DARKNESS

THE bus shrieked to a stop in Black Hawk and took on two more passengers, a plumply middle-aged couple. They overflowed the movable chairs in front of Penny, while Penny shrank farther into her corner, turned her face to the window, and closed her eyes.

She had probably two hours for grief. The bus was going to Boulder, and by the time she reached that point she must have herself in hand. She was to go straight to the station and take a bus for Denver and there change for a southbound one, which would put her down at the front door of the Home.

She would have to eat her supper in Denver. Mrs. Smith had told her where to go: a half block from the bus station, with no streets to cross, and a full steak dinner for twenty-five cents.

Penny had never in her life eaten in a restaurant. She tried to fix her mind on the delicious terror of going alone to McVittie's Restaurant, ordering her own dinner, eating it like a grown person. She tried to hold her thoughts to that and the excitement of reaching the Home, late that night. Miss Fleming and the kids would think she was pretty grand, with a fur collar and a suitcase and eating at restaurants.

She must live up to her new grooming, her suave brown clothing. She must speak properly, doing away with 'theseyeres' and 'hain'ts.' She must *keep* remembering that she was Penelope Adams, and came of decent folks with carpets to their floors. She must keep remembering that she was going to win through and *be* Penelope Adams, in spite of all the Mrs. Henleys in the world. Nor she wasn't going to have anybody pitying her, either.

But for all her self-admonitions, she was only thirteen and a half, and the Smiths and Napoleum and the New England house were steadily drawing away into a bleak Never. Vacation weeks — visits — they couldn't be the same as living with people. Penny felt that her own folks had cast her off. And what was a chance, compared to a family?

The woman passenger looked over her shoulder and met Penny's opening eyes. 'Ain't you afraid to be running around this part of the country with the bank bandits loose?' she inquired conversationally. 'You stopping at Boulder?'

'No, mom,' said Penny, and closed her eyes again.

Getting back to the Home —— She had presents for everyone: pine-cone turkeys for the smaller children. She and Virginia had made the grotesque birds for a Thanksgiving Camp Fire party, but Virginia said she could make more and Penny should take these. A balsam pillow and a glass of her own chokecherry jelly for Miss Fleming. A hop pillow for the cook. Balsam sachets for Maybelle and some of the other older girls. Pieces of peacock ore, splendidly iridescent.

She had her photograph to show them, too: at that thought her heart swelled like a balloon blown up almost to bursting. It popped her eyes open.

'You going on up to Cheyenne, maybe?' the woman pursued interestedly.

The man was gazing steadily out of the window, chewing with long slow motions of the jaw that crowded all his chins down over his collar.

'No, mom,' said Penny, and fastened her eyes on the driver.

He was rearing back in his seat, putting on the brake and shifting the gears and twiddling one gadget after another. The old car had balked at a hill.

'I suppose likely you're going to Denver, then,' the woman chased the subject down.—'Look out, Mister! You're awful close to the ditch.'

The driver was backing carefully down, watching the road behind him. The woman screwed around fatly and gave driving-directions, unheard through the glass pane. The car reached the foot of the hill with a relieved rock and grunt and the driver tried the ascent again. The car puffed laboriously up and coasted down the other side. Penny went back to her thoughts.

She wasn't going to — not ever — go caring for any family again. That would be easy enough, as far as the Henleys went. But she'd try putting even the Smiths out of her mind. Well, mostly. That is, she wouldn't think about them as being her own folks. Own folks didn't send you off like this — just because they couldn't give you a fancy education.

The woman was talking, a steady ripple with an occasional break filled in with the man's gum-muffled 'Eh-yah, I shouldn't wonder,' 'Ummm,' 'Naw, not hardly.'

'And so I says, well, pshaw, Mrs. Lanning — *Now*, what's struck the poor old wreck?' she demanded, as the car stopped once more.

This time the driver got out and pottered around the motor, scratching his ear with a puzzled thumb. He crawled under the car, and the woman opened the door on her side and leaned out to gaze at his dusty boot-toes. He crawled out, wiped his hands on his cover-alls, removed his cap to scratch the top of his head, replaced it.

'Not so good,' he acknowledged, with a general inclusion of the three passengers, 'but we'll make it down to Boulder.' He doubtfully returned to his seat.

The woman hitched herself back and banged her door shut, murmuring dissatisfaction. Penny shut her eyes determinedly, and the car rumbled on, along the curves and loops of the mountain road.

A squeal from the woman jerked Penny's eyes open once more.

'Charley, isn't that a man? Ahead there in the bushes. — No, no, this side.— My goodness, you don't ever see anything. An awful-looking man. I *know* it was.'

At the first sentence, Penny had peered through the side window, through the rear window. It *was* a man, but he was only tying his shoe. That might have explained his being up in the bushes, as if he had been hiding. As he stooped, Penny's quick eye registered all there was to see of him. A small man he was, with a face that tapered sharply below a bulging forehead. The large round lenses of his dark glasses made his aspect somehow unearthly. 'Like one of them skulls, seems like,' Penny thought, as a turn in the road cut him off from their sight.

She stirred uneasily at her own comparison. Who had said something like that lately? Grandpa.—'The least one alluz puts me in mind of a skull and crossbones, someway.' And whom was he describing? One of the

men that he and Mr. Smith fancied were spying on them.
It was an unpleasant coincidence. Penny remembered
that she'd broken the mirror in her cheap handbag. Just
a week ago. She'd hoped it wouldn't count, because of
being so small.

The bus went on, its motor unwilling. Again it stopped
and again. The middle of the afternoon was upon them,
and the air chilled as suddenly as if a door had been
shut. That was because the sun had dipped behind the
hills.

The man passenger pulled out his watch, his lower lip
out-thrust. 'By doggies,' he rumbled, 'this is too much
of a good thing. Hey, driver, what's the chance of getting
us to Boulder by four-forty-five? I've got to get to
Boulder by four-forty-five, no two ways about it.'

'My goodness, driver, I want to get out of these hills
before dark,' the woman screeched through the glass.
'I care more about that than I do about your old business, Charley. You're going to get us down before dark,
ain't you?'

'Ain't no spooks going to get you, Flora,' the man
passenger grunted. 'Too much of a load for them.'

'Spooks! Pshaw! It's those bandits I'm thinking
about.' She looked back at Penny, undiscouraged.
'No sense taking a chance with bandits, is there?'

The driver slowed up and addressed them through the
speaking-tube. 'This darned car,' he apologized. 'It
ain't my fault, Missis. I told 'em she needed new piston
rings and her valves ground, but they thought they was
so smart. I tell you what we could do, though, if the
Missis don't mind a little rough going. There's a short cut
here somewheres that ought to save us anyhow half an
hour. Frypan Cutoff.'

They all agreed to the bumps, and a few minutes later the bus turned into an abandoned mine road, yellow-paved with aspen leaves. Deeper and deeper into the desolation it jounced and jerked along. They met nobody; they saw nobody. An old shack, with boarded-up windows, a deserted car ——

'S-someb-body's had a wr-wreck.' The woman passenger's words were jerked out by the wild bouncings of the bus.

'Junked their — old car, more likely,' the man corrected.

' It ain't junked,' said Penny, looking back at it through the rear window. She had not offered a word before, but there was something about this car ——

'It's — got good tires and — nothing ain't been took off it,' she answered the woman passenger's questioning eyes, clutching the seat with both hands to hold herself down.

'What's the license? Can you make out the license?' the woman clamored.

Penny, her face bumping the window, shook her head. 'They — they ain't any. But they's a scraped place on the fender, and it — shows through green. And the far headlight — it don't match!' she said, with a catch of the breath.

· The driver was bending all his energy to the task of keeping the old bus upright and avoiding the worst of the ruts and stones, those that would endanger its springs. Penny and the woman stared at each other as they swung and shook and slid from side to side. When at last the bus came out on the highway, the woman moistened pale lips and spoke, pulling at her husband's arms.

'You never see anything! That car — it was the bandits' Studebaker sedan,' she stuttered. 'Don't look like I'm crazy. Ask the girl!'

He pulled his chins out of his collar and drew down his lips in a superior smile. 'By doggies! I wish I had a dollar for every time the bandits' car has been sighted in the last month. Only it never was.'

The woman hammered on the glass till the driver stopped. 'I tell you that was the bank robbers' car back there in the cutoff!' she whimpered at him, her face purplish. 'And I saw a man hiding in the bushes. They're waiting to hold somebody up, I'll bet any money. Oh, quit your grinning. You men always know so blame' much.'

The driver and the man passenger were exchanging tolerant masculine glances.

'You saw the man in the bushes, too, didn't you?' the woman demanded of Penny, over her shoulder.

Penny nodded, still pale.

'*She* saw the man. I warrant somebody's taking gold down to Denver tonight. Can't we telephone up to the sheriff first place we come to?'

'Heh-heh-heh!' the man chuckled fatly. 'Flora, you've seen more things that weren't there than I could shake a stick at. Always doing it. If we telephoned the sheriff every time some woman saw those bandits ——'

The driver joined in his laughter and drove on.

Penny was sitting tensely still. Likely, she thought, there wasn't anything to it. Probably it didn't join on at all, but it was queer that the man in the bushes should look like what Grandpa said about one of the men that had followed him and Mr. Smith.

Gold? Things did get out. Junior was such a chatter-

box. Easy for the bandits to find out that Mr. Smith
was planning to take his gold down to the Denver Mint.
They might suppose there was much more gold than there
really was. They might have men on both roads, waiting.
Penny knew that Mr. Smith had planned to take this
one, because it was not the direct route.

She could telephone herself from Boulder. She could
telephone Mrs. Sands. But would there be time? No
telling when Grandpa and Mr. Smith had got the blue
car running. At this very minute they might be rushing
straight upon the ambush, all of them.

What could Penny do? 'It's *not* my *fam*ily — It's
not my *fam*ily ——' The words clacked through the
rattle of the bus. 'I'll telephone soon as ever we get to
Boulder, and that's all I can do. It's not my family.'

Again the bus stopped. Penny gathered up her courage
and approached the driver as he lifted the hood.

'Couldn't we find a closeter place than Boulder to
'phone?' she begged.

''Phone who?' he grunted, engrossed in his engine.

'The sheriff, for one,' she said. 'Won't you *please*
'phone up the sheriff, Mister?'

He gave her a harried glance, rubbing his nose with
the back of a greasy hand. 'Say, young lady,' he snapped,
'I'd 'phone quick enough if there was anything to 'phone
about.' And he disappeared under the hood.

Penny drew a deep breath, slid her suitcase out when
no one was looking, and dodged into the cover of the
underbrush.

It was four o'clock, or just about that: she knew by
the shadows. The canyon was already filled to the brim
with them. She was miles away from Central City —
twelve or fifteen miles. And they were not level, easy

daylight miles, either. Penny didn't dare think of what they would be like when night blackened them.

She must follow this road and stop the blue car if it came. Lucky she knew the irregular cluck of the blue car's motor: even Napoleum, who could tell it blocks away, knew it no better than she. Lucky, too, that the Mister honked his horn around every curve: a funny horn that bleated long and loud with a crack at the end.

She sat down on a rock, opened her suitcase, and changed to her heavy patched shoes and cotton stockings. The suitcase she hid under the rock, poking it well out of sight. It hurt to leave it behind — with the picture and the new dress and all her presents. But she could not risk slowing her steps by carrying it. And she could find it again. The rock was a funny one with a darker slab stuck into its granite, and its side curved in to form a niche where she had thrust the suitcase. A mountain ash tree hung orange berries above it; and across the road stood the tumbledown red buildings of the old Loretta Mine.

With a last look at the hiding-place, she hurried on. For she must hurry — hurry! — over the four miles or more that would take her beyond the place where she had seen the man with the dark glasses. Throughout those miles she need not be much on the lookout for the blue car.

Penny was a sturdy hiker; but hiking at your own pace was very different, she soon found, from hurrying — hurrying! — with fear nipping at your heels and snarling out of the shadows that steadily thickened into dusk. At seven or eight thousand feet elevation, rapid walking is difficult, too. Penny's heart hammered and her breath stabbed her lungs.

She had to stop now and then, flinging herself flat somewhere out of view of the road, spreading her arms wide, and waiting so until her breath came normally again. She cringed at the thought of lying on the ground in her new coat. And maybe there was nothing *to* it. But then again ——

When she reached the point where the Frypan Cutoff emerged on the highway, she stole through the bushes on the farther side of the road, shaking with fear. 'Scarecat!' she called herself vehemently. But there was something real to be afraid of. Wild animals — it wasn't comfortable to think of them, and she alone and with no defense; yet it was unlikely that any would harm her. But these desperate men were another matter. They had held a woman bank teller in front of them to protect themselves from bullets. They had ——

By the time she drew near the place where the man had lurked, it was too dark to make her way through the undergrowth except by painful inches. It must be after five, and the clouds had deepened the dusk.

She stopped at the edge of the highway, dimly glimmering between black trees. Stopped because she couldn't go on. Terror squeezed her lungs like a clutching hand. She couldn't breathe. A little light scurry of breath was all that was left her, and her whole body ached with tightness.

She couldn't force her feet along that sinister stretch. They gripped the ground desperately. She felt as if she were caught midway of a shaky ladder, unable to go up or down.

Every black clump of bushes hid an armed man. When a car whirred up the hill, she was sure it was the repainted Studebaker. That light scurry of breath was

shut off and the hardness flowed out of her bones. The
bushes rustled sharply, and she was shaken from head to
foot by the sound.

The car went by, and a little breath returned. This
would never do. Time was running past her, and the
blue car ——

She set her teeth and stepped out into the perilous open.

'I ran off from school and I'm going home to Russell
Gulch,' she rehearsed over and over. That's what she
would say if anyone accosted her. If they gave her time
to say anything at all.

Her back crawled with the feeling of guns pointed at
it, and she dared not look behind her for fear of what
she would see. She must walk straight along — walk,
not run — as if she really was just going home.

Now, when a car approached, twin balls of green fire
sometimes flashed from among the trees. She didn't
let herself guess what they were. Coyotes were plenty,
and there were a few bears and mountain lions. Once a
deer bounded across the road in front of an automobile,
and crashed through the bushes where Penny crouched.
Once, when she threw herself down to rest, a small furry
creature ran squeaking across her body. Things scuttled
away before her in the fallen leaves. Birds flew up with
a whirr and clack of wings: doves, and sometimes great
ghostly owls. When there was no other sound, the tele-
graph wires sang overhead. Their loud hum comforted
her at first, for it meant that there were people still alive
in this mysterious world. After a while it deepened her
sense of desolation: somewhere there were people, and
fires, and supper smells, and safety; and the thought
only made Penny feel smaller and more utterly alone in
the endless dark.

By this time she simply plodded along, stepping out of the tunnel of light when the infrequent automobile did come. One foot after the other, hay foot, straw foot, one, two, three, three hundred, a thousand.— Wouldn't she feel like a fool if there was nothing to it?

She plunged into the bushes to avoid a car that rattled down the hill. As she shivered there, leaning against a tree-trunk, she saw a light high on the bank ahead of her. Strange, without moon or headlights to be reflected. Perhaps someone's dark lantern! She started convulsively at the thought, and turned to run back to the highway.

In her panic, her usual springy tread failed her. She had missed a thousand pitfalls that night; now she stepped on a stone which tipped and threw her backward with a violent twist of the ankle. She sat down heavily, sick with pain.

Clasping the wrenched ankle in both hands, she rocked back and forth there on the ground. At length she hitched herself over to a tree, pulled herself to a standing position, tried her weight gingerly on the injured foot. The pain sent her reeling.

For a moment she had forgotten the ominous light. Now she glanced back at the hillside. There it still shone, steady, unmoving.

'Great Jawns!' Penny muttered, 'it ain't nothing but a glowworm. Jest a little old worm that cain't even fly. And look what you went and made me do!'

Doggedly she began the last lap of that long, dark race. She had her knife, and Grandpa had sharpened it well for her. Half ashamed, she squeezed the rabbit's foot that lay in her pocket beside it. It gave her no assurance. Like enough Grandpa was right. If it was Grandpa, he'd be looking up and saying — well, anyway, asking for help from that big Someone who was all around and above.

'"Now I lay me"? No, Junior's prayer ain't hardly the one for now. "Give us this day our daily bread"? Golly poppings, it ain't *bread* I need. I'm jest too wore out to figure out the words. *You* know what I want to say, don't you?'

Feeling around in the dark she cut herself a staff of chokecherry. And labored on.

Surely the Mister wouldn't start later than this. But wouldn't he? You never could tell about the Mister. He liked night driving, and they could put up at an auto camp and take the gold to the Mint next morning.

So there was nothing to do but go on, hitch-tap-step, hitch-tap-step. She was like a frog, and a wounded frog at that, climbing up the side of the well. She didn't seem to make any progress at all. No longer did she notice the twin balls of green fire. No longer did she move an unnecessary step out of the road when a car sent its long beam ahead. No longer did she turn her head to look at it when the hum of its motor rose to a vicious whine in passing her. It was just eyes ahead, hitch-tap-step forever.

She was dully surprised when the first lights of Black Hawk jumped out at her around a turn in the road. She had stopped expecting them. She dragged her feet through the broad bright doorway of a livery-stable-garage and looked at the man who was greasing a car under the glaring light bulb.

'Can I use yore 'phone?' she gasped.

'Help yourself!' He jerked a thumb toward the wall

'phone, gaping at her as she looked up Mrs. Sands's number and called it in a shaken voice.

Brrrrr——Brrrrr——'I'll ring them again.'—— Brrrrrr —— Brrrrrrr —— 'I'll ring them again.' —— Brrrrr —— Brrrrrrrr ——

She fumbled the receiver back onto its hook. 'Will you tote me up to Central — quick?' she demanded, in a fluttering voice. 'To Mr. Henry Smith's, next door to Mis' Sands's?'

He backed out the car he was greasing and gave her a friendly lift and shove into the front seat, asking questions that Penny didn't even hear. He looked at her curiously, whirled the crank, jumped in, and sent the car up the winding street. Penny sat like a person in a dream.

Up the winding street. Into Central. Around the corner. Past the stores and the Teller House and the opera house and the Methodist Church. Still Penny felt that she, for all the chugging car, was slipping backward; as if the wheels spun uselessly.

'This the place, Sister?'

She was opening the car door. The Smith house was dark.

A car was standing at the curb in the shadows, but the garage man's headlight picked out a figure teetering on the curb talking to the occupants of the car, a shawl dragged close around its head and shoulders.

The figure turned its face toward them as Penny stumbled out. It was Mrs. Sands.

'Why, Penny Adams!' she cried.

XXII. THE HOME POCKET

'WHY, Penny Adams! Was there a wreck? Were you hurt? Penny, you are hurt!'

'It is our otto! It is!' Penny babbled, limping toward it as fast as she could. 'Oh, they ain't gone! Where were they going? Where was the Mister aiming to go?'

She had reached the side of the car, and all its occupants sat staring at her, dumb with amazement.

'Penny — darling!' gasped Mrs. Smith, pushing at the stubborn car door. 'You *are* hurt!' She was out, and taking Penny by the shoulders.

'You won't go? The Mister won't go?' Penny couldn't think of anything else to say. She stared and trembled and repeated it: 'You won't go?'

'Go? My gosh, with you getting into a wreck? Not hardly!' Mr. Smith assured her. 'That darn rickety bus. They ought to be sued. I ought to be kicked for letting you ——'

They were all out of the blue car, all crowding round Penny, helping her up to the house. 'I ain't paid the man,' she remembered, and held out her handbag to Virginia.

In the lighted dining-room, Penny repeated the question: 'Where was the Mister aiming to go? Was it — the gold?'

'Yes, yes. — My goodness, Papa, you better go out and bring it in. — Penny, honey, we couldn't just sit around. Not tonight. They got the car to going about dark, and we couldn't seem to settle down. — But what *happened?*'

'What in tunket happened, Penny, girl?' Grandpa begged. 'Where was the wreck at?'

'It wasn't a wreck. — It was the gold. — I mean, that queer-turned man like a skeleton — and the Studebaker sedan was painted over black, but it was green underneath — and the license plates gone ——' Penny looked at them piteously, her face screwed up like a small child's. Would they think she was silly? 'Those bank robbers, they had a Studebaker,' she said faintly, 'but I'm so cold I cain't get it straight ——'

When they had made up the fire and chafed her blue hands and put together what she was so desperately trying to tell them, Mr. Smith stood staring at her.

'It wouldn't make sense,' he said, 'if it wasn't that this bank gang's hard pushed. They'd — do anything for a few hundred; and on top of that, there might be one of the big mine men running some gold down tonight, besides.' He grabbed his hat. 'I'm going to the sheriff with this.'

He paused in the doorway. 'You say this car was in the old Frypan Cutoff, Penny?'

She nodded.

'Kid, how on earth did you get back from there?'

'Hoofed it.'

He went out, shaking his head.

'All alone in the dark?' Virginia's voice was hushed. 'Penny, I'd have died.'

'Wouldn't a cup of hot milk help the child?' asked Grandpa.

'And — Penny, how could you walk on that foot? The ankle's swelling like nobody's business.'

'It's jest turnt,' said Penny.

She sat sunk in a lethargy while they bustled around her, bringing hot milk, a hot foot-bath. 'Don't you, Virginia!' she deprecated, when Virginia knelt before her and took off her shoes and stockings. Lights wavered dizzily around her; hands touched her; Napoleum laved her foot with kisses as she eased it into and out of the scalding water; a great relaxed ache encompassed her; voices wove in and out of the roaring in her ears:

'Penny, how could you do it?'

'No flashlight — and cloudy ——'

'I'd have died then and there, Penny.'

'Did you see any bears? Was they any bears? Penny, was they?'

Penny only smiled vaguely. But suddenly her eyes widened.

'I ain't — oh, it looks like I tore my coat!' she whispered.

'Just a snag, Honey. I can fix it so it won't ever show. It's mostly the dust and burs and things that make it look so. We'll brush it up,' said Mrs. Sands. 'It's certainly high time I was getting home. I'll take the coat along.'

'And my suitcase,' Penny said, when the door had closed behind Mrs. Sands. 'I had to hide it by the road.'

The door opened again and Mr. Smith came in. He carried a squarish paper pail and a cellophane-wrapped cake.

'You sure set things going, kid,' he told Penny. 'Sher-

iff 'phoned down to Idaho and Boulder, and there's going
to be some tall doings if that Studebaker's still in Frypan
Cutoff. Likely Frypan Cutoff's where they've been
hanging out. Or one of the places.'

'Did you find out whether there was any other gold
going down tonight?' asked Mrs. Smith.

'You're darned right there was! One of the big mines.
Thought he'd kept everything so quiet, and that this was
the safest way. We mayn't ever know for sure whether
it was me they were going after or this big guy. Maybe
it was both. Anyway, Penny's going to be a popular
young lady around these parts.'

They stared at each other.

'It's peach!' announced Junior, who had tugged open
the ice-cream carton. 'It's my favoritest kind. -- It's
peach, I tell you. Hey, why don't we eat?'

Virginia served the cream, and they hitched their
chairs up to the table. Grandpa dropped his head and
murmured: 'For food and care, dear Father, make these
Thy children thankful.'

Junior exploded in a snorting laugh. 'Grandpa asked
a blessing on the ice-cream!' he gurgled through a mouthful of it. 'You don't have to ask a blessing on ice-cream,
Grandpa.'

'I never felt more like it, though,' said Mr. Smith.

Languorously, deliciously, they ate. But as Mrs.
Smith progressed more and more slowly with the last
quarter of her dish, her eyes, resting on Penny, sharpened
with sudden alarm. She looked at the clock.

'My goodness!' she cried. 'That matron at the Home!
What are we thinking of? She'll be sending out the
police when Penny doesn't get off the bus.'

Penny put down her spoon. Dearer than ever, this

circle round the table: Napoleum, sitting with his muzzle moist on her knee, waiting for her to drop tidbits of cake and cream; Mrs. Smith, rosy and comfortable-looking; Mr. Smith, beaming as he absorbed slow mouthfuls; Virginia, her clear little face sorrowful; Junior, tunneling industriously into his rosy cream and dragging his heaped spoon luxuriously through the circle of his lips; Grandpa, considering Penny over his spectacles.

Grandpa blinked rapidly and got up, helping himself with both hands. He looked sternly around the table. 'I — I — I don't see how we come to let ourselves do it. I don't care whether we've got any right or not. There's some things is human and some things ain't.'

'There, there, Paw.' Mr. Smith's cheekbones had reddened at the confused accusation, but he bit off another mouthful of cake. 'Better eat a little faster,' he advised, his voice muffled. 'You didn't dish out the whole two quarts yet, did you, Virginia?'

'I set it out with a wet cloth around,' said Mrs. Smith. 'But, Papa, this is serious. They'll think something's happened to Penny.'

'Oh, I guess they won't,' Papa reassured her, tantalizingly slow of speech. 'I guess they won't, Mamma. Because I sent Miss Fleming a telegram before I got the ice-cream and came home.'

Grandpa glared. 'Don't nobody need to pay no attention to me,' he croaked. 'But it does seem like Penny's earnt the right to starve along with the Smith family if she wants. And some day we're going to be mighty sorry if ——'

'Dad' — Virginia spoke tensely — 'I'm willing to work for Aunt Caroline and make my way through college. I'll even live in the house car. Dot Hooper thinks it would be great. That will take care of my college education, pretty nearly,' she hurried on, 'and when it comes Penny's time — well, why can't she do the same way? The gang can high-hat me if they want to,' she added recklessly.

'The old gang can go hang!' Mr. Smith rhymed jocosely; but his eyes rested more approvingly on his daughter than they were used to do.

'But, Dad! I don't think it's anything to laugh about!' she protested, half crying.

'Hold your horses, Ginny,' her father exhorted her gently.

'You — you said I'd be coming tomorrow?' murmured Penny. 'Or is my foot too stiff ——?'

'"Penny delayed. Will arrive same bus tomorrow"?' Mr. Smith asked facetiously. 'No, I splurged. Used fourteen words, I guess, and hang the expense. Let's see!' He fumbled for an envelope in his breast-pocket — 'How'd I word it? Here it is.'

But before he read his scrawled draft of the message, he looked hard at his family. 'I — sort of side with Grandpa. There's such a thing as — as being too sensible. We've been awfully lucky these six months. Only I reckon luck's the last thing you'd ought to call it. And — well ——' He blew his nose loudly and stared at the envelope, lifting it toward the light:

'"Find Penny is already member of family. Cannot give her away. Wish immediate adoption." There, now, you can say what you please, Mamma. No thirteen-year-old kid's going to do what she did tonight for anybody *but* her own folks.'

Junior broke the subsequent silence. 'You mean we got her for keeps, Papa?' he gasped. 'For keeps, huh?

Goody, goody, gander!' He galloped around the table and dragged Penny's head backward to smear her face with ice-creamy kisses.

'I'm so — *glad!*' Virginia said solemnly. 'Oh, Penny, I'm so glad!'

'Well, good land of Goshen, who ain't glad?' Grandpa demanded, sitting down again and taking a spoonful of melted cream. 'Now the Smiths'll alluz have their lucky penny. Yes, sir, we'll alluz have our penny for luck!'

THE END